THE DEAD WOMAN

Jennifer Samson

First Printing, 2018

ISBN: 978-1-988797-09-0

Published by Twin Crowns Press
twincrownspress.wordpress.com

www.arieswriting.com

Cover by Pholk Media

This novel uses Canadian spelling.

This novel contains depictions and mentions of smoking, illegal activities, sex, harassment, prostitution, drinking, smuggling, guns, murder and more.

For Hannah

1

The truck rumbled along the dirt road bouncing into every pothole it could find. Her limbs were sore from bracing herself against the walls of the cube truck. The air was stagnant and hot, the smell of sweat and human misery thick in the air.

The truck geared down, slowing, and she glanced at the others. It was far too soon to be at the American border.

The engine cut off. Both doors creaked open and slammed shut a second later. Everyone inside the back of the truck was as quiet as a mouse. The men had made it clear what would happen if there was noise.

Beads of sweat collected on her forehead and neck, plastering her hair to her skin. The heat was unbearable. She stood and stretched on the tips of her toes to see out the small grate that looked into the truck's cab, hoping for a little air. The men were gone, and she noted with annoyance they were stopped at a cantina.

They were locked in the back, sweating in misery and passing around a single jug of rapidly dwindling water while these pendejos stopped at a cantina.

She sat again, the metal floor hard and unforgiving. It was dark, a small swath of light shining in from the grate. A man sat across from her, the sheaf of light highlighting his bad eye, watering and rheumy.

The two babies were quiet and listless. When the water came around she gave up her sips in case the little ones needed it. It was a sacrifice she was used to.

It was almost a half hour later when footsteps approached and men could be heard talking outside the truck. She scrambled up to look out the grate again and relief flooded her—at least they wouldn't die on the side of the road in México.

1

The two men got inside, and the doors protested as they were pulled shut. The truck started a moment later, and the relief inside the back of the truck was palpable.

She sat, her nerves shot. The closer they got to freedom, the more nervous she was. The truck hit a rut and tossed them. She winced as her leg hit a piece of metal sticking out from the side—another bruise to mark her and remind her of this place.

She tried to fan herself, but it was useless, as the air was too stale and warm to provide any relief. She looked at the flushed faces of the people around her, barely visible in the darkness, and wondered how and why they had all agreed to this shared torture.

The big truck slowed about an hour later, and she stood again to peer out the small grate into the cab.

She slipped as the truck hit a divot in the road and someone hissed at her to sit before she was hurt. It was unnatural to hear another voice—no one had spoken in hours.

The signs on the road told her they were close to the American border at Nogales. They had driven over six hours out of their way to cross there instead of Mexicali or Tijuana, at Manuel's orders. While she understood the reason, the travel wore on her more than she wanted to admit.

She lowered herself from her tip-toe position. Sweat stung her eyes and she wiped them with the sweater tied around her waist. One of the men banged against the cab wall, and she jumped.

"Quiet back there," he said in Spanish, despite the fact they were silent. "You make any noise, and they'll open up those doors and shoot you all."

She rolled her eyes; Manuel would not have put her in this truck if that was a possibility. More danger remained in staying and being shot right where she was than at some American border.

A woman pulled on the hem of her dress to make her sit, and she looked at her coldly, even if she couldn't really see her in the dark truck. These people might be going to find their precious new lives, but if she was caught, she was dead. Her stakes were higher. She couldn't remember a time when they weren't.

She looked back through the grate. The truck slowed as they approached the crossing. Maybe Calderón's men would think she crossed into Calexico or San Ysidro and look for her there. Maybe they would think she tried to return home. If she was lucky, they would go south in search of her and spend forever in the scrub desert chasing ghosts. If she was unlucky . . . if she was unlucky, she would be dead so fast she wouldn't be able to think about it.

The truck approached the border crossing, and the engine slowed. The truck crawled forward at a snail's pace. Her nerves jangled, and she had visions of the border guards discovering them. The men up front seemed unconcerned, as if they always crossed the border with Mexican nationals hidden in the back of a cube truck, and maybe they did.

She knew Manuel was capable and knew what he was doing, but she couldn't help but wonder who else was in Calderón's pocket. Maybe he knew about Manuel . . . maybe he had someone paid off at the border. She peered out of the grate again.

"Sit down!" the woman urged. "Do you want them to see you? They'll kill us all!"

She sat, looking at the woman as if she was stupid. The woman shook her head, and lapsed back into her Ave María. Her own rosary beads were in her pocket, and she touched them as she watched the woman pray.

The men in the cab spoke in low voices to the border guards, impossible to hear over the sound of the diesel engine. A moment later the truck moved forward again, and she breathed a sigh of relief along with everyone else in the truck. No one protested when she stood to look this time. People began chatting with one another in relief, and one woman held her small child and cried. So many happy to leave México; she wished she could be one of them.

The two men in the cab spoke in rapid English, and she was thankful she knew what they were saying.

"Whereabouts are we headed again?" the man in the passenger seat asked.

"Las Vegas," the driver answered. "I don't have to tell you it's gonna be a dicey situation when we get there, do I?"

"Nope," the man said with a sigh. "It ain't usually a good time when you show up without the right merchandise. How I let you talk me into this, I don't know."

"Manny cashed his favour." The driver steadied the wheel with his knees as he tried to light a cigar and failed. "It was coming one day. Better he collect now. I reckon we won't have too much trouble. We'll drop these folks off at the waypoint like we're 'sposed to, then let this kid know his shit ain't with us."

"He's an ex-con, not some kid," the passenger said. He spit his tobacco into a metal coffee can. She shuddered with the memory of tasting chewing tobacco on someone's lips and the weight of a man on top of her, the feeling so intense nausea roiled her stomach. "An ex-con from Las Vegas, home of the mob. You want to tell him he ain't getting what he ordered? Because I ain't lookin' forward to that too much. He could be straight out of Chicago or some such, and bury us in the desert."

"Well, why don't we show up with this cargo, then?" the driver asked. "I'd rather him open the back up and see something rather than thin air. We tell him there was a mix-up. He won't have to know we were supposed to drop them. They'd be waiting at the waypoint overnight anyway since Manny sent us early. This con'll send us off with these folks, and we'll drop 'em at the waypoint on the way back. We'll blame Manny for the mix-up."

"Buddy, I like the way you think!"

The men lapsed into silence, and she sunk onto the hard floor, wiping the sweat from her brow. She remembered Las Vegas on the map, far from the Mexican border. Manuel promised she would get across the border, nothing more. She expected the men to drop them on the other side of the crossing and tell them to fend for themselves.

She hoped the man they were delivering them to would let them go. It would not do to trade one prison for another.

The truck hit a pothole, and she was tossed around the floor, a splinter jabbing into her finger. She was uneasy despite the fact she appeared to be heading for freedom.

María Guadalupe leaned her head back against the trailer wall and tried to sleep. Her sleep was fitful and her dreams unpleasant.

Friday, October 28, 1966

"They're late."

Tim Kelly opened the car door, got out, and braced his arms against the driver's side door of his Dodge Charger. He took one last drag from his cigarette, dropped it next to two others half-smoked, then ground the butt out with the heel of his boot. He hated he was antsy in such an obvious way and kicked some dirt over the butts.

"They'll be here," Bill said with confidence. "Mendoza said they'd be here around one, and it's barely that."

Tim paced. He hated waiting. He hated being out in the goddamn open like this. He expected a fleet of cops to come pouring out of God only knew where to arrest them. It would be better meeting somewhere hidden, like any number of abandoned warehouses near the railway tracks. Somewhere they wouldn't stick out like sore thumbs.

Instead, they were near the airport, waiting on a plateau of land where anyone could spot them from the road. The tree line was at least thirty yards away and was scrub brush and a few thin mesquite trees. Enough to hide a motorcycle cop, but not enough to hide his damn shipment if need be.

The sheriff had land out this way too, a whole damn cattle ranch, if rumour was right. He could picture the reaction if he got picked up for this on the sheriff's back doorstep.

He sighed and rubbed the back of his neck. It wasn't the first time he had bad feelings about the men Mendoza put him in touch with. The Castillos were Mexican, and even though they seemed to have the best merchandise available, they also were fond of speaking in Spanish to Mendoza when Tim was right there listening. He knew some Spanish, but these assholes knew he couldn't keep up with what they were saying. He knew they were trying to put him on edge, knock him off his game. He'd spoken up and told them English or no deal.

The men laughed until he'd presented half the money up front. That shut them up real good, and then there were cigars and tequila and talk of what they could get him for such a good price.

He picked up the duffel bag with the rest of the payment and hoisted it onto the car hood. The money made the pit of his stomach sour. All that work selling car parts, the break and enters, the small time loan sharking and the betting—he'd aimed to get a small apartment for his mother and sister to move into. He'd put down first and last month's rent, a damage deposit, and had a bit left over.

Then he'd told them.

His mother had laughed. "Timothy, I live here with your father, why would I leave?"

Why would she leave the man who drank their hard-earned money away, beat on her when he felt like it, and would sell his family down the river to earn a place with the Chicago Outfit? She'd been immovable—she wasn't going anywhere. Everyone would talk to see a married woman up and leave her husband, and there was no way a good Catholic like her would get a divorce.

All that work.

His sister Diana was seventeen and there was no way he'd let her live in an apartment alone. He offered her the bedroom and said he'd live on the couch.

Diana had rolled her eyes and said there was no way she'd live in an apartment with him.

"You'd be worse than a jailer, you know."

He would've made her do it, but he saw the look in her eyes—regret—and realized she wasn't saying no to him, she was saying no to leaving their mother alone.

So there he was, unable to do anything about his messed-up family.

He'd convinced the apartment super to refund his money—a handful of brass knuckles were persuasive—and he looked into what else Sam Wyatt had said.

He'd approached Sam about buying the slot machines in Everett's joint, only to find out Everett had somehow raised the money and beat him to it.

It took all Tim's control not to go and beat Everett's head in, but he tried to avoid Rett's place as much as he could these days. Looking at Rett's sister Ruby made his stomach turn in a way he didn't like. It was only a few months since their breakup, and the Vegas gossip mill was quiet now about her cheating on him with his sometimes-friend Jake Wheeler. It helped Wheeler had left town.

He didn't like spending time at Rett's roadhouse much anymore. It wasn't so much revulsion or hatred of Ruby for cheating on him, and he didn't like thinking about what it was.

So those slots were lost to him, and he needed other income. Wyatt had mentioned vending machines.

The biggest problem was vending machine companies knew they were a hot commodity with the mob, and all the old guys associated with Chicago were running them and wanted to sell at an absurd price.

They bought one machine themselves. A cigarette machine now sat in the middle of the warehouse, taunting him every time he went inside. He needed more machines, and he needed trucks to move them around town. To get trucks he needed money. He'd worry about drivers later.

With the remaining money from their work, Tim had contacted Marty out in Los Angeles, and Marty sent him straight to Tijuana and Rafael Mendoza.

Granted, Marty's last connection was that bozo Insane Wayne, who'd disappeared into the ether without paying him. Tim ran his hand along the car hood. He'd taken his payment anyway.

Mendoza was a bit player in the drug trade in Mexico. He had a business front in Tijuana and a junkyard across the border in San Ysidro. He introduced him to the Castillos, out of Mexicali, who were eager to make some American money to buy their way into the drug trade. Tim wanted cheap Mexican weapons, as his contact in Denver had already agreed to take any sight unseen.

Tim spent a few stressful weeks scraping together more cash without stepping on mob toes. Their best score ended up being a bet Jimmy Lewis made on a fight at the Hacienda. He bet the long shot, the long shot won, and Tim didn't have to murder Jimmy. He also had the money to make the deal.

Street gangs hadn't organized very much in Las Vegas yet, thanks to the Outfit. Sam Wyatt told him change was coming, the Outfit couldn't hold them back forever, and Tim hoped he was right. He'd broker this deal, make a good chunk of change, and get his ass into a vending company.

The Outfit was a problem, but Tim had asked Wyatt about that, too. The old Texan mobster recommended cutting the Outfit in on the take from this deal. He didn't like it, but giving them a percentage of his end was a price he had to pay. Paying it to Sam Wyatt to pass along to Johnny Moro didn't feel as bad as it could have.

A few minutes later Bill nodded toward the road, and Tim saw a cube truck headed toward them, kicking up dust as it rumbled along the unpaved road. The truck slowed and turned onto the hard pan, its rear doors facing them, and parked.

"You two from the Castillo outfit?" Tim asked the two men who climbed out of the truck cab.

Tim was surprised they were white. He expected Mexican nationals.

The two men nodded, but said nothing, looking at Tim with blank expressions.

"Well, open it up," Tim said. "Then you can get your money and go."

He tensed at the look the two men gave each other. Something was up. Tim reached around to feel the gun at his back and shifted it closer to his side. Something wasn't right.

He caught Bill's eye and nodded at him to step back while the two delivery men approached the truck doors at the back. The driver jostled the keys around with nervous hands, looking for the right one to open the padlock. Tim stood well to the side; he didn't want to get the stuffing shot out of him if the back of the truck was filled with armed men and not his shipment. Shit, it could be filled with cops for all he knew. White guys running with the Castillo boys didn't seem right, and Tim swallowed hard as he anticipated a flood of cops pouring out of the back of the truck with a nice prison sentence to cap off his day.

The lock fell off in the man's hands as he unlatched it, and he hooked the loop of the lock on his belt. Each man grabbed a door and swung it open.

"What the hell is this?" Tim asked.

Tim blinked as he looked in the back of the truck. Instead of wooden crates filled with weapons smuggled into Mexico and now the U.S., the back of the truck was filled with Mexicans.

He glanced at the two men, and went back to staring inside. Men, women, children . . . what the hell was this?

"I want some answers." Anger washed over him. Someone stiffed him. Half the money up front and this is what he got for his troubles. The cigar smoking joviality of the Castillos could have been a cover for stiffing him on this deal. He gestured at the duffel of money. "I came here with the other half of the cash expecting my shipment!"

"This is your shipment," the driver shrugged. "Everyone out! Vamanos!"

"Hell no, no vamanos!" Tim exclaimed as the people started pouring out of the back of the van, smelling like filth and looking like they hadn't bathed in a week. "Get the fuck back in there!"

Tim looked at the two men. One stared at the ground, while the other chewed on the end of an unlit cigar. Neither met his gaze.

"I paid half upfront for a shipment of weapons." He was about to run a hand through his hair, but stopped, not wanting to appear nervous. "Where the hell are they?"

The men shrugged. "I dunno. This is all we got. We showed up, and they loaded the truck with them. Can't tell you much more than that."

Tim whipped his Browning out, pointing it at the men. "I think you can tell me a hell of a lot more."

A woman screamed and spoke rapid, hushed Spanish. A prayer maybe.

"I swear I don't know what you were expecting, all I know is this is what we brought from Mexicali." The man swallowed hard. He held his hands out like he needed to keep Tim back. "There wasn't no weapons."

Tim looked over at Bill, who was as wide-eyed as he was. Tim had no idea how the hell this could have happened. It wasn't like someone mistook a gun for a Mexican.

"I want the rest of my money back or the weapons." He stepped closer, and cocked the hammer. "You've got five seconds to decide which."

"I don't have the money," the driver said. "That's a fact, you can search the truck. You gotta talk with the Castillo boys. I bet it's a mix-up."

"From what I heard they aren't in the habit of mixing shit up."

"You can keep these folks here and talk with the Castillo boys. Hold 'em like collateral," the driver said.

"What the hell am I supposed to do with a truckload of Mexicans?" Tim asked. His trigger finger itched. Jesus Christ, dealing with his own gang was enough to make him want to blow someone's head off at times, but this was ridiculous. "Do I look like the kinda guy who's gonna invite thirteen Mexicans over for dinner? You take them back and you tell the Castillos they give me my money or I come down there and blow their brains out."

The driver nodded and said something in Spanish. A second later two of the Mexican men in the group bolted, running through the brush toward a dry creek bed.

"I don't fucking believe this," Tim said, watching them run like jack rabbits.

The women were crying and huddled together. A small child hid in his mother's legs, snot running down his face as he screamed.

"Round them up!" Bill lost his composure as he gestured to the Mexicans. "Back in the truck!"

The driver and his passenger herded the Mexicans toward the back of the truck again. A flash of movement in the corner of his eye caught his attention, and Tim turned to see one of them, a woman, sprint for the trees. She had something in her hands.

"Shit!"

He tucked the gun back in the waistband of his jeans and ran after her. He forgot about the duffel bag, and now that bitch had his money.

Damn, she was fast.

He sprinted after her, his boots sliding on the hardpan. She was close to the trees, and he poured on a last burst of speed and tackled her. She didn't go down easy like he expected, either. She began screaming, kicking and clawing, not even minding the fact she was dirty as hell.

Bill hollered about the truck, but the duffel bag was more important than any truck. She wiggled out of his grasp again and grabbed the bag, but she got two steps before he was on her a second time. He pinned her hands to her sides, holding her legs down with his own.

"Quit moving," he grunted. She squirmed, trying to get away. "I got you; you may as well give up."

She kept moving, and he grabbed the gun and pointed it at her. Her movements slowed as she looked at the gun, her features impassive. She didn't cry or beg him like he expected.

"Get up," he huffed. He tucked the gun back in again and stood, a hand clamped around her arm. He was sick and goddamn tired of dealing with all this shit. One simple buy, that's all he wanted. One weapons buy to sell to an eager buyer who would overpay for them. It would've set them up nicely and was supposed to be an easy deal. Now this.

He hauled her to her feet. She resisted, and he was surprised at the strength she showed. She looked with a stone-faced expression, then glanced at the bag.

"Don't even think about," he said, shaking his head. He looked over at Bill jogging toward them, a slight limp in his step. It made Tim frown.

"The truck took off with the rest of them," he said. "So much for collateral. Jesus, she almost beat you."

"Fucking fantastic." The truck was speeding off into the distance, his collateral inside. He picked up the duffel and slung it over his shoulder,

9

squeezing her arm as she tried to pull away from him. "Shipment of weapons, and I got this."

Bill cracked a wry grin. "Ain't exactly an M-16, huh?"

Tim wiped the sweat from his brow. He had to get to a phone and call Mendoza about the Castillo boys and see where the hell his guns were. If they didn't make this right, he'd have to bust some heads.

Maybe that's what it was, some kind of test to see if he was a kid with no balls who'd stand for his money being stolen out from under him. They'd be surprised, then.

"Let's get outta here," Tim said. "We'll go back downtown, find a phone and call Mendoza. He turned us onto these thieves, so he better have some answers. I want the weapons or my money."

"What about her?" Bill jerked his head toward the woman.

Tim looked at her. She stared back with a mistrustful expression. She wasn't much in the way of collateral, but she was something.

Tim yanked her toward the car. "We'll see after we call Mendoza."

She looked at him, expressionless, and he pulled her to the car.

"Pendejo," she muttered.

"What did you say?" he asked. She glanced at him. "First a truck load of illegals, and now I get one with an attitude problem."

He ignored Bill's chuckle.

He put the bag of money on the ground to open the door. She kept her eye on the bag. Tim looked at the bag and then her, wondering how she knew what was in it.

"Hey," he said, shaking her. "¿Hablas inglés?"

She looked to the side, ignoring him.

"You do, don't you?" He took in her defensive posture and the way she tried to sneak looks at him. "You knew exactly what was happening, didn't you?"

She said nothing, and he wanted to shake her until his hands ached. If she spoke English, she might have heard something about what happened to the guns. Those two guys in the truck were way too cagey—they knew they were showing up with the wrong cargo.

"Come on, I don't have all day," he said. She looked at the duffel bag.

"If you think I'm giving you any cash, you've got another thing coming." He was amazed at her boldness. "You tell me what you know, and I'll think about dropping you at the nearest bus station instead of the Mexican border."

"Don't think he won't do it," Bill said, grinning from the other side of the car. "He's not real nice when he's mad."

The mention of the border changed her expression. She looked vulnerable for the first time, and he smiled to himself. It never failed. You waited long enough, and you saw the crack in the armour. She didn't want to go back to Mexico.

"Tell me what happened with the weapons, or I'll drive you back to Mexico so damn fast your head'll spin."

She pulled her arm out of his grasp and crossed them in front of her, trying to look at him with defiance, but she didn't quite get there. She tilted her head and looked him in the eye.

"I will tell you what you need to know." She spoke perfect, albeit accented, English.

"Go on."

"Later," she said. "I am a mess. I need to shower. They did not feed us. You do this for me, and we will talk."

"I find it awfully interesting you think you're in a position to bargain with me." He leaned against the car door and crossed his own arms in front of him. He didn't know what kind of game she was playing, thinking she could finesse him. "I'm the one with the gun."

"Yet you have not used it," she said. "And I gave you every reason to."

He stared for a moment, then glanced over at Bill, who shrugged. A hot shower and some food wasn't much if it would get his shipment back.

"Alright," he said. "Get in the car."

She hesitated as she looked at the Charger.

"Look lady, I don't have time for this." He yanked the driver's door open, putting the duffel bag on the seat. "You either get in the car or I put you in it."

She hesitated a moment before stepping toward him. He held the door open, moving the driver's seat forward. As she bent to get in, he grabbed her arm, and she flinched.

"I find out you're lying to me, you'll be back in Mexico so fast you won't know what hit you. Chew on that while we drive."

Her expression tightened, and he saw the tense worry shadow her face. Threats of Mexico was his leverage with this one, no doubt about it.

She got inside and sat rigidly in the back seat, as if preparing to drive to her own funeral. He looked at her for a moment before moving the seat back and getting behind the wheel.

Something wasn't right with this chick. If she had anything to do with his shipment not showing up, things weren't looking right for him, either.

2

Tim jerked the Charger into gear with more force than necessary. He gunned the engine down a flat stretch of road lined with mesquite trees, his mind reeling—he'd look like a fool if word about this got out.

He looked in the rearview mirror—the woman gripped the centre console, a mild expression of panic on her face. He pressed the gas pedal a little harder. So what if it was a petty move—she'd tried to steal his money.

"Where are you gonna take her?" Bill asked. Tim looked over at Bill, who lit a Chesterfield, bracing himself against the door as Tim took a fast corner.

Tim cranked his window, since she didn't exactly smell like a meadow, and glanced at her again. Her matted curls twisted around her in the wind, and she brushed the hair from her eyes and tucked it behind her ears to no avail. He guessed her age to be around twenty-one or two.

"My place," he said after a pause. "Your car's there, so we'd have to stop anyway. We'll call the Castillo boys from downtown and see what's going on."

Bill turned toward the backseat. "What's your name?"

Tim looked in the rearview mirror, and she glanced at Bill.

"Not a talker? She's not a talker, Tim."

"She'll be one in a little while," he said.

He pulled onto the Strip and slowed as he approached a traffic light, not in the mood to be stopped by a cop out for his monthly quota of tickets. He took another look back through the mirror. The girl stared out the window, her expression neutral, and he wondered for a moment if that's how he looked. Ruby used to tell him he looked like a stone statue.

He cruised toward downtown, turned onto North 15th and shot up across Fremont. Two-and-a-half blocks later he was outside the ramshackle shotgun house, one giant tree standing in the front yard hiding a multitude of sins. His father's car was gone, and these days he never knew if the bastard would be sober enough to get up and look for work. He had no idea why his father wasn't fired from his construction jobs more often, since he showed up late or hung over and ornery most of the time. It'd be better for all of them if he'd up and die.

He cut the engine and opened the door. He got out and slid the driver's seat forward. She struggled to get up and out of the car, using the seat for leverage. He watched her as she looked around at the shotgun houses, unkempt lawns and the construction going on around. Downtown wasn't far in the distance, and she stared at everything with little interest. He couldn't read her expression, and it bothered him.

He decided to let her loose a little and see what she'd do.

He walked toward the house, glancing back once to see if she followed. She did, but hung back, even after he opened the front door and went inside.

Bill followed him inside, and a moment later she crept up to the front door and looked into the house.

Tim rifled in the fridge and found two beers. He handed one to Bill.

"Go downtown, get all the info we got on the Castillo boys," Tim said, his voice low. "Anyone asks, don't tell them shit about what's happened."

Bill nodded and took off, his car starting up and roaring off a minute later.

The woman had ventured into the house and stood near the kitchen door, trying to appear like she wasn't nervous.

He opened the bottle of beer, the cap dancing onto the floor.

"Come on," he said, nodding toward the hall.

It took a moment before she followed, and he led her to the small bathroom. He got a towel from the linen closet and tossed it at her. She looked surprised and caught it before it hit her in the head. She tucked the towel under her arms and stood there and stared.

"What?"

"My clothes," she said. "They are dirty."

"Do I look like a fucking laundromat to you?" Tim was incredulous.

"What am I to wear after I shower?" she asked.

He sighed. She had a point. "Go get cleaned up. I'll find something."

He left the bathroom, and she shut the door behind him. He stood in the hallway and rubbed the bridge of his nose. This was one demanding chick. It burned him he needed whatever info she had. If she didn't have it, God help her.

He crossed the hall and went into his sister Diana's room. Clothes were scattered on the floor, filmy scarves stretched across the windows and posters of Mick Jagger hung haphazardly on the wall. He walked through the mess on the floor to her closet and flung the doors open.

He had no idea what a Mexican chick wore.

13

He picked through some of the clothes—clothes he knew he'd never seen before, and for good reason.

"What are you doing in my closet?"

His little sister stood in the doorway. She wore white go-go boots, a short skirt, and a sleeveless shirt she didn't have buttoned up high enough. Her hair was puffed up into a beehive she must've used an entire can of Aquanet on.

"Why are you dressed like that?"

"Everyone dresses like this," she said. "What are you doing in my room? And who's in the shower?"

"Why aren't you in school?"

"Time of the month." Her voice was sweet. He looked her over. At the rate she skipped school with that reason, she should be dying of blood loss.

"So who's in the shower?"

Tim took in a breath. Diana wasn't fond of girls he brought home, and this one would be a challenge.

He tossed a shirt at Diana and picked out a pair of blue jeans and tossed them at her too.

"What are you doing with my clothes?" She stood between him and the door with her hands on her hips.

He paused for a second and moved her out of the way and crossed the hall. He knocked on the bathroom door, opened it, and laid the clothes on the counter.

"Brought you some clean clothes," he said. She didn't answer. He looked around for a second, then gathered up the girl's filthy things, a dress and a sweater. He noticed there was no underwear amongst the clothes.

"What are you doing?" Diana asked, trying to look at what he held. She followed him out to the concrete slab that passed as a porch and over to the washing machine. "Who's in there? You don't have some floozy here again, do you?"

"Diana, buzz off," he said. He stared at the machine.

"Oh, this is rich. I bet you don't even know how to run that thing."

Jesus Christ, he didn't need this shit.

"Here," Diana said, maybe sensing he didn't have the patience to deal with her. "Put the soap in, put the clothes in, nice and even, then twist this around …"

She set to fixing the dials on the machine, and a moment later it started up.

"I swear to God, you are as useless as they come sometimes."

He said nothing, and she continued to follow him, trailing behind him in a way that made him remember her as a five-year-old kid, following him all over hell's half acre. He remembered ditching her more times than he could count, distracting her so he could get out of the house and get a moment's peace.

He sure could use that now.

"Who is she anyway?" Diana asked again. "Are you giving her my clothes? For keeps? It's not Ruby, is it?"

"Diana, go watch some television or something, I don't have time for this," he said.

The water was off in the bathroom. At least the broad didn't take too long in the shower. A hair dryer started up a moment later.

"I don't believe this!" Diana pouted. "Is she using all my things?"

"Diana, get in your room," he said.

He shoved her down the hall and into her room. Diana stood in the doorway, her anger visible in the frown on her face. He wondered again what it would be like to have a brother instead.

The hair dryer cut off a minute later, and Diana pushed past him toward the bathroom.

The door opened a second later.

The girl stood there in Diana's clothes, her hair looking longer and darker since it was wet. She looked at his sister with a curious expression.

Diana crossed her arms. "I never said she could have my clothes!"

"Shut up, Diana. Hers were filthy; you saw 'em."

"Who is she?" Diana asked.

Who *was* she? It was a damn good question.

"It's business, Diana."

"What, you finish with all the girls in Las Vegas and move onto Mexicans now?" she sneered.

Tim tried to shove her toward her bedroom, but Diana charged past him and went into the bathroom.

"You didn't touch any of my stuff, did you?" Diana asked, looking at all the things on the vanity. "Dammit, Tim, what're you doing bringing a girl like this back here? Does she even speak English?"

The girl tilted her head to the side, appraising Diana. "You are very beautiful."

Diana looked at her, her brows knitted together in suspicion. "Well . . . thanks." Her voice thawed a trifle. Tim watched the woman, wondering what her game was.

"Thank you for lending the clothes," the woman said. "I will return them."

"Well . . . the shirt doesn't fit no more, you know, in the bust?" Diana said. "And the jeans are old. You can keep them, I guess."

15

Tim looked at the woman. With a few words, she'd managed to calm Diana and had a new wardrobe. She was an odd one, and he figured at some point he ought to learn her name.

"Diana, get outta here," he said. "We gotta talk."

"First, I would like to eat," the woman said. She looked over, as if challenging him to go back on their deal.

"You better feed her, she's looking as skinny as you are," Diana said. "And that's saying something."

He went down the hall to the kitchen and tugged on the refrigerator door. He looked inside with a shrug.

"Help yourself to what you want," he said. "Leave the beer."

The woman hesitated for a split second before moving toward the refrigerator and flinging the door open wider. She took out some cold cuts, got bread from the bread box, then made a sandwich. Tim was surprised when she took out extra bread and made a second.

"You'll make yourself sick if you eat that much." He lit a cigarette and took out his switchblade, watching with pleasure as she jumped when he flicked it open.

"It is for you," she told him. "She is right, you are too skinny."

"Don't think I'm gonna forget what you did this afternoon because you're putting a sandwich in front of me." He picked underneath his nails with the blade. "My memory isn't that short."

She said nothing and laid the sandwich in front of him a moment later. She poured herself a glass of milk and sat at the table, said a soft prayer in Spanish and ate like she hadn't seen food in a good long while. Judging by her skinny arms, she hadn't.

He took another gulp of his beer. Diana hovered in the kitchen doorway. "Diana, get lost."

His sister put her hands on her hips. "I wanna know what's going on."

"Get lost," he said again. "She's helping me with something. Business. And we gotta talk. Privately."

"Right," Diana said, sarcasm dripping from the words. "Business. Like this business you have makes you so much money I'm rolling around in the lap of luxury living with mom and that drunken pothole."

She grabbed a pack of Winstons off the counter and went down the hall, her door slamming.

Tim turned to the Mexican girl.

"Now we talk," he said. Her gaze wavered as he stared at her. "Where the hell is my shipment?"

She tried to think of a good story the entire time.

She relished the shower and craved the food, but most of all, she needed the time to think. She couldn't tell him what Manuel did, because that would mean telling him why. God knew what he would do with her if she didn't give answers he liked.

He frightened her, his face a lopsided mess of scars on one side, his chin scarred, and his eyes untrusting and blank. He scared her with his fast driving and the switchblade. Despite that, she didn't think he would hurt her, not yet. He didn't remind her of Calderón, who was rough like this man, but had a sadistic streak that scared her. This Tim was angry, but his anger was purposeful. She could work with that.

She was glad the girl was in the house. It made her feel safe, even though the small girl wouldn't be able to help if something bad happened. The girl— he called her Diana—was a problem until she realized placating her vanity would win her over. The counter was littered with cheap perfumes, makeup and costume jewellery. She didn't lie in calling the girl beautiful; she told her what she wanted to hear most in the world.

"Well, come on." His voice snapped her out of her daydream. "Out with it."

"Your weapons are in a safe place." She chose her words with care. "The Castillos are aware you do not have them. You *will* have them, that much I know."

"Quit talking in riddles and give me some goddamn answers. Where the hell are they?"

She looked Tim in the eyes. "If I tell you, you will let me go?"

"You think I wanna keep you around here, you got another thing coming."

"You will let me go?" she asked again. He was adept at avoiding questions.

"I don't have any use for you once I get my hands on those weapons." He blew a stream of cigarette smoke toward her, and this time she tried not to flinch at his action. He hadn't answered her. She didn't think he would, so she weighed her options before speaking.

"There is a man who works closely with the Castillos. It was important his shipment get across the border first."

"The people?"

She nodded.

"So where are the weapons?"

"They are in México," she said.

"You know where?" he asked her.

She hesitated a moment and shrugged, not wanting to give too much away.

"Come on," he said. He ground his cigarette out in an overflowing ashtray on the table.

She looked at him in confusion, and he stood and grabbed her arm. She tried to yank it away, panic enveloping her. She imagined the knife, the guns—so many weapons for someone so young. He pulled her into the living room and toward the front door.

"Where are we going?" she asked, trying to keep the fear out of her voice.

"I've got a phone call to make and you're gonna be there, since you seem to know what the hell is going on."

Her legs tensed, and she contemplated running in a panic, but he tightened his grip on her arm. He took her out to the car and opened the passenger door. She glanced around the neighbourhood, looking for anything that might stand out to her, anything that could tell her something was wrong and she needed to run instead of get in the car.

"Get in," he said. "You don't much have a choice in the matter anyway."

She slid into the front passenger seat, hoping she made the right decision. He shut the door and circled around the car to the driver's side, and she flirted with the idea of running. She looked up and down the block—the streets were flat and empty, and there were few places to hide. He would catch up to her in a split second in the car, and he caught her on foot before.

She stayed in her seat.

He got in and started the car up and forced it into gear, tearing away from the curb. She said a quick prayer for her life.

"What's your name anyway?" he asked.

She hesitated again, unsure what she wanted him to call her. She went by many names over the years, some which brought fear and others that reminded her of home.

"María Guadalupe," she stated.

"Got anything shorter than that?" he asked, pausing at a red light to pop the lighter in on the dash.

She hesitated. "Lupe. You can call me Lupe."

"Loopy's about the word for you," he agreed. "You don't seem too sure of your name."

"It is my name." Regret at sharing her real name washed over her—she should have given a fake name. He could tell the wrong person on the phone, and it could be the end.

At least he wouldn't be calling her María.

"Your name is Tim?" she asked, desperate for a distraction.

He nodded.

She turned toward the window and cranked it down. She watched the scenery fly by, conscious of nothing but the wind on her face. She needed to get away from here as soon as she could. A little of that money would have gone a long way for her, much longer than the small amount she got from Manuel, who gave her American dollars in return for her pesos. She suspected he gave her more than her pesos were worth.

They drove down a street crammed with casinos. A giant cowboy towered up the side of one building. Binions, the Golden Nugget, the South Seas, The Mint . . . the giant signs, bright colours and flashing lights were overwhelming in the daylight and she couldn't imagine them at night. It was as if Méxicali's zona roja had grown into a huge monster.

He turned down a side street and into an industrial area, skirting along train tracks. They left the casinos behind and soon he pulled the car into an alley that butted up against a brick building. He got out of the car, and she hesitated until he came over and yanked the passenger door open.

"I'm not gonna get in the habit of opening the door for you, so you may as well learn to get out and follow me," he said. She stood, and he shut the door and turned and walked toward the building. He didn't grab her this time. She followed him, curious why he let her loose now. He paused and turned to her.

"You don't say one word about the shipment, the money, Mexico or everything going to shit, you got it?" Tim asked. "You do, and I swear to God I'll put you in the car and drive you to Mexico myself."

She swallowed hard, the thought of crossing back across the border terrifying her for a minute. Part of her wanted to go and retrieve the one thing she could use. She was naked, with nothing to bargain for her life if it came to it.

He waited for a reply, and she nodded her assent. It seemed to satisfy him, as he turned and walked toward the building again. She hustled to keep up with his long strides.

He walked toward a broken corrugated door set off its hinges. He moved it and nodded to her to come in.

The building was darker than the outside, and it took a moment for her eyes to adjust. Inside, there were a few young men sitting on old furniture in the centre of the large room, playing cards and smoking, candles and camping lanterns there for when it got dark. A few of them looked up as Tim came into the room, and they all called out greetings. He must be their leader.

"Where's Bill?" Tim asked.

"Your office," a handsome man with dark hair and brown eyes said, holding his cards close to his chest. "Who you got there?"

Tim looked back at her. "That's Lupe."

He asked her to keep quiet, so she did.

The dark-haired man's eyes had a wolfish look she tried to ignore. He looked at her with a piercing gaze, and she looked at the blue jeans and the shirt Tim's sister gave her. She looked like any other nice girl, even if she wore pants, and she was clean and presentable. His staring made her nervous.

"Who's got cigarettes? I'm out," Tim asked.

A few of the men patted their pockets and came out with a handful of cigarettes they tossed into a pile on the table. Tim picked one out, struck a match and lit it, cringing.

"Who's the asshole buying mentholated?" He crushed it on the table and picked out another.

"Lupe, huh? Where are you from?" the dark-haired one asked her.

She looked to her left, where he sat balanced on the arm of the old couch, his cards tucked into the pocket of his shirt.

"Can it, Ray." Tim walked over to what looked like a makeshift kitchen, hunting around for something in the cupboards. The bank of dirty windows lit the room with a yellow glow.

This Ray looked her up and down.

"You Mexican?"

She looked over at Tim. His back was to them.

Ray nudged the man beside him, a hulking blond with a thick brow and scowl on his face. Ray whispered something to the guy, and he looked her over too.

Something about their faces, something predatory, made her turn away and walk closer to Tim.

He turned back around, not finding what he'd been looking for. He turned toward a hallway, nodding at her to follow. She supposed the building was a warehouse in its past life, maybe a manufacturing plant, like the ones in Méxicali.

The hallway was littered with old newspapers and empty beer bottles. Tim opened a door and held it, waiting for her. His friend Bill sat behind a desk playing darts, his chair tilted back dangerously.

"What's up?" he asked as Tim came into the room, lowering the chair legs to the floor.

"Where's the phone? I couldn't find it." Tim asked.

Bill leaned down and picked up a black phone. The wires led out the back of it and up through an open window.

"It connects outside on the telephone pole," Bill said, noticing her gaze. He gestured at her to come near the window. The wires were strung right up to the box near the top of the pole. "Jesse, that's the blond out there that doesn't look like a Neanderthal, he's Tim's cousin, he climbed right up there to string those wires."

Lupe looked toward Bill. He was a little older than Tim, but his face was friendlier now. He had long sideburns and a quick grin.

"I'm Bill," he said, extending his hand.

She smiled at the gesture and shook his hand. "I am Lupe."

"Lupe?" he asked. "What's that, Spanish or something?"

She nodded. "It is in honour of Nuestra Señora de Guadalupe."

"I dunno what the hell that is," Bill admitted. "Sounds kinda nice."

"Our Lady of Guadalupe," Tim said. "The Virgin Mary."

"You speak Spanish?" Lupe was surprised he hid this bit of information, but maybe she shouldn't be. He was suspicious, and he talked little.

Tim shrugged. "Some."

"Learned it in prison," Bill said, winking.

She was inclined to believe him, considering this Tim bought illegal weapons and looked like he'd taken more than his share of beatings.

"Called Mendoza in San Ysidro, no answer," Bill said. "What do you want to do?"

Tim walked over and took Lupe's arm, using less force than before, and sat her on a ratty old couch.

"What we're gonna do," he said, "is I'm gonna call the Castillo boys direct and ask them what the hell is going on and see what they know about you."

"No. Please. I will talk to them."

Tim shook his head and picked up the phone, and she closed her eyes. Manuel didn't tell them anything about her. He was unsure the Castillos could be trusted.

She opened her eyes when Tim spoke and relaxed as she realized Manuel answered the phone.

"Yeah, well, I got a girl here who says otherwise," Tim said. He held the phone out to her. She took it, thinking about what she could say to help herself.

"Manuel?" she asked.

"Lupe?" he asked. "What happened? Who is this man?"

She spoke to him in rapid Spanish, hoping Tim couldn't keep up.

"They did not let us out like they said they would," Lupe said. "They took us to Las Vegas, and the man you are talking to is the one who expected the guns."

"Dios," Manny swore. "What have you told him?"

"Nothing," she said.

"Start speaking English," Tim said. He tapped his fingers on the table.

21

"I told him the Castillos know he does not have the weapons," she said in Spanish, watching Tim's brows knit together in frustration. "I told him I knew where they were. If I tell him, I think he will let me go."

"Be careful," Manuel said. "Calderón's men are asking questions in town again. The Castillos suspect, but I don't think they'll tell. I have heard they are eager to take Calderón's territory. There will be a war, and they will not risk anything right now. I believe they are to be trusted."

Tim snatched the phone out of her hand.

"I said English," he told her again.

"He does not speak English well," she lied. "He was confused."

"Then you ask him about my shipment," he said.

Lupe nodded.

"He wants to know about his shipment. What should I tell him?" she asked Manuel.

"Tell him where the shipment is. The Castillos won't be angry if he comes for it himself. If he's so concerned about it, he'll leave you to come for it," Manuel said. "Stay away from México, Lupe. Stay safe."

She handed the phone back to Tim, and he spent another frustrating minute trying to get the same info out of Manuel before he got fed up and hung up the phone.

"Well?" he asked, looking tense and angry. His agitation had started the moment she spoke Spanish. She remembered how frightened she'd been at the Casa, when the men who spoke English would come. She had not known what they'd said then, and the terror and frustration of not understanding what would happen to her drove her half-mad.

Tim did not look like the kind of man used to being uninformed and in the dark.

"Your weapons are at the Castillos' warehouse in Méxicali," she said. "You can come for them."

"I can come for them?" he asked. "You've got to be fucking kidding me. They mess things up, and I have to go pick up my own shipment? No . . . that's not how it works."

"Why the hell was there a mix-up anyway?" Bill asked.

Tim looked over at Lupe, and she shrugged.

"You did not tell me to ask that."

"Yeah, you spent an awfully long time chatting. What the hell were you saying?" Tim asked.

She froze, and Tim stood and moved in front of her.

"I'm tired of your bullshit." His voice was low and angry. "What did you say to him?"

She weighed her options.

"The men driving the truck were supposed to let us out along the way. They were to come to you empty-handed and tell you about your weapons," she said. "They decided otherwise as they drove. They thought it better to have something than nothing."

"Where were they supposed to drop you?" Bill asked.

"Manuel did not tell me. He said we could be let out anywhere," she said. "I assumed a city, but it could have been the side of the road."

"Is Manuel the one who put you in the truck?" Tim asked. "He's the one trafficking illegals over the border?"

She said nothing, but he nodded anyway.

"That's what I thought," he said. "So now you can tell me what the hell the game is, because it doesn't make any sense."

She swallowed hard and looked around the room. There was no way out, and she didn't like the look of him right now. She looked at the scars on the left side of his face and chin, the off-kilter look of his face doing nothing to soften the hard look in his eyes.

"Bill, take a walk," Tim said, not breaking eye contact with her. "Lupe and I need to have a talk."

Bill got up to leave, and Tim noticed, as he always did, whenever his right-hand man sat too long it took more time for him to rise out of a chair. A bullet in the leg did that to him, and it was one Tim put there. Even though necessary, he didn't like the constant reminder, and the slight limp Bill got when it was damp or cold was a reminder.

Tim watched Lupe's expression as Bill shut the office door behind him. The fear was plain in her eyes, and he could use that. She stared at the door, like she might try to make a break for it, and he moved so he was in front of it.

"I want you to tell me what the hell is going on," he said to her.

"There is nothing," she said.

"Oh, I think there's something," Tim said. "You don't ship a truck full of illegals over the border out of the goodness of your heart. They pay for the luxury or you ship them over to a factory or something—they go to someone. So if they weren't going somewhere specific and someone out there didn't get their weekly order of Mexicans, then this was a cover for something."

Her eyes darted from side to side.

"Lupe, out with it, alright?" He was tired of all the talk. "This cat and mouse is getting old."

"Cat and mouse?" The confusion on her face was genuine.

"This game," he said. "Why'd this Manuel ship these people over the border and into thin air in place of my weapons?"

"You would have to ask him," she said.

"You know I can't do that, since you said he doesn't speak English." He moved closer to her. "Which is bull. He'd need to know English to deal with the border guards, the paperwork and his contacts in America."

"He helps people. Sends them over the border for money," she said. "That is all I know."

"You know a hell of a lot more than that." Blood pounded in his ears. She double talked like the best of them.

She looked at the floor, steeling herself for something, then looked up at him through her lashes. He was surprised when she moved closer to him.

"I was eager to come to America," she said. "I have been told much about it."

Her voice was soft, and she closed the distance between them considerably. The sudden change in her demeanour was odd.

"I do not know anything about weapons." She stepped close to him and placed a hand on his chest. "But there are other things I know of."

She ran her hands down his chest. He stared at her and was startled when her hands skirted his midsection, and she reached for his belt buckle.

"What the hell are you doing?" he asked.

"It is alright," she said. Her body shook almost imperceptibly. "Perhaps I owe you this after all the trouble."

He pushed her hands away. "Cut it out."

He remembered a girl like her, Rosa from the ranch in California where he'd met with Insane Wayne. Something else danced on the edge of his mind, a memory he didn't like, so he shut his mind to it.

"Many men like for me to do this," she said. "It will not cost you anything. A favour."

"You gotta be kidding me," he muttered. He grabbed her wrists, harder than he meant to, and she cried out—in pain or fear, he didn't know. "What the hell did you do in Mexico?"

"I work," she said.

"Yeah, and I bet I know where." He pushed her away from him. "Christ, not only do I pickup a thief with an attitude, she turns out to be a whore, too. Lemme guess, like Boy's Town?"

She frowned and nodded. "Sí. It is called the zona de tolerancia. A zona roja. Red zone."

He rubbed his eye. He gave his sister's clothes to a prostitute. Not to mention he brought her to his house and now his headquarters. He was soft in the head.

24

"Most men are happy to find this out."

"I'm not most men," he said.

"I can see."

He sat in the chair, trying to figure out what his next move would be. He'd feel like a punk going to get his own shipment, and there was the convenient fact he'd get caught red-handed heading over the border with it.

He needed to talk to Mendoza and find out if this was a set-up.

Then there was the matter of what to do with Lupe.

He looked over. She had moved herself closer to the corner of the room, her back near the wall, her arms crossed like she wanted to stay warm. He didn't get it. One minute she tried her best to stay fifty feet from him, the next she crawled all over him like a disease.

She got in a truck with twelve others and rode with little food or water to get here and claimed the truck had no destination to let everyone off. No one to meet them, no one to put them to work.

In his experience, that added up to something wrong. The fact she left home with no known destination made that something wrong only one thing.

"Lupe." She looked at him, and he wondered if she was as old as he thought. "Who are you running from?"

3

Lupe frowned at his question.

"I am not running." Her voice trembled when she spoke, and that was all he needed to confirm his suspicions.

"Bull." He leaned forward. "You get in that truck, knowing you'll be let off in the middle of nowhere in a foreign country to fend for yourself. That's a stupid way to start a new life. People desperate enough to do that are running from something. Pimp?"

She shook her head, her brow wrinkled.

When he served time, the Mexicans in for pandering called each other something. He struggled for the word.

"Padrote?"

She hesitated a moment. "Sí. Yes."

"Great," he muttered.

"Manuel promised he could get me to America. I asked no other questions."

"Yeah, well you should have," he told her. "Stupid as hell to not know where you're going."

"Away," she said. "That was all I needed to know."

She paced over to the window again. The sun was setting, bathing the room in a dim gold light. It would be dark soon, and there was no light in the building at night, save for candles, lanterns and some flashlights.

He leaned back in the office chair, wondering what the hell to do with her. He didn't want to let her go yet. Mendoza may learn something useful about her that would help him. For all he knew, Lupe could be running a scam herself. Better to keep a possible problem close in case it ran out of control.

He'd spent plenty of nights in the room down the hall. He crashed there most of the time now, since it wasn't at home with his old man. It was a good place to rest up after a fight, or a place to bring a girl when Rett's was

26

too crowded. He watched Lupe's shoulders rise and fall as she breathed. She was nervous.

"You can stay here tonight. There's a room with a mattress you can use." It'd taken awhile to find another after he almost bled out on the other mattress a few months back.

"Am I not free to go?" She turned around and looked with a mixture of anger and fear.

"No sense in going anywhere if I'm offering up a place to stay, is there?" he said. "There's nothing stopping you from picking up and leaving in the middle of the night."

She said nothing, but Tim sensed he hooked her. She looked undecided, but there was tiredness in her face. He wondered when she last slept.

"The room's clean," he said. "May as well stay here than on the street. No one can find you here."

He buried that nail last, satisfied when she nodded.

"Alright," she said. "I will stay. But only for tonight."

Tim nodded and kept the tight smile to himself.

Lupe followed him out of his makeshift office toward another door farther down the hallway. He opened the door and waved her inside.

She was surprised; it was nicer than the room she shared at the Casa.

A mattress, in good condition, sat on the cement floor. An overturned orange crate sat next to the bed, with an ashtray and empty beer bottle on top. Newspapers were scattered around the room, and she noted some of the crossword puzzles were filled in and wondered if he did them.

Tim waved a hand toward the bed. "Blankets are pretty clean."

"There is no . . . " She frowned, not wanting to ask him. "To shower? Or . . . "

"Oh. Right."

He gestured for her to follow him, went into the hallway, then turned toward a large metal door at the end of the hall. A key hung beside it.

"The building next door has a working bathroom," he said. "It's used as a warehouse, so I cut a deal with the manager, he leaves this door unlocked from his side. Use the key to get in, the bathroom is the first door on the right. Warehouse is busy by seven in the morning; they clear out at four in the afternoon. Don't be in there when they are."

He unlocked the door and opened it. She went into the bathroom, which contained a sink and toilet. She attempted to brush her teeth with some water and her finger. She was dismayed at her appearance in the small mirror above the sink; she looked tired and old despite the shower and new clothes.

She used the toilet, washed her face and tried to comb her curls. Tim waited in the hall, knocking a few minutes later.

"Hurry it up, I don't have all night."

She opened the door and followed him back into their side of the building.

"Always lock it." He did so and hung the key on the nail again.

"I will be here alone?" she asked.

He shrugged. "Some of my boys may be here, but they won't go in the bedroom. They know better than that."

She followed him back toward the makeshift bedroom, and he stood outside the door as she went inside.

"I'll be back tomorrow," he said. "If you leave, you leave."

She nodded. "And if I do not?"

"Doesn't matter to me either way," he said.

She wasn't sure she believed him. She wasn't sure if she believed anyone these days. He had a suspicious look in his eye, like he knew she lied about everything.

He nodded and left without a goodbye.

She shut the door, happy to see a slide lock on the back, but it was loose and wouldn't stay bolted. She gathered up the blankets and shook them out; they were clean like he said. They smelled like the aftershave she detected on his skin. She frowned, steeled herself, and smelled the blankets. She was relieved when she didn't recognize the scent.

She could sleep in these.

She laid a blanket on the mattress, then covered herself with the other, unable to sleep without something covering her. The warehouse was cooler than she expected from the hot temperature outside. She turned over a few times to get comfortable, then stared at the wall. The room had no windows and it was as dark as a tomb, but somehow it reassured her.

For the first time since she left México, she relaxed.

Tim was unsure, and if there was one thing in the world he hated most, it was feeling unsure.

Bill was out in the main room playing poker with the rest of the guys. Jimmy was missing—his old man had him work at the Lucky Lady tending bar on busy nights.

Tim waited until Bill looked his way and nodded at him. Bill folded—a lousy hand since he'd never fold otherwise—and joined him near an old icebox they kept a few beers in when they had money for some.

"She's a prostitute."

Bill raised an eyebrow. "Do I wanna know how you know that?"

Tim pressed his lips together. "I want to go call Mendoza. But not from here. I don't want the boys to hear this."

Bill glanced over his shoulder to look at the crew, and Tim did the same. He frowned at Ray Roth, who had wandered toward a table close to him and Bill and grabbed an ashtray, despite there being two already on the table they were playing at. He waited until Ray sat again and looked over the group.

They were tough as nails and had followed him into things that had put them up against the Chicago Outfit. It took a lot of guts to run on your own when the Outfit was in your way more than the cops. Each of the guys had their purpose.

Carl Hamilton was all hulking intimidation, and he had the muscle to back it up, if not the brains. No one wanted to go toe-to-toe with him.

His cousin Jesse got in more fights than Tim could count, mostly for dumb reasons. He couldn't control his mouth, and it got him in fights and locked up more than anyone else. He didn't have the control to be ruthless, and sometimes Tim thought it might be for the best.

Pete Malcolm brought guns and technical know-how, although his nervousness made everyone else nervous. He always looked a second away from passing out with his pale skin and twitchy demeanour.

Jimmy Lewis, absent tonight, handled money and betting like he was born to it, even though his penchant for women meant he was tangled up in a lot of ways he shouldn't be.

Adam Barnes was all fists and good nature, and sometimes that got the job done better than a gun or intimidation. He wasn't around tonight, and neither was his brother Dale, who worked late managing the bowling alley at the Showboat. Dale was a bit older than the others, and not cut out for a life of defying the mob, but he had brains, and Tim let him hang around, even if he wasn't part of the inner circle.

It was the same with guys like Eddie Demarco, a valet on the Strip who drove getaway better than anyone, or Dave Brown who was tops with any lock, while Tommy Martin could hotwire a car in the blink of an eye. Frankie D, a captain at the dining room at the Dunes, kept him apprised of all the mob comings and goings he heard, and Joey 'The Rat' Dunn . . . well, he came by his name honestly, trading information like he was born to it.

Those guys weren't the inner circle though - not in the group, but not on the outside, either.

Guys like Bill and—he hated to admit it, Ray Roth—were thinkers, who used their brains as well as their fists. Everyone had a place, and his was to lead.

It bothered him to feel like he was set adrift at sea and something loomed on the horizon—a storm maybe—and there was no way to fight it.

"Keep these guys busy for a bit and make sure they all leave—all of them," Tim said. "I don't want anyone getting any ideas with her here."

Bill frowned. "You think they'd try something?"

"She might. She's running from a pimp or something. Could be trouble."

"Will do. There's a blackjack tourney going on at Binion's, I'll convince them to go up there."

Tim nodded and left the building as quietly as he could, letting the boys continue their game of five card draw.

He got in the Charger and drove toward Fremont, pulling into a gasoline station and parking the car near a pay phone. He grabbed a fistful of dimes from the glove box. The neon station sign hissed and popped as he opened the door to the phone booth and jammed it shut. He plunked his dimes in and dialled the number in Tijuana, Mexico. Bill had tried him in San Ysidro, but Tim had his other number across the border.

"Mendoza," the man's familiar voice answered.

"It's Kelly," he said.

"Your shipment arrived alright?"

"Not even close." Tim let him know about the situation.

"Give me a half an hour. I'll see what I can learn."

Tim gave him the pay phone number and hung up the phone, then sat in the car for awhile, his head aching. A half hour later the pay phone rang, and he wasn't surprised at Mendoza's news.

"Your shipment is sitting in Mexicali," he said. "The Castillos have it."

"I figured. Some guy named Manuel sent the illegals over. I didn't get a last name. I need you to find out who he is. Lupe said he didn't speak English, but you know as well as I do that's bullshit."

"Lupe?" he asked.

"One of the illegals. They took off without her and a few others that ran off," Tim told him. "Something's up with her. She said she worked in something like Boy's Town, and her pimp was after her, so she ran from him."

"Not unusual," Mendoza said. "Many girls will come through the border to escape them."

"Something isn't right with her," Tim said. "She knows too much about that shipment, and this truck full of illegals wasn't headed anywhere. I think she knows more than she's telling. I'm not about to haul my ass down to Mexicali and get caught bringing my shipment through or get involved in some Mexican gang war that isn't my business."

Tim could hear Mendoza puff on a cigar. He had only met Mendoza in San Ysidro, and the air in his tinny auto parts building was always thick with cigar smoke.

"Juan goes to see his family in Mexicali often. I'll send him to ask about her in their zona," he said. "We will find answers for you."

He said goodbye and hung up, more in control now he had feelers out. Mendoza was motivated—he'd only been paid half of his fee for connecting Tim with this job. The other half would come after the deal was complete.

If anyone could find out information about what went on in Mexicali or Calexico, Mendoza would. He had connections with gangs, criminals and plain average people; he was a good man to go into business with.

Tim got into the car and leaned forward, resting his head on the steering wheel for a moment. He remembered how Lupe changed tactics with him, her look seductive, her hands roaming. It made his skin crawl and reminded him too much of Rosa. The Californians he worked with a few months back thought it was something to have a Mexican whore at their place, but she was trouble. He was glad he didn't have to work with them now. He wondered if he didn't guess Lupe's profession, if her actions would have turned him on, Mexican girl or not.

Some other memory tried to force its way into his brain, but he shut his mind to it.

Lupe was worse than Rosa in some ways. Rosa stayed with Wayne and his right-hand man Sykes. He imagined Lupe, working at a place like Boy's Town, was passed around a lot more than Rosa was. He was relieved things had fallen out with Wayne—the upside to losing that operation was no longer dealing with that sneaking whore. He'd come back on his last run with fifteen dollars missing from his wallet, and he was sure she snatched it from him somehow.

He opened his eyes. The neon from the gas station sign stung his eyes, and he waited a moment before he started the car. In the past he'd spend the night at Rett's, but not since things went south with Ruby.

Instead, he pointed the car down the street and headed to the Galaxy Motel for the night.

Saturday, October 29, 1966

Lupe gasped for breath and bolted upright, brushing hair out of her face, the vestiges of her nightmare clinging to her like sweat.

She looked around, but it was pitch black. Panic swept her as she tried to remember where she was. She turned over, tangled in the blanket, and the memories came flooding back—she wasn't in the Casa; she wasn't at la zona. She was somewhere safe.

That word sounded foreign in her head.

She lay back on the pillow, willing her heartbeat to slow. The blankets were clenched in her fists, and she made herself loosen her grip and wiped her sweaty palms on them. The nightmare was always the same: Calderón's weight crushing her; his grunts, the cloying, nauseating smell of cigars and cologne mingling with the pain when he entered her. She wanted to throw up.

She knew it was a dream and tried her hardest to wake up each time. She would break through the fog, open her eyes and take a breath, relieved to wake from the horrible nightmare, then look up and see him standing in the doorway, loosening his belt; a nightmare within a nightmare.

As her heart slowed and her breathing returned to normal she allowed herself a few moments of leisure before getting up. She could tell it was morning from the light under the door.

She left the room and walked to the big metal door, took the key ring from its peg and listened. She heard no noise and opened the door cautiously. The warehouse was deserted, so it must be before seven o'clock. The sky was lighter, but it wasn't yet dawn.

She went to the bathroom, washed her face and drank her fill of water before she returned to the bedroom. She curled up on the mattress again and dozed. It felt safer than anything since she'd left, but she couldn't relax. México slipped away from her as slow as molasses, and, in rare moments, she pretended there was nothing to go back to. She pretended she was happy with running.

She wiped tears off her face.

A metal scraping noise echoed through the empty warehouse, and she froze. Her heart pounded in her ears, a rhythmic swish she tried to quell so she could hear better. She slowed her breathing; Calderón's men wouldn't laugh and joke if they were coming for her, like these voices were. They would creep in with sick efficiency and kill her in her sleep. She crept toward the door and listened for a moment, unsure if she should leave the room.

Her stomach growled, and she placed a hand over her midsection. It was as good a reason as any.

She opened the door and made sure the clothes Tim's sister lent her looked presentable. She knew her hair was in desperate need of a comb, but her fingers would have to do. She stopped grooming herself when she realized it was what she did in the Casa and la zona, before the men came for her.

She walked into the cavernous room and saw some of the men from the night before. The dark-haired man, Ray, was there, along with two others, the hulking one and a pale blond. Before she could melt back into the shadows of the hallway, Ray spotted her.

"You're here," he said. "Good."

Why that was good, she didn't know. She did know the look in his eyes made her back up against the wall.

"Come over here, sit for a minute."

She didn't reply.

"Maybe she doesn't speak English," the pale one said.

"She does."

"How do you know?"

"Tim doesn't speak Spanish very well."

Ray put his hands in front of him in a conciliatory gesture and took something out of his pocket. Cookies.

She knew better, but she approached the table anyway. Food and shelter always made her stupid.

"Lupe, right?" Ray said. His voice was smooth, buttery . . . too nice. She'd seen men like this all her life. A kind word, a nice smile, all to hide the violence beneath them.

She reached for the cookie he offered, and he grabbed her wrist. She tried to yank it away, but he was stronger.

He was looking over her arms.

"No tracks," he said.

She tried to yank her arm away again. He traced the outline of pale scars on her wrist.

"But it looks like she doesn't stay where she's told."

She looked into his eyes in alarm.

He grinned at her like a shark.

"I heard Tim tell Bill you're a whore." He yanked on her arm. "What do you think, Carl? She fit in?"

Carl nodded. "Not sure how much market we'd have for a Mexican though."

"She's got light eyes. Lighten her hair up a bit, maybe, I think she'd do okay."

She pulled away from Ray's hands, caressing her hair.

"What are you talking about?" she asked. Her voice sounded scared, and she hated that.

"Tim isn't going to do much with you. Word has it he needs some information from you or something. Why he wouldn't beat it out of you and get it over with is beyond me. But that'd ruin the merchandise."

She swallowed hard. She let her body relax as much as she could. It wasn't the first time men had come for her like this, and it wouldn't be the last. She could tamp down the fear and use it to make them go away.

She tried to change her expression and move closer to Ray. He stopped her before she got there.

"I'm not that stupid," he said. He shoved her back into Carl. "We either take her now and tell him she took off or we can wait and see what he does. And you know me. I hate waiting."

Carl's grip on her wasn't as strong, and she elbowed him in the gut and ran for the door.

Ray was on her a second later, grabbing her by the hair and yanking her back toward him. He took her wrist and bent it at a painful angle. She cried out despite her best efforts.

"What's going on here?"

In the doorway was the blond—the one Bill called Tim's cousin—and another man she hadn't seen the night before. He had dark hair and a handsome face, a scar on one cheek. He walked into the room, his eyes troubled and his expression holding warning in it.

"I don't particularly like walking into a room and seeing anyone with their hands on a woman."

"Ah, get lost, Jimmy." The hulking one—Carl—stood taller, but Jimmy didn't back away. She liked him already.

"From what Jesse told me, this young lady came in here last night a guest of Tim's." He circled toward Ray. "Be a shame to tell Tim you were less than gentlemanly. If I remember right, he knocked you out once for putting hands on Ruby, and he didn't even know her then. Be interesting to see what he'd do for someone he trusted enough to let stay here overnight."

"Yeah." Jesse's tacked on response was almost comical. He seemed younger than the others, but he was on the right side, and that said what she needed to know.

She yanked her arm out of Ray's grasp and hurried closer to Jesse and this other man—Jimmy.

Ray spread his hands. "No need to threaten, Jim. Me and Lupe were just having a chat."

"Pendejo," she muttered.

The corner of Jimmy's mouth rose.

"You should get lost before I decide you backing off isn't enough." Jimmy looked over at Ray coolly.

"I'm gonna pick Diana up anyway, she wanted a ride," Ray said.

"Tim finds out you're seeing her, and you'll be pissing blood," Jesse remarked.

"That's why no one's gonna say nothing," Ray said. "She's a big girl; she can take care of herself."

"You sure about that, Ray?" Jimmy asked.

"None of your business, Lewis." Ray bumped Jimmy's shoulder as he walked past.

"We're outta here," Carl said. He followed Ray to the door, with the pale one close behind.

She let out a breath when the corrugated metal door was shifted back into place.

"Don't mind them," Jesse said to her.

"No, you mind them completely," Jimmy countered. "Shouldn't be here on your own. Where's Tim?"

She shrugged. "He allowed me to stay. I do not know if he will return."

"Hey, you speak English!" Jesse said.

She nodded at Jesse.

"Thank you both," she said.

"What were they on about?" Jimmy asked.

She looked at the door. She wondered how much Tim knew about these men and their ventures. As nice as these two were, it might be safer to keep the information to herself.

"I do not know," she said.

Jimmy looked at her, and she avoided his gaze.

"Hey, Jesse? If I remember right, that icebox was pretty empty last time I looked. Maybe you oughta go over to the gas station and get some ice so we can put some beer in there later."

Jesse looked at Jimmy in annoyance but nodded. "Yeah, alright."

He loped out of the building.

"Where from?" Jimmy asked her, tucking a cigarette behind his ear.

"México."

"Oh, I figured that. Tijuana?"

"Méxicali."

"Good Chinese food down there."

She frowned, a smile threatening her lips. Most people didn't know how influential the Chinese had been in Méxicali unless they had visited.

"I was born in Calexico," he said, answering her unasked question.

"We are neighbours, then."

"Seems so." He looked her in the eye. "So what was Ray on about?"

Lupe looked at the couch.

"Look, Tim needs to know if something's up with that yahoo," Jimmy said. "Ray's been seeing his sister, and there's not a guy alive here who wants to tell Tim about it. It's easier to tell him if Ray is up to something else and let it go from there, you dig?"

"I am not sure I know what this Ray is doing."

Jimmy studied her for a second. "I think you've put it together. Haven't you?"

She shrugged. "It was little things the big one said. He said he was not sure if there was a market for a Mexican girl like me. Not a store kind of market. I think he meant demanda."

"What kind of demand?" Jimmy's eyes had narrowed.

"They check my arms. They said I have light eyes, which is good. I know when a man is pricing me." She held out her wrists, where scars from thin ropes weren't as visible now as they were when she was younger. Calderón hadn't seen need to tie them up after the first year. "He knew what these were."

Jimmy reached out and took her wrist, gently running his fingers over the pale, white scars.

"Someone tied you up," he said, his voice emotionless. "For a long time."

"Sí," she said. "Ray, he said they could take me now or wait to see what Tim did. He decided not to wait."

Jimmy let go of her wrist and walked over to the couch. He took the cigarette from behind his ear and lit it, taking a quick drag.

"He wanted to try and prostitute you. You think he has other girls?" Jimmy asked.

Lupe nodded. "I guess as much. He asked if I would fit in. That would only be a concern if there were others."

Jimmy nodded, deep in thought, and smoked for a minute.

"Don't tell Tim what you told me," he said.

Lupe couldn't hide the surprise from her face, and Jimmy's grin was guileless.

"I know, I know," he said. "Dangerous territory, right? Look, Tim's got a blind spot to things going on under his nose, because if he saw them happening, it'd mean he didn't have control over everybody, you dig? And he can't have that."

She nodded. "So what will you do?"

"Find out what Ray's up to. Get enough proof and tell Tim when the time is right. It's the only way."

"You have known him a long time?"

Jimmy shrugged. "Moved here in middle school. Tim hung around the gym my old man worked at. I just fell in with him. What about you? Rumour has it something got messed up with Tim's deal."

She nodded. "It is complicated."

"And you don't wanna tell me in case Tim finds out." Jimmy ground out his quarter-smoked cigarette. "Smart girl."

A minute later Jesse came back into the building with a block of ice in a cardboard box.

Jimmy smiled. "I'll have Jesse stay here until Tim arrives. He's alright. Ten cuidado."

Be careful.

"You learned Spanish in Calexico?" she asked.

He shook his head. "My mother's Mexican. Well, hell, I guess that means I am, too."

He winked at her. He didn't look Méxicano, despite his black hair. His eyes were light, and his complexion could pass for a nice tan.

"Stay here," he said. "I'll find Tim."

Whether that was good or bad, she didn't know. Jimmy said a few things to Jesse before he left.

Lupe returned to the couches and sat. Ray had taken the cookies, of course.

"Lupe, huh?" Jesse asked, coming over and sitting on the arm of the couch farthest from her. "What's it mean? In Spanish?"

"It is in honour of the Virgin Mary," she said. "María Guadalupe is my full name."

"Maria's like Mary, huh?"

Lupe nodded.

"What's my name in Spanish?"

"Jesse?" she asked. "It is Jesé."

She pronounced the J as they did in Spanish. He looked disappointed.

"You are Tim's cousin?" she asked. He nodded. "How old are you?"

"Twenty. You?"

"Seventeen," she said.

He looked up from lighting his cigarette.

"No shit? You look a lot older, like Tim's age or something."

"How old is he?" she asked, even though she remembered the men in the truck said he was in his twenties.

"He'll be twenty-five in a few days. Sometimes he seems older than that to me."

"Why is that?" she asked, although she agreed with him.

Jesse shrugged. "I dunno. You ever watch his eyes? It's like knows too much. Kinda creeps me out, if you wanna know the truth."

His accent was different than some of the others and she said so.

"Was born in Chicago," he said. "That's up north, you know it?"

She nodded.

"I got into some trouble back there, so my mother, she sent me down here to live with my dad a couple years ago. Dunno why she thought it'd be better for me, I get in more trouble here than I ever did in Chicago. My folks, they got divorced. Helped my ma out some with me living here since I got two younger brothers an' a younger sister back in Chicago. Tim's mom, she's my aunt. I'd say they look out for me, but truth be told, I think she forgets I'm here half the time. Not that I can blame her."

She looked at him quizzically.

"Never mind," he said. "So you're from Mexico, and you're up here now, and you're doing something for Tim. Why'd you leave Mexico?"

He offered the pack of cigarettes to her.

"No," she said. "But, thank you."

Her stomach growled again, and she settled her hand over it, her smile shy.

"Hey, you hungry?" he asked. "Come on. Jimmy was right about the ice-box being empty. If I had half a brain I would've bought something at the gas station, but I know where we can find a bit of food around here."

She stood and followed him straight toward Tim's office.

"It is locked," she said. "I watched him do it last night."

Jesse looked over and grinned.

"That's what he thinks."

He kneeled and took a thin piece of metal out of his pocket.

"Watch this," he said. He slid it between the wooden door frame and the door, then took another piece of metal out and put it in the lock. She was fascinated as he jiggled it around, then shoved the metal piece down. The door lock popped open.

"¡Qué chido!" she exclaimed as he opened the door and ushered her in. "Does he know you do that?"

Jesse shook his head. "Don't say anything, I'm not eager to get my ass kicked."

She smiled.

"He's got some stuff in the desk here." He waltzed over to the desk where Tim had sat. Jesse rifled through the drawers.

"Got a bottle of pop here." He put it on the desk, then dug out a can of peanuts a second later. "Sorry, it ain't much."

"It is fine," she told him.

"Wait!" he exclaimed. "I gotta candy bar."

He pulled a candy bar from an inside pocket in his jacket. It was a warm day; she had no idea why he wore the leather jacket with the chain hanging off it. The candy bar he handed her was soft and pliable from the heat. She read the name on the wrapper: Almond Joy.

"Do you have that one in Mexico?"

"No," she said. She hoped he wouldn't ask her which candies they had in México. Calderón sometimes gave them wafers of Ibarra chocolate. She never had anything like this.

She followed Jesse back out into the hall, and he pressed the door knob button in on the knob facing into the room and pulled the door shut behind them.

"Where did you learn that?" she asked. "To open the door?"

He grinned. "Tim taught me."

She laughed this time. "I am thinking he did not intend for it to be put to this use."

Jesse shrugged. "What he won't know won't hurt him, I guess. You never told me what you left Mexico for."

She had hoped he'd forgotten about their conversation. She liked him; he was nice to her, and it was a relief to have someone not know her history. Tim didn't know even half of what she was. To be a girl in the zona roja was one thing . . . her history was so much darker, and from Tim's reaction, she didn't want to tell him the rest.

Perhaps Jesse would feel the same way. She detected hatred in Tim's eyes when he told her to stop, pushed her away and looked at her in disgust, like some of the people in Mexicali did when they saw her in the back of the truck heading back to the Casa. People on the street looked at them with hatred in their eyes, and Lupe sensed the same hostility from Tim.

It was strange he hated it. Most men didn't care; many men liked it. They liked it for one reason, of course.

Jimmy was different also, but he was older than Jesse, she could tell. Maybe it was their common heritage, but she felt safe telling Jimmy things she would hide from everyone else. Jesse was nice, and nice people were a rarity in her life. She didn't want to risk him leaving her here alone, and if he knew the truth, he might.

She studied Jesse's face for a moment and tried to come up with a lie.

"I left someone," she said.

"A boyfriend?" he asked.

She nodded.

"Tough break," he said. "He ain't gonna follow you here?"

"Not if God is willing." She took the lid off the can of peanuts and poured some into her hands. "I pray he does not."

"What are you? Like, praying-wise?"

"Catholic," she said. She crunched on the peanuts and realized how hungry she was. The salt stung her lips.

"Same here. I don't go to church much though, not anymore. My mom isn't so big on church since she got divorced. They weren't real nice to her about it, even though she had good reason to leave him."

They were quiet as Lupe snacked on some of the peanuts and attempted to eat the melting candy bar, sharing a hunk of it with Jesse. The chocolate was good, and inside was coconut and almonds. She didn't think she ever tasted anything better. The Pepsi tasted far different from the kind in México, and the sugar gave her a headache.

"So the guys are saying Tim had some kind of a shipment and it didn't come."

Lupe said nothing.

"I get it, he told you not to say anything."

She smiled in response.

"So where'd you learn English? You talk kinda funny," he said. "Like a teacher or something."

"I learn from people, Americans like you," she said, licking chocolate off her fingers. "There are many in Méxicali. It is right next to the border with America."

She didn't want to tell him why she had learned English. She looked around the dirty table and spotted a stack of playing cards and picked them up, hoping to distract him.

"You play poker?" She shuffled the cards. She watched many games between the guards as they waited to take the girls to the brothels under Calderón's control in la zona. Cards interested her; so many Americans came and played with Mexicans in the cantinas, neither understanding the other, but everyone understanding the cards.

"Not good. Well, pretty bad," Jesse admitted. "Rett Gordon, he's this cowboy who has a bar up past Fremont, he has these big poker games all the time. He never lets us in on them. Sometimes Tim or Bill, but never any of the rest of us. Well, never me, I should say. But I can't play, so it's not like I'd ever get to join anyhow."

"I can teach you." She shuffled the cards. "It is called five card draw."

"Now we're talking," Jesse said. He shook some peanuts out of the can and divided them up. "How about we use the rest of these peanuts to bet?"

She smiled, and her smile faltered as she remembered the girls at the Casa. They would make up games and beg Lupe to play to pass the time.

"Alright," she said, pushing their voices out of her head. "I will be the dealer."

Tim left the motel early and went home to shower. His father had already gone to look for work, and Diana got in a screaming match with their mother over her clothes.

Tim agreed with their mother, her skirt was too short, and her top too revealing, but he knew better than to side with anyone against Diana unless he wanted a screaming banshee on his case for the rest of the week.

He planned to stick around until Diana left for school, but with time ticking away, and Diana insisting a friend would pick her up, he couldn't spare anymore time to baby-sit and make sure she looked presentable when she left the house, so he left it up to their mother.

He got in the Charger and drove downtown. He needed to find a way to keep Lupe around. He hoped the bed convinced her to stay at least another night. Mendoza would have information for him by then, and he'd know whether he'd need her to get the shipment back.

Tim stopped at the Round-Up for some food and spotted Jimmy Lewis in the parking lot. Jimmy waved him over and moved around the side of the building, away from everyone.

"Ray got handsy with the Mexican girl," he said. Tim didn't bother to ask how Jimmy knew about her, since he hadn't been there the night before. His boys were bigger gossips than any girl he'd ever met.

"And?" Tim asked.

"I took care of it, but . . . "

"But what?"

Jimmy shrugged. "Something's up with him, that's all. I don't know what, but I don't like it."

"Something's always up with Ray. She there?"

"Was when I left. Jesse's with her."

God help him. Tim nodded a goodbye and went inside and ordered some burgers. Food might be persuasive if he needed to convince her to stay. She only ate the single sandwich and some milk the day before.

He drove back to the warehouse and parked the car in the alley. He moved the corrugated door aside. He heard laughter, and it sounded like Lupe's. Jesse's voice was louder.

"Alright, well say something worse than that," his cousin said. "I need to know all the worst ones."

She laughed again. Tim walked inside, moving the door back to its place. Lupe and Jesse sat on the couch facing each other, playing cards. Lupe's face was red from laughing.

"I have already told you all of the bad words," she said.

"Well, how about something like 'suck my cock, motherfuckers,'" Jesse said. She yelped, both laughing and horrified.

41

"Jesse," he said.

His cousin turned to look at him. Lupe looked over as well, trying to smother her smile.

"Stop bothering her," he said.

"He is not bothering me," she answered.

"Lupe knows a ton of curses in Spanish, Tim," Jesse said. "It's great. We can cuss out the cops, and they'll never know it."

"You said you would not do that!" Lupe said, pretending to be angry, her smile giving her away.

"I can't promise a thing when it comes to the law," Jesse said.

"You ever think the cops might know some Spanish too, Jesse?" He didn't expect an answer. "I brought some food."

He handed the bag from the Round-Up to Lupe. She looked at him in surprise, then opened the bag and pulled out a hamburger.

"Gracias," she said. "Thank you."

"I didn't figure you'd stick around." He sat on a chair, the stuffing coming out of the arms, and lit a cigarette.

"Jesse has been keeping me company," Lupe said. "And you were right before. I have nowhere to go."

"You better figure it out before you go," Tim said. He was pleased he wouldn't even have to finesse her much. She seemed to have made up her mind pretty fast.

Jesse snuck a few fries from the bag, and Lupe tried to slap his hand away. Jesse smiled, and his stomach lurched for a moment. Jesus Christ, trust Jesse to fall for a whore.

He reached over and took a hamburger from the bag for himself and ate it. Lupe and Jesse continued to play cards and share French fries, their voices more subdued with him here. When Jesse was done eating Tim tried to get him to leave.

"Jesse, take off for a bit," Tim said.

"What for? I'm having fun," he said.

"Just take off." Tim's voice was edged with impatience. Lately, it seemed all Jesse did was question why Tim asked him to do this and that; a damn pain in the ass.

"We can play another time," Lupe told him.

"You gonna stick around here?" Jesse asked. "Or skip town or something?"

Tim thanked whoever was up there for putting the question on Jesse's lips.

"I think I will stay," she said. "I do not know if it will be here ... "

She nodded toward Tim, and Jesse bade his goodbyes and headed outside.

"He is very nice," she said, staring at the door Jesse left through.

"You try any of your tricks with him?" He rested his feet on the makeshift table.

"What tricks?" Lupe asked, her brow wrinkled in confusion.

"You try and get him in the sack like you did me?" He took a long drag on his cigarette. "Cuz I'm gonna tell you right now, you knock that shit off with him and anyone else in this gang or you'll be out on your ass."

Lupe stood and looked at him, her cheeks flushed and her eyes narrowed.

"I did nothing of the sort," she said. "He is a nice boy. He does not need to know of things like that!"

Tim tried not to laugh at her words, but couldn't help himself.

"You're a piece of work," he said. "Try and play all high and mighty right now after you were so quick to try it with me yesterday."

"I do not understand you. You are a man. You push me away when I try to come to you." She crossed her arms and looked at him with a raised eyebrow. "Perhaps there is something wrong. I have seen it before."

Not only a whore, but one who insulted his manhood. Tim was about to say something to her, but she turned around and marched away from him, down the hallway. He heard the bedroom door slam shut.

He paused, remembering the sound of doors shutting and the raucous laughter of women. He remembered the long drive with his father, excited to go out of town with him and wondering where they were headed. They always stopped on the way home no matter how late it was. He remembered the long dry road to the house with no neighbours around, but an airplane landing strip right outside. He remembered watching the sky for planes, but none ever came. He remembered the cars parked outside. He remembered the smell of perfume, and the woman at the desk at the front who gave him peppermint candies. Peppermint made him gag.

He remembered the women, but not their faces. Sometimes they were the same women, some with blood red lips and thick eyelashes, breasts pushed up to the heavens. Sometimes they would say hi to him, coo over him and ask him why he couldn't smile for them. Sometimes they would ignore him. But they always asked for the money up front.

He didn't understand why they went here, he didn't understand why he waited in the hallway, listening to noises that confused him and sucking on peppermint candies. He could've been outside watching for planes. He didn't understand why they stopped at the truck stop so his father could shower before they returned home.

One fateful trip his father skipped the shower in his hurry to get home. He remembered his mother's screaming, the dishes shattering against the wall and her accusatory voice, asking him why he hadn't told her what was going on. Why, Timothy? Why did you go there with him? How many times have you been there? Why did you bring a boy there, Frank? Why? Why? Why?

He remembered her crying most of all.

It was years before he understood what it was all about. All he knew then was it was the night his old man had beat his mother for the first time.

He took a breath as the memories faded, got up and walked down the hallway and opened the door to the bedroom. She was on the bed, her back to him.

"I don't get you," he said.

He heard her sniffing.

"I do not understand." Her voice sounded tiny, like a child's.

"I don't get how women like you can do it," he said. "Fucking anything that walks in and waves a dollar in your face. You ever think about who these men are? They don't give a damn about you, you know that?"

She turned over and looked at him, her face streaked with tears.

"I know better than you think," she said.

"Yeah, I'm sure you know a hell of a lot of stuff."

"Things you probably cannot do." Her voice was arch. "Perhaps that is why you are so angry."

"You're a real bitch, you know that," he said. "I told you once back there, you keep your hands off my gang. They're not buying what you're selling."

She said a soft "Hmm."

He left the room and went to the office. She was so much damn trouble he should've turned her out on her ass when he figured out what she was. Let her fend for herself.

He sat and opened the desk drawer and swore.

"That stupid kid," he sighed.

"You know?" She looked at him from the doorway.

He was surprised to see her there. At least she didn't sit in that room and stew like a girl all afternoon.

"I taught the kid how to pick locks, of course I know he swipes my shit," Tim said. "He's lousy at covering his tracks."

"He would make a terrible spy," she agreed. "But he is loyal to you."

"And who are you loyal to?"

She raised her chin as she looked him in the eye.

"I am loyal to no one but myself," she said.

He stared back and didn't believe it for a second.

He left Lupe alone at the downtown place, confident she wouldn't leave. They didn't speak to each other after their exchange, and she spent most of her time dozing in the bedroom.

Tim called Mendoza again, but he had no news.

"Juan is in Mexicali," Mendoza said. "He has not discovered anything yet, but there are many cantinas in their zona roja, and many women who work there in the brothels. There are also private cantinas that allow women in the zona roja, and there is a new compound there. But do not worry—he will find something. She may be lying, Tim. I do not know. Hold onto her until we know for sure."

Tim was uneasy and wondered if he had all the angles. It disturbed him to think she hid things from him, and he was sure she was.

He found Bill at Jimmy Lewis's place. His old man had poured everything they had into the Lucky Lady, and it did decent business thanks to the food and generous pours.

Part of him missed Rett's. He went there on occasion—Rett did run some decent poker games—but it wasn't a habit anymore.

He'd see Ruby behind the counter and felt nothing for her, but he couldn't stand her staring at him all the time, and he was sure she did, even though he never caught her at it.

"I dunno, Tim," Bill said. "You think any gang down there's gonna trust her? You said it seemed like she was on the run, and she probably is. If a pimp's after her maybe she stole all his money and ran."

"Yeah, and that's why she runs off with our bag of dough? I don't believe she's got a cent to her name," Tim said. "She's not telling us the whole truth, I know that much. I wanna keep her around until Mendoza gets me word on what her deal is. After that she can go wherever the hell she wants."

"You better hope an angry pimp doesn't show up at your door," Bill grinned.

"No one'll find her. They weren't even supposed to bring the illegals up this way anyhow," Tim said. "No one'll be looking for her in Las Vegas."

He drove the short distance back to the warehouse. He went down the hall and the door to the bedroom was closed. He was about to knock and settled on barging in. It was his place, after all.

"You staying here tonight?" he asked.

She looked at him. She held a copy of Seventeen Magazine, and he wondered where the hell she got it.

She noticed his gaze.

"Jesse gave it to me," she said with a smile. "He said I can learn better English. He says I talk funny."

"Are you staying?"

She hesitated a moment. "Will you let me?"

He nodded. "For now."

"Then I will stay. Thank you." She turned back to her magazine.

He left her alone in the room.

4

Lupe slept in fits and starts, her sleep punctuated by strange dreams. She tossed and turned most of the night, unable to rest.

She stared into the darkness, wondering about Tim. He acted strange toward her. She could tell from the way he looked at her he didn't like her, like she was dirt under his nails. She was used to that, in some ways. But the hatred was so pure from him, and she didn't understand it.

Most men gave in to her touch. It was all she had, and if he wouldn't let her repay him like this, she didn't know how she would be expected to.

The men who looked askance at her in the border towns Calderón took them to were the religious men. Some of them faltered and came to la zona roja to sin their night away. She never met a man like Tim, one who lived so clearly on the wrong side of the law and turned down a willing woman. She admired his resolve, but didn't understand it. There was no reluctance. There was hated, pure and simple, and she didn't know what she did to offend him so much.

After she used the bathroom and freshened up, she found Jesse waiting on the couch, ready to learn more poker.

They played cards, and he shared a sandwich he brought with him. Bill came by, but only nodded this time. Ray said he overheard Tim tell Bill what she was, so she wasn't surprised Bill no longer spoke with her.

"Tim does not like me." She shuffled the cards together and prepared to deal.

"Tim?" Jesse asked. "He don't like many people. Don't take it personally."

"No," she said. "It is more than that."

Perhaps one day she could tell him the truth, but not now. He would hate her too, since he seemed to do whatever it was Tim wanted him to do. Jesse was nice to her and talked to her like a normal girl. It was a refreshing change, and she vowed to keep it that way.

Jesse left her in the mid-afternoon, and she wandered around the building restless and bored. She read her magazine and tried to siesta, but her mind was too active to sleep. She didn't venture outside, fearful someone would see her. She knew Las Vegas was a big city, but at one time she thought Mexicali or Tijuana could hide her.

In the late afternoon, the corrugated door was moved aside, the metal scraping concrete, like it was moved with effort. She was surprised to see a girl step inside.

She hadn't seen a girl in the building the entire time she'd been staying here. Tim's sister never came by, and no girlfriends appeared either. So this blonde girl was a surprise.

"Who're you?" the blonde asked, her voice cold, her high heels clicking on the concrete.

"I am Lupe." She looked behind the girl, wondering if one of the men would follow, but no one was there.

"Where's Tim?" The girl crossed her arms. Her blonde hair hung loose, a bobby pin caught in a curl. She had dark roots growing in, and her clothes were rumpled as if she slept in them.

"I do not know where he is."

"Sure." The blonde's voice dripped with sarcasm. "I'm gonna believe the reason he didn't show up at Castaways last night—like he *promised* me— was because of business and not you? Bill lies worse than anyone I know. Tim was supposed to be with *me*."

The girl staggered forward on the last word, a challenging look in her eye.

"I do not understand," Lupe told her.

"Honey, you keep your claws outta Tim," she said. "I've seen a lot of girls come, and they all go. He *always* comes back to me."

Lupe sighed; she encountered this before. Angry wives, angry girlfriends . . . they all came to stake their claim. Calderón's men were good at keeping them away from their girls in Calderón's zona, but they couldn't control the crowds outside of it. Many women waited outside the cantinas and brothels to catch their men leaving.

"It is not like that," she said.

"Tim and me, we go back a long way," she said, stepping closer to Lupe. The blonde was taller than her, and Lupe stepped back a little. The girl's breath smelled of alcohol, and Lupe wasn't prepared for a fight.

"I am not here for him," Lupe said.

"Oh yeah?" she asked. "Where're you staying?"

Before Lupe could answer, the girl charged toward the hall, and Lupe followed.

"What are you doing?" Lupe called out. She wondered who this woman was and what her problem was.

"You're staying here with him?" The woman had barged into the small room she slept in. "So now you're a liar and a thief!"

"Thief? I am no such thing!"

"Tim," the girl said. "Hands off. I don't care what he says about it. As a matter of fact, I think it's time you beat it outta here."

Lupe was startled when the woman reached out and grabbed her by the arm, yanking her down the hallway and into the main room. Lupe stumbled against her and cringed at the alcohol on her breath.

She was unsure whether to fight back or not, but was relieved when the girl skidded to a stop. Tim stood in the doorway, looking at the scene with a blank expression.

"What the hell are you doing here, Carrie?" he asked, his voice rough and angry.

"Carolyn, you jackass," she said. "You didn't show last night!"

"I sent Bill to tell you I was busy." He sauntered in the room like this she-devil wasn't clamped onto Lupe's arm like a bloodthirsty starfish.

"'Business' is what he said," she told him. She yanked on Lupe. "This doesn't look like business to me. She's staying here with you!"

The girl let go, and Lupe stumbled before righting herself. The blonde walked up to Tim, and she was surprised the girl raised her hand to slap him. He caught her by the wrist.

"You're drunk." His voice was flat. "Drunk and acting like a damn lunatic."

"You are such a jerk!" she said. "And sleeping with the likes of her! Didn't know you liked Mexican girls, Tim."

"It's not your business, Carrie, but I'm not sleeping with her," he said. "You know better than to come around here without asking."

"You didn't have a problem inviting me before," she said, pouting. "Send her away, Tim. Get her out of here, and we can have some fun."

The girl leaned up and kissed him as Lupe watched, aware the girl did it for her benefit. She saw much of that too, from women coming to collect their husbands at the cantina or the other girls staking their claims on the customers. She wondered if this girl worked at a club.

"You need to go," Tim said, pushing her off him. "I told you I was busy."

"Not with her," the girl whispered, running her hands up his chest. Lupe looked at the girl's clothes—a short skirt, a low cut blouse and high heels. She was dressed like any working girl in la zona. Lupe frowned, wondering why he would let this girl stay with him, yet he refused her offer of payment.

He steered the girl away from Lupe and toward the door, but she planted her feet and refused to go any further.

"You are such a jerk," she said. "I make time for you, and all you ever do is push me aside for someone else."

Tim looked at this girl with a blank expression. "Carolyn, go home and sober up."

"Why? So you can take her to bed instead? You're slumming now?"

Lupe stared. Tim looked from her to Carolyn.

"Let's go, Carolyn," he said. "Out."

"You're kicking me out over *her*?" she screeched. "You can't be serious! I'm never going to speak to you again!"

Tim grabbed her wrist and pulled her toward the door, but the girl yanked her arm away.

"Don't touch me!" she said. "I don't want your hands on me, you are such a jerk. I am never coming around here after you again!"

Her skirt rode up her legs up as she struggled against Tim, and she slid out of her left heel. She tried one last time to convince Tim to keep her around, sliding a hand around his neck. He peeled her off and gently pushed her out the door, sliding the corrugated metal across the opening.

Lupe heard her screaming threats through the door, then sobbing, and finally it was silent a moment later.

He made no apologies and walked past her into the hallway and down to his office.

She followed.

"Thank you," she said.

"Don't bother." He searched his drawer and came out with a half empty pack of Pall Malls. "I didn't do it for you. She's drunk and angry, and she isn't fun to be around when she's like that. I'd have thrown her out whether or not you were here."

"Still," Lupe said. "Thank you."

She walked over to him and placed a hand on his arm. She ran her hand up his arm and across his chest, fingering the lapels of his jacket.

"Let me say thank you."

"Jesus Christ, you don't quit do you?" he asked. He moved her away and sat in his chair, huffing out a breath. He pressed his fingers to the bridge of his nose. "You learn as fast as she does."

He stood again, cagey and angry.

"I do not understand you," Lupe said. She placed her hands on his chest. "That girl was not so different from me, yet she said you have spent many nights with her. And you still refuse me."

He took her by the shoulders and shoved her back.

"I said to get your hands off me. I'm not asking again. What the hell makes you think I'm gonna want to take you to bed?" His gaze was steady, and she tried not to avert her eyes. "Carolyn isn't a whore. She may look like it, but she sure as hell doesn't open her legs for money."

"Why is this so upsetting to you?" she asked. "Even when the most religious of men shame us in the streets, they still come to la zona."

"I don't have a dollar to spend on you." His eyes were cold, and she couldn't read his expression.

"But it would not cost you anything," she said, confused. "Most men would not turn me away." She had nothing, no way to thank him, no way to earn her keep here.

"I'm supposed to be impressed?" Tim asked. "You've got some screws loose in your head if you think that."

She must be missing some vital words in English. When men turned her away, she always knew they didn't mean it. His hatred was real—he turned her away twice now. She could think of no other way to repay him for the room and letting her stay. This was all she had, and he threw it in her face and made her feel bad for it.

"I do not understand you. You are not like them," Lupe said.

"I'm not like who?"

"The men that come to la zona roja. The men will always say the right things in the streets, or in front of their wives or family, but in the end, they always come to la zona."

"Those men are weak and stupid, and I'm neither," he said, as if challenging her. "You're as bad as they are, worse maybe. You mess with everything they have for a few dollars."

"They come to me!" She couldn't hold back the anger. "I did not ask for this."

"Then what the hell do you do it for, huh?" he asked. "You like being a paid home wrecker?"

"I know these men are not doing what is right, but I cannot stop them. It is not my fault they are there," she said.

"Yeah, well do me a favour and keep your whoring hands off me," he said.

"You treat me worse than dirt." The bitterness in her voice surprised her.

"Well, you act like it."

She wanted to slap him. All the years of not talking back, not reacting, not fighting—she wanted to slap him so hard everyone would feel it.

Instead, she turned and left the office, slamming the door so hard the thin walls vibrated. The door opened behind her and she hurried to the bedroom and slammed that door too, managing to force the slide lock into place. His heavy footsteps followed and he tried the knob, but she held onto it so it wouldn't turn. He pounded on the door, making her jump.

"You don't go slamming shit around this place," Tim said, his voice controlled, but angry.

"I will do whatever I please!" she shouted back. She looked around the room, wishing there was another door out. It wasn't worth it to stay and hear the things he thought about her. She did what she had to, what she was taught.

She slumped against the door.

Maybe it wasn't normal to use sex the way she did. It was all she knew. The men she learned from and the women in la zona were her guides, and she knew inside they were wrong. God punished those who sinned. She remembered that much from church.

She grasped the rosary beads in her pocket. She had slipped them out of her dress before Tim washed it, keeping them hidden in case he wanted to take them. Men took *everything*.

She wiped tears off her cheeks. Things were so mixed up.

"You know, you oughta be grateful I'm helping someone like you anyway," he said. He had stopped banging on the door.

Lupe said nothing. She *was* grateful, how could he not see? A moment later his footsteps retreated, and she relaxed.

It was mid-afternoon. She would stay the night and leave in the morning, and she would be rid of Tim and his insults for good.

Tim drove home and found the house empty again. His mother worked the cages at the Stardust, from three in the afternoon until midnight. His father would be home soon, in a bad mood despite spending most of the evening at a bar. His job at Caesars had ended when construction finished, and he had yet to find another job.

Tim found it easier to be out of the house than deal with him sitting and drinking his life away in the recliner. The more he drank, the angrier he got, and Tim was like a beacon to him—they argued, they fought, and it made everything worse for everyone. So he stayed out of the way as much as he could.

Of course, doing that left Diana and his mother open to his anger. No solutions presented themselves, not since his mother shot down his offer to move out. They were trapped like fish in a barrel.

Tim got out of the car and slammed the door, angry at Lupe.

He didn't get her. He didn't have one clue what made her think she could pull one over on him. She might be pretty with her curls and full lips, those eyes giving come hither looks, but he bet she thought if she slept with him, he'd do whatever the hell she wanted.

He went to his room and was startled to see Lupe's clothes sitting on top of his dresser. Diana never would've done it, so he suspected his mother had finished laundering them. How she knew they didn't belong to Diana he didn't know. The dress was ragged, the material thin and worn, and the sleeves stained from when he tackled her. The dress and sweater had no tags and looked homemade.

He lay on his bed and closed his eyes, feeling a headache come on. He needed word from Mendoza, but they weren't scheduled to talk until eight o'clock that night.

Tim showered, then dozed for awhile. His father came home and made Diana heat up the plate their mother had left for him. Diana ate in Tim's room with him. Leftover meatloaf and wilted vegetables.

He checked the time. It was fifteen to eight. His father was parked in front of the TV waiting for something to come on. Diana was in her room, the Rolling Stones coming from her record player. He walked a couple blocks over to the laundromat where there was a pay phone outside. He'd memorized the number to give out if he needed to, and it rang five minutes after he got there.

"We may have trouble, my friend," Mendoza said, his voice thick with worry.

"I knew it," Tim sighed.

"Juan asked around Mexicali, and some men who are associates of José Calderón were interested to hear about this girl," Mendoza told him. "They were looking for a woman named María."

María Guadalupe; he remembered she hesitated about her name.

"Why? What'd she do?"

"Juan could not find out. They were . . . how do you say it? Tight-lipped," Mendoza finished.

"Is this Calderón a pimp?"

"No, not entirely," Mendoza said. "He is what they call El Camarilla."

"What the hell is that?" Tim asked.

"A criminal organization, the largest in the area. Calderón is the suspected leader. You will understand not many talk openly of the El Camarilla. He has a big operation—prostitution, yes, but mostly drugs. He controls much of the Baja region and is moving into Sonora—he already has his women working in the zona roja in San Luis Río Colorado. He exports marijuana, but he has been moving into the heroin trade. He is ruthless. The men pressured Juan about what he knew of this girl when he began asking them questions."

"What's your take on it?" Tim asked, a gnawing feeling in his stomach.

"A bad feeling," Mendoza said. "I have a bad feeling. If she is running from them, you all may be in danger. El Camarilla doesn't take lightly to any threat, perceived or otherwise. If she worked for them and decided to leave, she will learn there are no decisions to be made when you work for Calderón."

"Would she know?" Tim asked.

"How dangerous Calderón is? Of course. That he is El Camarilla? Most likely, if she is working for him. He is well known here. If she is running, there is a reason."

Tim cursed after he hung up the phone. The bitch was done with her lying. He'd make sure of that.

Lupe stayed in the room, leaving once to drink water and go to the bathroom. Her stomach growled. Jesse had brought her a snack, but it wasn't enough to sate her appetite. She didn't think Tim was inclined to return and feed her, either. He would prefer she starve to death.

She would go at first light, so she could have most of the day to travel. She had little money, but there were ways to get around. If she learned one thing from Mexicali and her life, it was everyone had a price—and men more so than anyone. She would use her power this time; use what she was taught, and this time for her own purposes. It would be *her* sin this time, but she thought God would forgive her. He would understand the situation she was in.

She sat on the mattress and thought about her options.

The now-familiar sound of Tim's footfalls echoed in the building a short time later. His boots made staccato raps on the cement floor. From the way he walked, he was angry.

She sighed. That wasn't new; he always seemed to be angry with her for something. His footsteps got closer, and she stood, anticipating he would try the door without knocking. The slide lock was in place but it was flimsy, and she had no doubt he could break it if he tried.

He pounded on the door and tried to knob.

"Open up, Lupe, I know you're here," he said.

She remembered the footsteps of Calderón, coming heavy into the casita, or down the hallway in the main house, a sound that made everyone look at each other with fear in their eyes. She remembered the sound of the door opening and what it meant. She was so far from that now. She'd come so far.

"I do not want to open the door." His voice made her feel wary.

"Lupe, you don't open this door right now, I'll break the thing down," he said. His voice was measured, and to the average person it may not sound threatening, but she knew sometimes the worst threats were hidden behind the quietest of requests.

She took a deep breath and pushed on the door and moved the slide lock. He was in the room before she could step back.

"I wanna know what the hell is going on," he said. "No more lies, no more bullshit."

"What are you talking about?" she asked. "I have not lied."

"José Calderón."

She froze.

"That's what I thought," Tim said. He grabbed her upper arm and pulled her out into the hallway and took her out in the front room of the warehouse. No one else was there.

"What are you doing with me?" she asked. She noticed a bundle in his hands. "What is that?"

He held up her dress and sweater bunched in his hand. "Your clothes. I want you to tell me who he is and why you're tied up with him, or you're out on your ass and can fend for yourself."

"How did you learn of him?" She yanked her arm away.

"You don't get to ask the damn questions, you answer them," he said.

"How?" she yelled. "Tell me how!"

"My contact in Tijuana, the one who set me up with the Castillo boys," he said. "He sent a man asking about you and got an earful about—"

Before he could finish speaking she darted back toward the bedroom, Tim following behind her. She made it to the bedroom, shoved her hand under the mattress and pulled out her rosary beads. She was in the hallway before Tim stopped her.

"Let me go!" she yelled. "Let me go! He will find me; you have ruined everything! He will kill me! Let me go!"

Tim pushed her back toward the wall and held her by the wrists.

He had her clothing tucked under his arm—the things she ran away from México in, the dress that reminded her so much of the Casa. She gagged for a moment, and she gulped in air.

"Please let me go, he will find me," Lupe said, beginning to cry.

"Who is he?" Tim's breathing was heavy.

"He is Satan," she said. "He is the devil."

"Not the answer I wanted. Who?"

"He is a bad man." She shivered, despite the warmth radiating from Tim's body. "The worst kind of man."

"I got that part," Tim said.

"Please, let me go," Lupe begged. "You say your contact knows of me? Then Calderón knows as well. He knows I am here."

"Then I'll get you away from here, and you tell me everything I wanna know," Tim said. "That's the deal."

Lupe nodded, and he let her go, stepping back and giving her space. He held out her clothes, and she took them, hugging them to her. He kept a hand on her arm and pulled her toward the doorway.

Her breathing returned to normal when they entered the alley. The night air was cool, and Lupe shivered again, this time from the cold.

She jumped when she heard the noise, and it was a second before she realized the loud bangs were gunshots.

The devil had come.

5

It took a moment for Tim to recognize the sounds as gunshots. He was around guns more than most people—he had one tucked into an ankle holster at the moment, and another in the car—but the muted pops were nothing like the deafening roar of the gun he shot Bill with months back.

After the first two shots, all he heard was Lupe's screams.

"Christ!" He yanked her back and ducked into the doorway as a bullet ricocheted off the brick façade, leaving a ragged chunk missing from the place his head was a moment ago.

"He is here, he is here!" Her voice was high pitched and hysterical.

"Shut up," he said. "Go!"

He pushed her back into the building and moved the corrugated metal across the opening. Men's voices shouted in Spanish from the end of the alley. They could get away if they ran fast enough, and Tim had the benefit of knowing the building. He grabbed the small Colt from his ankle holster and cursed himself for leaving the Browning in the car.

She paused inside, unsure where to go, and Tim shoved her toward the back. She didn't move.

"You want them to get us? Move, for Christ's sake!" He shoved her forward again. "The door."

She looked at him in confusion.

"The door!" he urged.

Her eyes widened as she got his meaning. They dashed toward the hall, and as they passed the bank of dirty windows, movement out of the corner of his eye caught his attention. He grabbed her hand and yanked her to the floor as a shower of bullets and glass rained on them.

He crawled past her, glass crunching under his arms, and he cringed to think of the state his jacket would be in after this. "Come on!"

She crawled with him until they reached the hall, then he pulled her up. He heard the screech of metal on concrete as the corrugated door was moved.

"Hurry!" Lupe said. She held her clothes against her chest like they would protect her from the bullets.

He pulled the key off the wall, got the door open and pushed her through. He looked back and ducked as one of the men spotted him and got off a shot. He levelled the Colt, not taking the time to aim, and fired wide. He hoped it was enough to get them to retreat for cover.

Their gunshots were muted compared to his; they must be using a silencer so they wouldn't draw as much attention. It was a bad sign.

Lupe pulled his hand as another pop rang out. She screamed and ducked, and there was a thunk as a bullet slammed into the wooden door frame. He pushed the big metal door shut as the men rushed toward them. Tim locked the deadbolt.

He said nothing as he grabbed Lupe's hand and pulled her through the big warehouse. It was Sunday, so the building was dark and empty. He knew it like the back of his hand from all the time he spent lurking around here after hours, and he pulled Lupe around the machinery in the cavernous room with ease. The only sounds were their footsteps and her hiccupped breathing.

He paused as he opened the front door, looking up and down the street. The mercury vapour lights glowed bluish-green on the street, but no one was around. The front of his side of the warehouse had been boarded up for years, so the hitmen put all their energy into heading around back. They hadn't even left a lookout—a sign of a bad leader if there was one.

"Come on," he said. "The car's around the corner."

Lupe's tennis shoes were quiet on the pavement. His boots were loud with every step, and no matter what he did, he couldn't silence them. His solution was to run faster.

He reached the car and opened the door, shoving Lupe in the driver's seat where she climbed across to the passenger side. He expected gunshots and shattering glass, but they were inside the car and speeding off a moment later.

Tim rocketed through the streets of Las Vegas, turning left and right whenever he saw a well-lit street. He checked the rearview mirror every few seconds to see if they were being followed, but there was no one there.

He pulled into the parking lot at Sills and stopped the car at the side of the building, half-hidden by a Dumpster in case they knew what his car looked like. He pulled the Browning out of the glove box and stuck it in the back of his jeans.

"Where are you going?" Lupe asked, her voice high-strung and strained. Her face was streaked with tears. "What are you doing?"

"I'm calling Bill," he said. "Stay in the car."

She looked ready to protest, so he shut the door. He went to the pay phone and called Bill's house.

"We've got trouble," Tim said, glad Bill had answered.

"Pimp come after you?" Bill joked.

"Worse," Tim told him. "Mendoza's man asked around about Lupe, turns out some big crime boss is after her. Some guy named Calderón."

Bill whistled. "What's it mean for us?"

"A lot of trouble. A bunch of Mexicans showed up at the warehouse and started shooting. They almost blew our damn heads off."

"What?!"

"I need you to tell the boys to keep an eye out," Tim said. "But I want everyone to clear away from the warehouse for now. I'm hoping these guys are coming after me because I was with her."

"There's gonna be a lot of questions from the boys about this," Bill said, his voice tight with concern. "We shouldn't have brought her to the warehouse."

Tim huffed out a breath at Bill's use of "we." It was his own decision that opened this can of worms, and Bill knew it. He also hated it when Bill was right.

"Don't say too much about it all," Tim said.

"I'll make sure Pete brings in some firepower just in case," Bill said. "Are they on your tail?"

"I don't think so," he said. "They might stake out the warehouse, that's why I don't want anyone there for awhile."

"Okay," Bill said. "Tim, we're gonna have to tell them what's up if we're gonna tell them to keep their eyes open and stay away from the building for a few days. Some of them may be slow, but they're gonna notice Mexican hitmen."

"Do what you have to," Tim said. "Don't get anyone killed. I have enough trouble keeping tabs on the boys we got. I don't wanna have to recruit again."

Bill's chuckle had no humour. "You must be panicking if you're cracking lame jokes like that."

"Get Jesse to keep an eye on Diana and my mom," Tim said. "I don't think these guys would know where I live, but it's possible they've been following us. If they do show up, tell him to blow their damn heads off."

Tim felt his pocket for his cigarettes and came up with a thin pack of Pall Malls. Two left. Great.

"How many were there?"

"I didn't get a good look," Tim admitted. "At least two, I think. I don't know if these guys have been on my tail for a few minutes or a few days, but I don't wanna risk it."

"Got it," Bill said, his voice sober. "What do you want to do about the Outfit?"

Tim paused. Christ.

If the Outfit had given these guys the okay to come after him he was dead. If they hadn't . . . well, that might help him out. Tim wasn't the Outfit's favourite person, so there was only one place he could go.

"Let me take care of it," he told Bill. "I'll be in touch. Stay close to the Lucky Lady tonight, I'll call you there."

He hung up and went inside the restaurant and bought some food. Lupe was hunched in the front seat like she didn't want to be found, clutching her old clothes like a life preserver. The left knee of her jeans was torn and bloody, but she'd made no effort to clean it up. He opened the passenger door.

"Here." He shoved the bag at her. "Food."

"I am not hungry," she whispered, her voice strained. She made no effort to reach for the bag. He put the bag on her lap and shut the door harder than necessary.

He walked around the car, got in, and tucked the gun back in the glove box, since he couldn't sit with it against his back. He drove around the streets, circling around and trying to get the prickly feeling between his shoulder blades to go away. If those men had followed them, they would have killed them back at the restaurant.

He couldn't figure out how they found her; she had been at the warehouse since he brought her there. If they knew she was there any sooner, they would have gone after her when she was alone. He relaxed a bit at the thought; that meant the chance they'd seen where he lived was slim.

Goddammit, she should have told him the situation from the beginning. Now everything was going to hell in a bucket. If he knew she was wanted by some gang he never would've taken her with him, information about the shipment or not. He could have cut her loose, and she could have been on her own with these guys.

He glanced over. Her face was impassive, but there were tears on her cheeks. She said nothing, and he turned his gaze back to the road.

He headed into a back alley off Fremont and cut the engine. The South Seas was busy, and people came stumbling out a side door, laughing loudly. It wore on his nerves.

"Stay here," he said.

"Where are you going?" Her voice was panicked.

"Gotta see someone," he said. "Relax. No one knows where we are. If it makes you feel better, crouch down so no one can see you."

He got out of the car and shut the door. He headed into the side casino door and down a warren of hallways. A redheaded man with an acne-pock-marked face tried to stop him.

"I need to see Sam Wyatt."

"You'll have to make an appointment."

"Yeah, well if I'm dead in the morning because the Mexican hit squad operating here got me, an appointment won't do me any good."

The redhead looked at him for a moment, then nodded.

"This way, Mr. Kelly."

He didn't bother to ask how this man knew his name. He was ushered into Sam Wyatt's opulent office, and the man didn't look up as Tim sat. Tim waited until he raised his head from his paperwork.

He wasn't sure what Sam Wyatt expected to hear, but "Some Mexican mafia tried to shoot me at the warehouse" probably wasn't it.

"What now?" Sam asked.

"I need to know if Chicago sanctioned this." Tim looked at Sam, who was confused.

"Start at the beginning."

Tim reminded him of the deal about the weapons going to the buyer in Denver. Sam nodded.

"I remember. You gave them their end up front. The boy's learning," Sam said. He explained about the truck showing up, Lupe, and everything else, and Sam looked downright thunderous when Tim got to the part about some Mexican nationals shooting up the warehouse.

"And you say they're after this girl?"

Tim nodded.

"Let me make some calls," Wyatt said. "Where can I reach you?"

He thought for a moment. "Reach Bill, he'll be at the Lucky Lady. He can get a message to me."

Tim left the office and got turned around once in the halls before he found his way back out the side entrance. Lupe was crouched low in the passenger seat, trembling. He started the car, unsure about where to go.

He decided to do what the Bible said and head for the hills. He got on Lake Mead Boulevard and headed east between the mountains. Sunrise Mountain was on the left, Frenchman Mountain on the right. He pulled off onto a gravel road heading toward Frenchman and took a few more turns for good measure until they were deep in the hills. He pulled the car in behind some large boulders and cut the engine. It was quiet, aside from Lupe's ragged breathing and the ticking of the engine as it cooled.

"What the hell was that?" he asked her.

She shifted in the seat. "I told you. It was Satan, come straight from Hell."

"I want you to tell me the truth," he said. "Swear it. Swear it on those rosary beads you carry around. They must mean something to you if you stopped to get them. Swear on those."

She fingered the delicate beads and looked over at him.

"I swear."

"Why are they after you?"

"Because I escaped," she said. "I left the Casa, where they keep us. Calderón does not take kindly to that."

"Sending hitmen after some whore who left sounds like an awful lot of trouble." Her gaze flicked over to him at the word 'whore.'

"I am what they made me," she said. "I ran because I finally could."

"I don't get how you wake up in the morning and look at yourself every day," he said. "Blaming everybody else because you open your legs."

"I do not look at myself," she said. "I cannot. It is the only way to get through this hell."

"Hell? You call it hell, yet you're out there taking their money for what? A good time isn't worth the money. If it's hell, why didn't you get out before? Why get in it in the first place?"

She had a strange look on her face. Her expression softened.

"I am seventeen, Tim." Her voice was quiet. "I am no woman. I am here because I tried to get out. I am running because they will not let me go. I got into nothing myself. They came to my village and took me at gunpoint. I did not know why, and I was not permitted to ask."

He took a deep breath. Seventeen. Jesus Christ, he figured her to be twenty-one or twenty-two.

"Bull."

"It is the truth," she said. "These men are evil. They keep the girls to work; we are like slaves. I see none of the money. I am watched at all times. It was luck I escaped and by chance I could find my way out of México."

This was not right. This wasn't the story in his head; this wasn't what women like Rosa came from. He looked at Lupe again and wondered how he missed her true age.

"For all I know, you could be bullshitting the hell outta me with that sob story." He almost tasted the peppermint candies.

"I am not, but you will believe what you will." She looked out the window toward the scrub.

"So why do they care about you so much? You lose one whore, you pick up another. No great loss."

"Will you stop calling me that?" Her voice was weary and tired.

"Answer the question. Why are they after you?"

"I did not leave empty-handed," she whispered.

He knew all along there was something more going on. She might have lit out with all their money.

"What?" he asked. "What did you take? Money? Drugs?"

"A microfiche," she said. "It is like a little piece of film."

"I know what a microfiche is. What's on it?"

"I do not know," she said. "I had no way to read it. Calderón guarded it with his life. It was in his shirt pocket at all times, in a little envelope. I thought . . . I thought if I took it, they would make a trade. My freedom for the microfiche."

"Only they didn't wanna trade," Tim said. "And you don't have any idea what was on it?"

"No," she said. "I did not think it would cause this. I did not think they would try to kill me. Twice they have tried. I hid the microfiche away so they would not get it. I realized it was important. I wanted to get it to my cousin Ramón, but . . . he had seen me in the zona roja three months earlier. He told me I was la muerta—a dead woman. Dead to him."

There was more to her story, much more. It felt like something huge ready to burst out of the ground below and swallow them.

"Start from the beginning, Lupe," he said. "The very beginning."

Lupe didn't want to tell the story. Saying it made it true.

Tim did not react well to what she did in México. If he knew everything he was liable to throw her out of the car and let her fend for herself. She avoided ending up on the side of the road with a bullet in her head by dumb luck before. She wouldn't be that lucky again, not without help.

She glanced over at him. Tim looked impatient waiting for her to start talking, his brow furrowed and his eyes angry. She took a deep breath. Maybe it would be better if they killed her. She could stop running for once in her life.

"The men came to my village one day," she began. "They took me and another girl. A third girl tried to run. They shot her in the head."

It was burned in her mind forever; Marta's head exploded in front of her, and the girl's small body was prone on the ground in seconds. The night-mares had lasted for months. She shook her head, trying to lose the image.

"They took us to a place we called the Casa," she said. "We lived there. Calderón . . . he . . . he . . . it was the beginning of it all. He would beat us . . . he hurt so many. "

Tim was quiet, and she snuck a look at him out of the corner of her eye. She couldn't read his expression.

"When I turned sixteen, they brought me to the zona roja in Tijuana, I suppose because I looked older than my age. The men they bring to the Casa do not go there for the women they can find in la zona," she said. She raised her gaze and looked him in the eye. "They are looking for girls. Young girls."

Tim raised his brow. She continued, glad he understood her meaning.

"Calderón's men would take me from the Casa to a zona, sometimes in Tijuana, sometimes in Mexicali or San Luis Río Colorado. There was always a guard with me. They would keep us there to work in the brothels or the cantinas under Calderón's control where they allowed women, but there was a guard on us at all times. We would work all through the weekend and they would take us back Sunday night for Calderón.

"I thought I could get away in la zona, but I could not. I had so much hope when I saw my cousin Ramón in Mexicali, but when he saw me . . . when he saw what I had become, he turned his back on me. He cried, for the first time I saw him cry since his mother died. I wanted to leave, but I had nowhere to go. My family would not have me back, and if I ran, it would be the first place they would look. I needed a way out."

"This microfiche."

She nodded. "I was sure Calderón would value it over me. I was not his favourite by far. A woman in la zona got me a drug, and I slipped it into Calderón's drink when he had me brought to him one night. He passed out in the bed, and I took the microfiche from his pocket. Security was not as heavy at the Casa. It is far away from the city, and no one dares go there without Calderón's permission. I found my way out of the compound on a laundry truck. I hid the microfiche in case they caught me. Later, I knew the men were looking for me, so I telephoned him and told him my freedom and one thousand pesos, and he could have his microfiche back."

"What did he do?"

"He laughed." Her voice sounded far away, even to herself. "He laughed and told me I would be dead before the sun rose. I was afraid—he is El Camarilla and does not threaten lightly. I have seen him kill many men. For a moment I thought I might go home, even if he found me there and killed me. But to go home to my family . . . that would have been worse than death, I think."

She opened the bag of food and took out some cold French fries, nibbling on them. Her hands shook, and she tried to stop them.

"How'd you get across the border?" Tim asked. He reached over and pulled a lukewarm hamburger from the bag.

"Manuel," she said. "He was a client, a friend."

Tim shook his head. "Figures."

"It was not like that," Lupe said. "Manuel came to la zona . . . Manuel is . . . maricón, they say."

"Maricón?" Tim asked.

"He does not like to be with a woman," she said. "It is a sin."

Understanding dawned in Tim's eyes.

"He would come to la zona roja and pay for a woman, but we would talk. It was a way for him to hide," she said. "He became close to me. A friend."

"That's why he changed out the shipment."

She nodded. "He hid me when I returned to Mexicali after Calderón's men tried to kill me. He promised to get me across the border. He smuggles many people to America to work in factories or in fields. He often gets the papers for the Castillo family when they need to ship things and the border guards cannot know. He knew their truck was scheduled to ship your weapons. He put us in the truck instead."

"What the hell were you going to do?" He lit a cigarette. "Spend your entire life wandering around America hoping no one came to kill you?"

"I do not know," she said. "I thought far enough ahead so I would not be dead."

"You should have told me," he said. "Now I'm fucked as much as you are."

"I did not intend this," she said. "I did not tell you because I did not trust you. When I did trust you, I did not tell you because I feared for you. If they found out you knew, they would kill you. They will think I told you where it is."

"And let me guess, you're not gonna tell me?" he asked.

"No," she said. "You can threaten me all you like, but I will not. I will not get you killed over my mistake."

"I can tell you what's likely on that microfiche," he said. He blew a few smoke rings. "I bet he's got all his contacts, information about every operation he runs, names, telephone numbers, drop locations—you took his entire operation away from him. I almost have to admire the guts."

"I did not know."

"That's why I said almost," he said, the hint of a smile on his lips.

"I do not know what to do now," she said. "I am sorry."

She leaned her head back against the seat and closed her eyes, then cried.

Tim hated it when chicks cried. Tears got you nowhere, whether you were a girl or not. He could understand why Lupe did it, but dammit he hated being around it.

"I'll think of something," he said. "I'm neck deep in this now."

He took another drag on his cigarette. There was a lot to think about. They needed a place to hide first, and it would be damn hard to hide in a car as rare as his, but the one saving grace was it was black and it was night.

"We'll stay here tonight," he said. "In the car. They won't find us. The car's pretty well hidden, and it'd take a local to know how to get here. It'll give me time to think."

She nodded, wiping her face, and looked out the window again.

"Your cousin, this Ramón," he said. "You think he'd help you at all? If he knew you had Calderón's information?"

"Ramón is policía," she said. "He joined right before I was taken. He may not help. His shame may be too great, I do not know. He is only a cabo, a corporal."

"He's a cop? Great," Tim sighed. He did the math. One promotion in six years. Some help he'd be. "Even so . . . he wouldn't step up for his family?"

He couldn't imagine a cop standing by and letting his own family do what Lupe had done. Another reason he'd never trust the cops.

She looked at him. "Perhaps things are different in America, although from listening to you, I do not think so. I am an outcast. Ramón turned away from me in la zona; he told me I disgraced the family. He is as tolerant as you are."

"If it was my sister—"

She laughed. "You would sooner cut off your own manhood than have that happen in the first place."

"Damn right."

"There was no one to stop them." Her voice was thin and tiny. "When the men came into town, there was no one to stop them. My father, he is not well, he was unable to fight them off. The women cried and begged, but they would not listen. Calderón and his men lied at first and said we would be taken to the city to work in a factory. Some parents gave their girls willingly. The ones who refused, he threatened. Then Marta ran . . . and they shot her. And the parents, they screamed and he threatened to kill us all. There was no one who could stop them."

The sick feeling growing in his gut as she spoke made him ask the question.

"Lupe." He waited until she turned to look at him before he continued. "How old were you when they took you?"

She smiled a regretful, sad smile. "I was eleven."

Tim closed his eyes. "And Calderón, he . . . "

66

"He raped us all that night. He brought clients the next." Her voice steady. "I was not the first to come to the Casa, Tim. I was not the youngest. And I was not the last."

Eleven.

He remembered Diana as an eleven-year-old, unaware of what makeup was, playing with a Barbie doll she'd since relegated to the trunk in her room, yet hadn't thrown away. A couple of years away from short skirts and men paying attention to her a little too much. Way too young to be doing anything more than that.

Lupe watched him, studying his face.

"You hate me," she said. "You hate me, and I do not understand."

"I don't understand why you're using it," he said. "You were ready and willing to pull that shit with me."

"I know of nothing else. Perhaps now you see, a little. If it was not for Calderón, I would not be what you hate."

Hours later, he was in the front seat, his head against the window, unable to get in a position that would allow him more than ten minutes of sleep at a time. Lupe was asleep in the back. He folded down the rear seats, which combined with the armrest in the middle, created a long, flat space she could sleep on. She was curled up in a ball, a hand tucked under her cheek, an old blanket covering her.

Her curls spilled onto her cheek, her eyelashes fluttering as she dreamt. She looked like she was in her twenties before, but as he watched her sleep, he wondered how he could have missed it. She seemed younger asleep, and he watched her quiet breathing for a moment, her chest rising and falling.

His mind spun with images: men firing guns into the night, men with weapons stealing little girls, men having sex with little girls, Lupe in the back of a van.

He reached into the glove box and took out the Browning. He racked the slide and emptied the chamber, then took out the magazine.

Lupe stirred at the noise. Her eyes were open, and she stared at him.

"I hope you were not going to kill me in my sleep," she said. He couldn't decide if she was serious or not.

He held out the empty gun to her, and she sat up, startled.

"This is the one you wore the day you chased me," she said.

He nodded. "Stupid of me to leave it in the car."

He motioned for her to take it, and she hesitated before doing so. He pulled out the small gun in his ankle holster, a Colt Detective Special.

"You are prepared," she said.

"Not tonight." It burned to say that. He prided himself on being prepared for things and he'd been taken by surprise.

She was quiet, and sat forward on the seat, leaning her head against the passenger seat. He looked over, her expression tired and some of the fear back in her face.

"I try to be with you because it is the only way I know how to repay you," she said quietly. "I have nothing else to offer. I need a place to stay; I need a place to hide. When you need things where I have been, they come at a cost. I do not like it, but I am prepared to pay it."

He looked back at her.

Currency.

Sex was her currency, and she had tried to pay him. He looked out the windshield at the dusky sky full of stars, wispy clouds covering them now and then.

"You get my shipment back, we'll call it even," he said.

"You would do that?" She was surprised.

He said nothing else and concentrated on the gun. He pushed out the cylinder of the Colt and checked to make sure it was loaded. "You ever fire a gun before?"

She shook her head. "No. My father, he hated guns. Calderón would have been stupid to give any of us guns."

"How many were there? Girls, I mean. How many did he have?"

"Many," she said. "When the girls are too old, like me, they are sent to the zona de tolerancias in the cities to work. Some are lucky. They receive freedoms. In the past, those freedoms would make them run, but by the time they are given them, they have nowhere to run, and they know this. Most of them stay in la zona in Mexicali, or Calderón has them travel to other border towns to work. None go home."

"Why not?"

"He will not let them," she told him. "And if he did, it is like I said before, there is great shame. We are Catholic. The Bible says you are to be a virgin when you marry. Prostitution is a sin. When your family learns you have done this, many turn you away."

"You said you haven't been back," Tim said. "How do you know they'd turn you away?"

"Ramón did," she said. "I have no doubt my family would. My mother, she would be sad, but she would not be permitted to have me back. My father would not allow it."

"Any brothers or sisters?"

"Three sisters, all younger."

She was quiet, and he wondered if she ever thought the same thing he was.

"You ever think Calderón will go back for them?"

She wiped away tears.

"I think about this every day. If I saw him bring one of them, I would put a knife through her heart and then my own."

"Are there many girls there now?" he asked.

"Nine." She began crying in earnest. "Florencia saw me leave, she begged me to take her, but I could not. It was difficult enough getting out on my own. I hear her calling for me. This guilt is something that eats your soul. I know what they endure every day, and I feel sick, but I cannot do anything."

Tim felt sick himself.

Lupe's face shone silver from the moonlight shining in the car. Her cheeks were wet with tears.

"It isn't right, your family not taking you back," he said. "Still . . . you don't know if they would or not."

"They would not," she said.

"Well, I guess it wouldn't hurt to try, seeing as there's nothing to lose."

"If it was your sister . . . "

"It wouldn't be my sister."

"If it was," Lupe said firmly. "What would you do?"

"First, she wouldn't get into that kind of trouble," Tim said. "Second, if anyone showed up and tried to take her from here, they'd be bleeding on the floor and praying for God to let them die."

"If she left here and one day you learned she has done what I have done, what would you do?" she asked. "You hate so much of it; I can see that in your eyes."

He spun the cylinder of the gun, watching the .38 Special bullets rotate. He imagined Diana in the doorway of a brothel and it was too easy to imagine the men who would look.

He imagined for a second, then closed his mind to it.

"You cannot even bear it," Lupe whispered.

He couldn't think of it anymore, but the anger coursed through him. He would race to Diana, pull her out of whatever trouble she was in and make sure she never did it again. If someone had made her to do it, he'd kill them without a second thought. But he wouldn't turn away from her.

"I wouldn't leave her," he said. "Not for a second. If she took off, came home and told me she made her living doing that while she was gone, I'd set out first thing and blow the head off the guy who made her do it."

"You are so sure she would not do it on her own."

"She's proud," he said. "Too proud to do it."

"I am not?" Lupe asked.

Tim studied her. Despite the tears smearing her cheeks, there was defiance in her eyes. This was a woman who would not rest until she was away from these men, he could see that. Hell, she came across the border in a delivery truck, stole from a crime lord and had the wherewithal to hide the evidence. Lupe was proud all right, and he nodded. She had fire in her. Calderón hadn't put that out, not yet. It might be her saving grace.

"I wouldn't leave her," he said again. "Gimme the gun."

She handed him the Browning.

"Tomorrow you're gonna learn how to shoot."

"Me?" she asked.

"Yeah, you," he told her. "I want you to carry the Browning, so I'll teach you on that. I know a place we can go, they won't find us. I'll get you shooting targets. If these guys show up, I want you able to protect yourself. Can you do that?"

She swallowed hard and nodded.

"Good." He snapped the cylinder back in on the Colt and tucked it back in his ankle holster. He put the magazine back in the Browning and stuck it in the glove box. "They show up, I want them dead."

"Have you killed a man before?" she asked, her voice low.

His gaze darted toward her. "No. But I've shot someone."

"Could you?" she asked. "Kill a man?"

He locked gazes with her. "Yeah. I could. Can you?"

She glanced away, then looked him in the eyes again. "I do not know."

Tim nodded. "Get some sleep, Lupe."

She nodded back, then paused before she settled into the back again. She put a hand on his arm.

"Thank you," she said.

He didn't pull away this time. "You're welcome."

6

The night air in the desert was cold, and when Lupe awoke, the car windows were covered in condensation. She shivered under the thin blanket, curling up tighter in an effort to stay warm.

Tim was asleep, his seat reclined and his head leaning against the window, his jacket jammed between the seat and window to create an uncomfortable-looking pillow. Frown lines creased his forehead, and he looked tired, so she decided to let him sleep. She had to pee, her stomach growled and her head ached, but she felt better than she had in a long time.

It was a relief to pour out her story. Manuel knew it, of course, but it was different to tell it to someone who never saw her in la zona and didn't know what she was. Tim had an imagination that could fill in the gaps quite well, but somehow sharing with him had lightened her burden.

She sensed a slight thaw in his behaviour; perhaps he didn't hate her any longer.

She wondered why he hated prostitutes so much. He was not a religious man from what she could see. He drank, he swore, he smoked, and, from the looks of the blonde girl who had come looking for him, he was no virgin himself. The girl looked as much a whore as she did on her worst day in la zona.

She was scared to hold a gun, and the weight of it surprised her. She didn't know if she could shoot a man in cold blood. Murder was one of the worst sins.

But then, she liked to think God had forgiven her for a multitude of others. He put her on this path for a reason, and if He wanted her to learn to shoot it made sense He brought her to Tim.

"What are you thinking about?"

She looked at Tim's profile, startled to hear his voice. His eyes weren't even open.

"How did you know I was awake?" she asked.

"Your breathing."

"I was thinking of God," she said. "He has put you in my path for a reason."

"Yeah? Well, today's reason is to learn how to fire a gun. While you're at it, tell Him we might need some help if those Mexicans show up again."

"I have told Him." She was serious.

Tim cracked a grin. "You sound like my mother."

"She is religious?"

"Catholic," he said. "I am too, I guess. Don't go to church much. Old man never put much stock in church. Hopefully it's the only way I take after him."

"You do not believe?"

"I dunno." He opened his eyes. "I'm not one to believe anything I can't see. I'm surprised you would, though, after everything."

"God did not do this," she said. "This is the work of Satan."

"No," Tim said with force. He looked back. "This is the work of men. Nothing else but men. And we're gonna take them down."

She was surprised at his use of we; she assumed he meant his gang.

He got out of the car and disappeared behind some large boulders, returning a minute later.

"Go on." He nodded toward where he'd come from.

She got out of the car, her body aching from sleeping in the hard rear of the car. She went behind the rock and did her business, finding leaves of the gordolobo to use. She was comforted to see plants she recognized.

She returned, and Tim cranked the engine.

"We need bullets," he said. "I need to make a stop before we go out to the place I'll teach you to shoot at."

"They will not find us?" she asked.

"No."

He pulled out of their hiding spot, yanking the wheel to one side and turning the car. For the first time she realized the breakneck speed he travelled was his regular way of driving and had nothing to do with anger or fear of being followed.

He headed back into town, making lots of turns in case anyone followed them. He pulled up at a gun store ten minutes later. He told her to stay in the car, then he walked up the craggy concrete walk and knocked on a door at the side of the building. The pale blond from the warehouse answered, and Tim disappeared inside with him.

She glanced around the neighbourhood. It was industrial, with a plumbing store, a refrigerator repair place and a locksmith nearby, but a few houses were scattered amongst the businesses, and they were all run down, the yards unkempt. A sheen of neglect hung over the entire area.

A train whistle blew nearby. She had heard them at the warehouse and wondered how far they were from the railway.

Tim came out the front door a few minutes later, a large paper bag in his hand. He handed the bag to her when he got in the car, and she peeked inside to find a package of cookies and two apples.

Underneath the food were boxes of ammunition, paper targets, and a bag of cotton balls. She took the boxes out and looked at the numbers. One said 9mm and the other .38 Special.

"The Browning is a nine millimetre," Tim said. "The gun is bigger, but you'll be able to shoot it easier."

"And the other?"

"I'll use the Colt," he said. "It's a .38 Special, a little harder to fire since it's a snub nose. Your hands are small, the Browning will be better for you."

"You know a lot about this," she commented.

"I've been around guns since I was a kid."

"Does your father shoot guns?" Lupe asked.

Tim nodded. "He was in the service. You wouldn't know it to look at him now. Pete, that was his old man's gun store back there, he's always brought guns around. I'm a decent shot."

She watched the scenery fly by as they headed into the desert. Tim pulled into an abandoned ranch twenty minutes out of town.

"What is this place?"

"It belonged to Pete's grandmother. She died awhile ago, and they're trying to unload the property. It's quiet, we can shoot out back and no one will bother us."

They got out of the car once Tim had parked it. The house, weathered white and creaking in the wind, was empty. The barn was in disrepair, boards missing, and the post and rail fence had fallen in more than one location. Desert scrub had grown its way into what was once a garden, and the land around the ranch held cholla and sagebrush.

Lupe followed him, but looked back to the road, her brow wrinkled.

"Would you quit looking over your shoulder?" Tim asked. "They're not here, and there's no way they can find us here."

"I would not be so sure," she said. "I did not think they would find me in Las Vegas."

Tim walked toward a fence post some distance away and set a can on top of it. She sat on a tree stump in the abandoned yard, hoping it would warm up soon. The wind was cool, but the sun wasn't up high yet. She guessed it was early morning.

"Stay there," he said.

He stood facing the fence, the small Colt in his hands. He put cotton in his ears before he pushed out the cylinder of the gun and spun it, then clicked it back into place. He aimed the gun and fired. The can flew off the fence post.

She relaxed. At least he wasn't lying about being a decent shot. He had missed the men in the warehouse, and she was afraid he had never fired a gun before. Her hopes rose, knowing she was with someone who knew the business end of a gun, perhaps as well as some of the El Camarilla foot soldiers.

"Come here," he said. He pulled the Browning out of his waistband.

She approached him, a little afraid of the gun.

"Here. You press this button and pull out the magazine like this." The button was on the side of the gun, behind the trigger. "The bullets are stacked like this."

He removed some from the magazine and re-loaded them, by pushing them in one by one. He handed her the magazine when he was done, and she took out the bullets and placed them back in.

"You insert the magazine like this." He popped it into the handle of the gun and used the release switch and took it out again.

He handed her both the gun and the magazine. She looked at him for a second, then put the magazine in the gun like he showed her.

Her hands were shaking, and she swallowed hard. He handed her some cotton balls and she put them in her ears. She could hear him speak, so she didn't know how well they'd protect her hearing.

"Good." Tim stood behind her. "Now, raise your arms up. You're right handed?"

She nodded, holding the gun in her right hand. She couldn't figure out what to do with her left hand.

"Here." He put his arms out alongside hers and covered her right hand with his own. "You hold the gun in your dominant hand. Finger on the trigger, other fingers curled around the grip, like that. You want your thumb on the left. Now, your left hand covers the grip on that side, line the thumb up. Make sure you don't stick your thumbs up, the slide could pinch it."

He walked to the side and looked at her holding the gun out.

"Whatever you do, don't shoot me," he said, approaching her and moving her fingers. He readjusted her grip until he was satisfied.

She took a breath when he stepped behind her again.

He adjusted her stance, kicking her feet apart a little, then ran his hand down her back, pushing her between the shoulder blades. She wasn't sure, but it seemed his hand lingered on her back longer than it should have.

"Don't hunch," he said into her ear, his breath warm. She swallowed hard. "Shoulders straight."

She took in a breath as his hands moved down her sides and stopped at her hips. He turned her to face more toward the other can he had stood on the post. "Feet should be a shoulder width apart."

"I do not see what it will matter," she said. "They will not give me time to do things right."

"I know. But you learn right and everything else comes." He stood back and looked at her. "Okay. The Browning is a single action pistol. You need to rack the slide or cock the hammer before you take the first shot."

She shook her head.

"The hammer." He indicated the small thing sticking out of the back of the gun. "It needs to be cocked back to shoot. Usually you do that by racking the slide when you put the magazine in."

He took the gun from her and slid the top part of the gun back and forth.

"It loads the bullet," she said, understanding. He nodded.

"You can also cock the hammer all the way back yourself. You don't do it, the gun won't fire when you pull the trigger."

"And if I forget? I will be dead before I can do any of this."

"No. You load the magazine, you rack the slide. Safety goes on here." He flicked a small switch on the side of the gun upwards. "Flick it down, safety is off. Flick it up, safety is on and you can't fire. Carry it cocked and locked."

"So it will always be prepared."

"Exactly. After the first shot, you'll be able to re-fire without doing that. Whenever you're ready, squeeze the trigger. There's gonna be some recoil."

"What is that?"

"You'll feel the gun kick back in your hand from the force of firing the bullet. Don't loosen your grip, but don't hold on for dear life, either."

She nodded, then adjusted her grip and stance again. He stood back observing and told her to move her feet and straighten up until he was satisfied.

"Whenever you're ready," he said.

She nodded, said a short prayer, and squeezed the trigger. She yelped a little when the gun fired, the hammer catching her skin between her thumb and index finger. She looked at the circular red wound on her hand, then looked at the can. It sat on the fence post.

"Lupe," Tim said, the hint of a smile on his lips. "You might wanna open your eyes next time."

An hour later, Lupe wasn't any closer to hitting the can.

Tim had no idea what her problem was, but noticed before she fired she tended to close her eyes, and she didn't breathe either.

"You're doing it again," he said, his frustration growing.

"I do not mean to. My hand is hurting."

He walked over and looked at it. "Hammer bite. The hammer catches you when it fires."

"Make it stop."

"Hold the gun better." He adjusted her grip a little lower on the weapon, then stepped back.

"It feels wrong there." She adjusted her grip back and fired again. Wide.

"You closed your eyes again."

"I do not mean to. It just happens," she sighed.

"You have to breathe. You have to breathe like normal, and you've got to keep your damn eyes open. I don't get what you're closing them for."

"Perhaps it is because I am imagining what I am shooting," she said without humour.

"Well, use it. Imagine Calderón's fat head is over on that post and blow the damn thing off!"

"It is not that easy," she said.

"Sure it is. Ready, aim, fire, dead as a doornail. Are you telling me you wouldn't kill him if he was in front of you?"

She looked at the ground. "I do not know."

"After all he did to you? The man takes you away from your family, rapes you every night, gives you up to anyone with a peso hanging out of his wallet, and you'd look him in the eye and what, Lupe? Maybe you're not such a victim like you think. Maybe you care about this Satan you keep talking about."

"No!" she said. "Stop it!"

"It makes sense." He cupped his hand around the tip of his cigarette and flicked open his lighter, closing out the wind. He continued to bait her. "He's had you since you were a kid. Maybe you got some kind of attachment to him, despite what you say."

"No!" Tears were in her eyes.

"Then fire the gun."

She stood there, breathing hard, her eyes dark and angry, and he waited for her to turn the gun on him. She stood still, so he marched over and pointed her toward the target, raising her arms.

"He doesn't think you can do it," Tim said into her ear. "He's counting on it, because he knows you can't walk away from him. You don't *want* to walk away from him."

The gun roared as it fired, and Tim smiled when the can finally fell.

So had Lupe.

She was on the ground at his feet, the gun discarded at her side. She cried, her shoulders wracked with each sob.

He leaned over and pulled her up, trying to show her the fallen target, but she pressed herself against him and cried into his shirt instead.

He stood there for a moment, unsure what to do. He put an arm around her with trepidation. "You got the target."

She nodded against his chest. "I want to walk away. I want to *run* away."

"So do it," he said. He made circles on her back, her tears slowing.

"It is not that simple."

"Nothing ever is. But can you do it?"

She looked at him, her eyes wet with tears, and for the first time, he noticed her eyes were not brown like he would have thought, her being Mexican and all, but green, like his own.

"If you will help me, I think I can." She looked young. It took him a minute to recognize the look on her face. Hope.

"Pick up the gun. You got a few more rounds to shoot."

Awhile later, Lupe rubbed her hand; the wound was worse now.

She sighed. She hadn't hit the can again after that lucky shot; hadn't even gotten close, according to Tim. He tacked up paper targets on the side of the old barn. They were larger, but she had yet to hit the paper at all.

"I am not good at this."

"No, you're not," Tim agreed. "So you have to hope he's close to you when you pull the trigger."

"How close?"

"On top of you'd probably give you the best chance."

She looked at him and pursed her lips. "You are making fun of me."

"I don't make fun."

"You do not have it, either."

"I have fun," he said. "That's fine coming from someone who's been locked up all those years."

"You seem angry all the time," she said. She squeezed off a round. The pain in her hand made it harder. She was afraid each time she fired the gun that it would take off more skin. With her aim as bad as it was, it didn't seem worth it to keep practicing.

Her index finger was sore from pulling the trigger, and her ears were ringing from the noise. The gun was large and heavy in her hands, and Tim said it would help her aim straighter than the smaller gun. She vowed to hit at least one target. She would settle for hitting the damn paper.

Tim stared at the hammer bite on her hand. "I would've taken my old man's Colt, but it's a .45. It can bite too, especially with your high hold. You wouldn't be able to handle it."

"I cannot handle this one."

She sighed, fired the gun and missed. Again.

"So what'd you do anyway?" Tim asked.

She looked over her shoulder at him, unsure what he meant.

"In the boy's town, the zona you talk about. I know what you did, but I mean …"

"How it worked?"

He nodded.

"We would leave the Casa on Friday mornings. We would never know which border town we would go to, but more often than not it has been Mexicali, especially of late. His men would bring me into town and I would stay in a small room. In Mexicali, Calderón has built a place, like la zona in Nuevo Laredo. We stay there, sometimes with others who Calderón controls. They would leave men behind to make sure we did not leave."

"Not the greatest security."

"No," she said, lowering the gun. "The threats were enough. We would sleep late and then get dressed. Sometimes they would take us to the market, it was a treat reserved for the ones who brought in the most profit. In the evening, we would get ready and the cantinas would fill. We would be brought to the brothel which is under Calderón's control. His men would be everywhere. The men would come—many Americans would come from Calexico. They would choose a girl, and they would come to the room. One of the guards would follow in case of trouble."

"What kind of trouble?"

"If the man was rough or would try to rob us," she said. "It frightened me. In some way the Casa was safer, because it was controlled, although Calderón was not concerned with what these men were like with us, as long as they were happy. Men who come for children are . . . they are frightening in a different way from the men that come to la zona roja. The men that came to the Casa were all bad men. You knew what to expect. In la zona, you never knew who chose you. If he was a crazy man or just lonely."

"What kinds of men would go there?"

She rubbed her palm on the jeans she wore, which were now dirty with dust and grime. "All kinds. Religious men with families, Americans that come to have a good time, criminal friends of El Camarilla. Single men, married men, divorced men. Old men, young men. Everyone."

Tim sat on a rusted piece of ranch equipment. "Any of them bring kids?"

"Children? For what purpose?" She frowned, trying to figure out if she had misunderstood his question.

"Bringing them along, you know?"

"Some men would bring their sons. When they were sixteen or seventeen. To have a woman for the first time."

"No, little kids. Did any bring little kids?"

"No," she said. "I never saw any children. Most of the men that came would leave all of their family behind at home. Coming to la zona was a great secret."

He was folding the foil wrapper from his cigarette pack over and over, a nervous gesture that surprised her. She walked over and sat next to him. A water blister had formed on her trigger finger. "Do you know of men that bring their children? Here in America?"

He glanced at her, and she wondered if she said the wrong thing.

"You better lay off shooting for a bit. We'll pop the blister. I think there's a bandage in the car."

He got up and went to the Charger, and she sat for a few moments longer and wondered about his questions.

7

They spent the entire day at the abandoned ranch. The sky had darkened by the time they left the country. Purple streaked across the sky, and a brilliant orange and yellow sunset faded behind the mountains in the west. When they reached downtown it was dark, and he was confident no one was coming after them—at least tonight.

"Where are we going?" Lupe asked "I hope for food."

"I don't know yet. I need to make a call."

He pulled into a Mobil station and headed to the pay phone. He dialled the Lucky Lady and got Jimmy's old man. He grunted and handed the phone to Bill.

"Chicago is not happy," Bill said.

"This wasn't sanctioned?" Relief flooded his system.

"Not from what Wyatt said when he called. He told me to tell you to keep your head down while they deal with it."

Fat chance when those Mexicans were out there hunting for him.

"Jimmy spotted them at the warehouse last night, and Jesse said there was a sedan watching your house for awhile this morning. Nothing happened though. Adam was pretty sure the same sedan was outside of the Lucky Lady earlier tonight."

"We need a plan," Tim said. "Meet me in an hour."

"Where?

"Rett's," he said. "Make sure you aren't followed."

"You sure about that? Rett's?"

Tim looked at a car full of high school kids that pulled into the gas station, everyone in costume.

"Yeah, I'm sure. What day is it?"

"Halloween," Bill said. "Happy Birthday, by the way."

He'd forgotten. "Yeah, some birthday. Rett's in an hour or so."

He hung up the phone and got back in the car. He stopped at McDonald's and picked up hamburgers, shakes and fries, and they ate in silence in the parking lot.

When they were both finished he pulled out of the parking lot and onto the boulevard, stopping at a red light. People in costume crossed in front of them.

Lupe looked at them with a strange expression.

"It's Halloween," he said. "You celebrate that?"

"No," she said. "In the south of México they celebrate Dia de Muertos this time of year, to honour the dead. Some do in the north. My mother, she would take us to the cemetery to lay wreaths for those who have passed. We would go to church and pray."

"No costumes? No trick or treating?"

Lupe frowned.

"Kids dress up and go door to door, asking for candy."

Lupe laughed. "No. And there was nothing of the sort at the Casa. But . . . I think the children would like that."

Her voice had taken on a sad tone.

The light changed.

"Where will we go?" Lupe asked.

"A bar I know," he said. "They won't know it, even if they've been following me. I haven't been there in awhile."

"Is this where the cowboy has poker games? Jesse told me of it."

Tim nodded.

"Then I will change," she said.

"Into what?"

"I have my dress." She lifted up the bundle of clothes. He'd forgotten about them. She moved into the backseat.

He looked through the rearview mirror. "You're missing a few other pieces of clothing if I remember right."

"I was embarrassed and kept my underclothes and washed them in the shower with me, then dried them with the hair dryer. The dress will be alright?"

"It's not a fancy place by any stretch of the imagination, you're fine in blue jeans."

"You do not wear pants to a club," she said.

"It's not a club, it's a bar," he said. "Like a cantina."

"Women are not permitted in most cantinas. But Jesse tells me they are here. I want to look proper."

He didn't bother to argue. He flicked his gaze up to the rearview mirror when he saw a flash of fabric. Lupe was in profile, the streetlights highlighting her skin as she changed out of Diana's shirt. He looked at the road for a moment, then glanced at the rearview mirror again as she pulled the dress over her head.

He drove up along the railway tracks and pulled off into the gravel lot at Rett's. The neon beer signs flashed in Rett's windows and a large crowd of costumed people milled around the parking lot. Nothing seemed out of place, so he drove around back and parked in a way that would make it easy to leave if he had to, then cut the engine.

They got out of the car and headed around the building to the front door. Bill's Bel Air wasn't there yet.

People greeted him as he approached, and he began rethinking his idea to meet here, since everyone he'd ever met seemed to be milling around. But maybe it would help him. He could count on some backup from these people if trouble showed up.

Jake Wheeler was nowhere to be found. He'd taken off a week or two after their big fight a few months earlier and no one had seen him since. He was glad Jake had left, it was nice not seeing his face around town, but truth be told, he wouldn't mind having him back him up tonight, just in case.

But Jake was on the rodeo circuit, so the gossip said. He wondered if Wheeler would ever come back. With his girl Darla gone, maybe he'd head west to Los Angeles and chase after her. Better for all of them if that happened.

Well . . . maybe not Darla.

He didn't stop to shake hands with anyone as they made their way toward the entrance. A few people were staring at Lupe, and he realized she stood out, a Mexican amongst them all. It would've been better if he'd found a costume for her, but there wasn't any time.

The inside was noisy and raucous, "Monster Mash" playing on the jukebox and costumed people dancing and drinking everywhere. He couldn't remember the last time the place was so packed. Lupe looked around with obvious curiosity.

"Sit up at the bar for a minute," he said to Lupe. "Don't talk to anyone."

She nodded, and Tim shooed someone off a bar stool so Lupe could sit. She looked around at the people and the commotion, and Tim wondered if she was reminded of the zona roja in Mexicali she mentioned.

He spotted Rett in back emptying coins out of one of those blasted slot machines that should be his, then saw Ruby out of the corner of his eye. He couldn't stop himself from turning to look.

She was dressed in her everyday clothes, a blue and white checked shirt and tan jeans, but had a black cowboy hat on her head and a studded belt.

The last time he was here they interacted like they'd never met before. After he learned she'd slept with Jake Wheeler, he took a girl upstairs right in front of her. Sometimes he remembered her expression, the wounded look she deserved, yet never made him feel any better.

Since then, they'd maintained a cordial peace, but hadn't spoken more than a few words to each other. He found that harder than hating her, and spent the last few months at the Lucky Lady instead.

Ruby put beers on the table for a ghost, the devil and Cleopatra, then turned.

She paused for a second when she saw him, the surprise evident on her face, like everything she felt. She recovered quickly and headed toward him and the bar.

He leaned against the wall near the entrance to the bar and waited for her.

"Hey," she said, her voice neutral.

He nodded. "I'm gonna need a room upstairs for tonight."

She paused a second before nodding at him. She took a piece of paper out and wrote out the room number and his name and tucked the paper in the register, then handed him a key in exchange for the few dollars he forked over.

She used to take everyone up and unlock the door for them, make sure the room was in decent shape. She didn't anymore, and he was the reason why.

She didn't ask why he was here or why he needed a room, even though he knew she was curious. It relieved him she didn't look at him with that wounded expression anymore. Maybe she sensed he was done twisting the knife.

"Why didn't you dress up?" he asked.

She deflated right in front of him. "I did. I'm Cat Ballou."

Tim looked her over and smothered a smile. "Shoulda worn her hanging dress instead."

The pursed lips and eye roll she gave made him forget about her and Jake for a minute. He wondered if he'd ever be able to look at her lips and not want to taste them.

"Bill was in earlier," she said. "He was looking for you."

Tim nodded. "Where's he at?"

"He was in the back room, but he took off for awhile, said he'd be back," Ruby said. She put a hand on her hip and looked at him, as if trying to decide whether to say something. "Jesse's back there playing poker with a few regulars. I don't think it's goin' so well for him. He's already lost five dollars."

"Figures," Tim said. "He learned the game the other day. I'll be in back. Send Bill back there when he shows up."

He glanced over at Lupe, who watched them with interested eyes.

"Get her a drink." He nodded at Lupe and plunked some coins on the bar. "Whatever'll calm her down fastest."

He turned away from the bar, not wanting to see Ruby's expression or answer the questions he knew were on her lips.

Lupe was at home amongst the loud music and the people. It reminded her a little of the busy streets of cantinas and clubs of the zona roja, but not in a bad way. She had always liked the liveliness and activity, a stark contrast to life at the Casa.

People were dressed in all kinds of costumes, from elaborate to put together at the last minute. She stood out in her street clothes, even though she'd changed into her dress. She pulled her sweater tighter around her, feeling out of place.

Tim stood at the other end of the bar talking to a raven-haired girl. They stood apart from each other, yet there was a closeness she could see. The girl's gaze was on Tim's lips rather than his eyes and was full of want.

She was sure this girl loved him, but she couldn't read Tim. He seemed unconcerned with her—but he seemed unconcerned with everyone else in the room as well. She never met anyone who was so detached from people.

Tim looked toward her once as he spoke with the girl, who was dressed like a cowgirl. Tim headed into a hallway, and she had no idea what to do with herself. He said to sit at the bar, so she'd sit at the bar.

"Tim said to get you a drink." The raven-haired girl was in front of her. "What are you drinking?"

"Tequila, if you have it," she said.

The girl poured her a shot of tequila and set it in front of her. Lupe waved away the salt and lemon and took the shot straight, grimacing a little at the burn.

"Do you know Tim well?" Lupe asked her. The girl turned around, her expression guarded.

"I've known him for awhile," she said.

"He is . . . complicated," Lupe said.

"You can say that again," the girl said, her voice low. She looked at the empty shot glass. "Another one?"

Lupe nodded her head. She would have one more, since she needed to have a clear head in case something went wrong. The girl poured the tequila—not a good one—and she finished the shot.

"How did you meet him?" the girl asked.

Lupe looked at her and wondered how much she should say. Tim seemed to play his cards close to the vest, so she would too.

"We met because of business."

The raven-haired girl raised an eyebrow and wiped the counter.

"So you haven't known him long," she stated.

"No," Lupe said. "Long enough to know he is complicated."

"Be careful with him." The girl had stopped wiping the counter and studied her. "He ain't all that . . . uncomplicated. Ever."

Lupe looked at the girl and wondered what she meant. The last thing she wanted was an angry girl—another one—bothering her and Tim.

"It is not like that," she said. "He is helping me with a problem."

The girl's eyebrow rose again. "My, isn't he being generous."

Lupe gave a small smile. "It might not be entirely his idea."

"I don't doubt that," the girl said.

"It is not like you think," Lupe said.

"Yeah, how do I think?"

"You think I am sleeping with him."

The girl looked at Lupe in shocked surprise, perhaps not expecting her to come out and say it.

"I wasn't—"

"You were wondering," Lupe cut in. "I can see it in your eyes. You were lovers?"

The girl blushed at Lupe's words, and for a moment, the full weight of her time at the Casa and in la zona was on her shoulders. She blushed herself, embarrassed she hadn't realized how forward she must sound. She wondered how long the things she learned at the Casa would stay with her, and how much they would make her stand out.

"Not anymore," the girl said.

"This saddens you," Lupe said, more as a statement than a question.

The girl didn't answer, but the way her gaze swept lower before she continued wiping the already clean counter gave Lupe her answer.

A moment later she heard someone say "hello" in her ear. She turned, expecting a man to be there, ready to proposition her, as if he read her soul. Instead, Tim's friend Bill was behind her.

"He's waiting for you in the back room," the girl said, taking the shot glass away from in front of Lupe.

"Thanks, Ruby," Bill said. "I'll take a Bud if you got one."

Bill grabbed the beer she set down and motioned for Lupe to follow him. She slid off the stool and looked back at the girl again.

"It is not like that," Lupe said.

"No," Ruby said. "Not yet. But it doesn't matter anyhow. It was a long time ago."

Lupe smiled. A long time, but not forgotten.

Tim marched into the back room and put an end to the poker game—and a good thing too, since Jesse was down. The guys at the table collected their winnings and left. Jesse had a few coins left in his pile.

"Aw, Tim, I had a good hand this time," Jesse whined.

Tim picked up the cards—a pair of twos, a seven, a jack and an ace. He rolled his eyes and tossed the cards back on the table.

"What's going on?" Jesse asked.

"Gonna figure that out," Tim said.

Bill opened the door to the back room a minute later. Lupe trailed behind Bill, out of place in her dress and pale blue sweater, which looked like it belonged on a child. He had trouble imagining her as a prostitute when she was dressed like that.

"Did you win?" she asked, sitting next to Jesse at the table.

"Nah," he said. "I'm not good at bluffing, like you said. I kept giving it away. I'm not too swift on the math part either, I keep forgetting when to fold right away."

"We can work on that." Lupe smiled at Jesse.

"Not right now we can't," Tim said. He got up and shut the door to the back room. He noticed Lupe didn't seem so jumpy and figured whatever Ruby gave her had done its job.

"Your girlfriend does not like me," she said.

"Girlfriend?" Tim asked.

"Behind the bar. The girl with dark hair you were speaking to."

"Ruby?" Tim asked. "She hasn't been my girlfriend in a long time."

"So she was, then?"

Tim let out a breath. He'd walked right into that, and Lupe looked pleased at the fact she'd pulled the information out of him.

He sat at the table. Lupe's gaze was on him, a smile playing on her lips. Anger washed over him for some reason. She needed to mind her own damn business.

"I could have seen it blind," she said. "From the girl, yes, but also you."

"You wanna quit analyzing me? We're not here to talk about me, we're here to deal with the shit you brought in," Tim asked. "Anyway, I broke it off with her over four months ago, and it's nothing now. At least nothing some two-bit Mexican prostitute needs to know about."

He regretted the words the minute he said them.

"What?"

Jesse looked over at Lupe, his brow wrinkled in confusion. Lupe's mouth was open, a perfect expression of surprise on her face.

"¡Culero! ¡Vaya al diablo!" She cursed at him. She got up from the table and pushed back her chair so hard it toppled over. "You are a horrible man."

She flung the door open and headed out into the hallway, pushing past Ruby who stood in the doorway with more drinks.

"What's wrong with her?" Ruby asked.

Tim shrugged. "Leave the drinks."

Ruby exchanged a look with Bill, then she left the room, her tray sitting on the table.

"Is that true?" Jesse asked. "Is she a prostitute?"

"Yeah." Tim wasn't sure he wanted to get into the story, but maybe it was best Jesse learn the truth now.

"Wow," Jesse said. "She seemed so nice."

Tim didn't think Jesse knew about the drives he used to take with his father. Yet somehow, he'd come to the same conclusion about prostitutes to please him. It rankled for some reason.

"The men after her are from some kind of Mexican mafia," Tim said. "The leader, Calderón, took her from her family when she was eleven."

"Took her for what?"

Tim looked at Jesse pointedly.

"Eleven?" Jesse asked, his face contorting in disgust. "Jesus Christ, an eleven-year-old kid ..."

"Calderón sent those two men who shot up the downtown place," Bill chimed in.

"She didn't have a choice if some asshole's making her do that at eleven," Jesse said. "Holy shit. And you had to go and say that to her. Bet she feels real nice about it right now."

Tim stared at his cousin.

"Well, come on, Tim." Jesse's voice was loud. "You've never made it a secret you hate girls like that."

"Yeah, with good reason," Tim said. "You remember me telling you about Rosa and how she stole money straight outta my wallet. Hell, Lupe tried to rip us off the second I saw her."

"Well, why are you helping Lupe if you hate her so much?" Jesse asked.

The bastard had him there.

"I thought she was a real nice girl before," Jesse said. He was quiet for a moment. "I guess I still do. I'll go find her. If I bring her back in here, you better be nice to her."

Tim watched his cousin leave the room. Maybe there was hope for him yet.

"You got a plan in mind?" Bill asked.

Tim nodded. "Yeah. But she's not gonna like it."

Lupe pulled the sweater tighter around her legs. She had tucked her knees up to her chest while sitting on the back porch. A cool wind blew, making her shiver. The raucous laughter and screeches from the party made her cringe.

"Here."

She looked and the raven-haired girl held out another glass of tequila.

"Might not make you feel better, but it'll keep you warm," she said.

Lupe smiled wanly and took the shot.

"He is very cruel," Lupe said, her voice hoarse from the effort of not crying.

"Yeah," the girl said. She sat next to Lupe. "I know. But he doesn't know any other way to be, I don't think. If it makes you feel any better, I think he regrets things the same as anyone. He just hides it better."

"He will not regret this," she said. "He hates me."

"I bet he doesn't," she said. "I'm Ruby. What's your name?"

"María Guadalupe. They call me Lupe," she said.

"Lupita," Ruby said.

Lupe looked over at her, intrigued this girl knew the pet form of her name.

"I lived in Del Rio, Texas for awhile, with my grandparents," she said. "They had a local girl come to help with the laundry. They called her Lupita. She told me it was short for Guadalupe."

"My father would call me that, Lupita." The word brought tears to her eyes. She looked at the heavens. "I have not heard that in years."

She leaned her head against the wooden post.

"I saw you rush outta there," Ruby said.

Lupe nodded. "Jesse is a very nice boy. I did not want him to know something, and Tim told him."

"Told him what?"

Lupe glanced over at the girl. She didn't care what anyone thought anymore. No one would ever think of her nicely again. It didn't matter.

"He told him I was forced to work as a prostitute in México," Lupe said. The girl was quiet. Lupe looked over.

"You may go now," she said with a sigh, "if it bothers you."

"Well, I can see why Tim ain't too happy. He's got a thing about . . . girls like that," Ruby said.

Lupe's smile was wry. "I had not noticed."

She was surprised at the level of sarcasm in her own voice.

"There was this one girl on a ranch in California, she worked there. And by work, I mean . . . well, you know what I mean. She was a sly one. She'd hang off him right in front of me and drive me 'round the bend. I never wanted to slap someone more," Ruby said. "She had a lot of nerve. Rosa was her name."

Lupe knew the women she talked about. Some were like that in la zona. Aggressive, challenging and forward. Lupe thought they were coarse and cheap, but their hard push to sell paid in results. She always sensed some of these women enjoyed what they did. Perhaps they used it, as she had tried to. Used it for power.

"He did not like her?"

"He hated her," Ruby said. "I never understood why. It wasn't like he was a stickler for things like virginity."

"Perhaps . . . " Lupe said. "Perhaps he had a poor experience."

Ruby laughed. "He'd never go to a . . . a professional."

"No, I do not mean that. He asked me a question. He asked me if men brought children with them," Lupe said.

"To prostitutes?" Ruby asked, her eyes wide. "What in tarnation would they do that for?"

"That is what I asked him. I thought perhaps he meant a father bringing a son when he was . . . ready to be a man," Lupe said, trying to bring a bit of civility to their conversation. "But he asked about them bringing young children, their children."

"Hmm."

Lupe looked at Ruby, who was deep in thought.

"You know much about him," Lupe said.

"As much as he let me." Her voice was tinged with sadness.

"Do you know about his father?"

Ruby shook her head. "Never met him. Heard stories, though. I think he kept me away from him on purpose."

"He thinks of you," Lupe said. "He does not like to admit this, but I can see he thinks of you often."

Ruby smiled, then stood and brushed her jeans off.

"Come on back inside if you get too cold," she said.

Lupe nodded. She heard the door open, the sounds of the party floating out to her, then they quieted again as the door shut.

He waited for Jesse to return, and when he didn't, Tim left the back room and headed into the party to find Lupe. He circled around the main floor, checked the kitchen and the bathroom and looked out front, but there was no sign of her. If she'd taken off somewhere he was in for it.

He spotted Jesse by the bar and his cousin shrugged—no sign of her.

Tim sighed. Women were too much trouble.

Someone grabbed his elbow, and he turned around to find Ruby standing there. She pulled him toward the stairs.

"She's outside."

Tim moved toward the back door, but Ruby stood in front of him and held out a hand to stop him.

"I'd give her a minute or two."

He looked at her, those dinner plate eyes staring at him, and for a minute, forgot what he was doing.

"She out there crying?" he asked.

Ruby's brow knitted together and she put her hands on her hips. "So what if she is? Sounds like she was justified."

So Lupe had told her. He could imagine what Ruby thought about all of this.

"Don't get involved, Ruby."

"That's rich coming from the guy that brought her here in the first place." She shifted over when he attempted to get past her. "Look, whatever you need her for can wait a minute or two. Let her get it out and let her come back in herself."

"And if she doesn't?"

"She will," Ruby said. "But if not . . . send Jesse."

He could stop the wry smile on his lips. Send Jesse.

She smiled back. "He's a little more . . . "

"I get it, Ruby."

She nodded at him, hesitated a minute, then plunged back into the crowd. He tried to stop himself, but he turned to watch her go.

Lupe wiped her face with the sleeve of her sweater and prepared to go back inside. She would face Jesse, face Tim, and help him get that shipment back. Then she would disappear into the ether and no foot soldiers would find her. She could be free.

She was about to stand up when she heard the door creak open. Part of her hoped it was Tim, hoped he had come to apologize, but he didn't look like the sort of man that ever did that, even when he was in the wrong.

She looked over her shoulder and tried to keep the dismay from her face—Ray.

She stood and turned to face him, then backed down the stairs. The hulking one, Carl, was behind him. Her stomach soured. Apology or not, she wouldn't mind seeing Tim next.

Ray came down the rickety stairs, hands in his pockets and a smile on his face. The pale one, Pete, followed Carl out the door and shut it behind him.

90

"Saw something interesting at the warehouse," he said. "Bullet holes riddling the place. That's something new."

He walked closer, and she backed up further. She looked over her shoulder and saw she was penned in by some garbage cans.

"Then we got Bill telling us to stay away, keep an eye out for some Mexicans in a sedan. All that traces back to you."

"I do not know what you are talking about," she said. Her voice was low and reedy, the fear in it easy to hear, and she cursed herself for being so weak.

"I checked around. Outfit isn't too happy we got Mexican hitmen working this city without their say so." He leaned closer and she tried not to shudder. "They don't like it when folks get murdered in the city. Scares the tourists."

"Ray, let's just take her and go before Kelly gets out here," Carl growled.

"Take me where?" Lupe asked.

"The Outfit's gonna take care of those hitmen, and when they do, no one'll be looking for you," Ray said.

He didn't elaborate, and she didn't ask what he meant. She didn't want to know. She tried not to shudder and went to step back.

Before she could, Ray's hand snapped out and grabbed her wrist, yanking her toward him. She pushed against his chest, and he lost his footing. She turned and ran into the alley, but he was on her a second later. He grabbed her by the hair, yanking hard, and she cried out.

"Pete, go bring the car around." The pale one hurried around the corner and out of sight.

Ray wound his hand into her hair and pulled her closer, his breath on her neck.

"You gonna take her to the Bar S?" Carl asked.

Ray nodded. "Johnny wanted a look at her first. One day I'm not gonna have to run everything by that asshole, but until then . . . "

Lupe struggled, but Ray had a good grip on her. He let her hair go and grabbed her arm.

"Let me go or I will scream!" Lupe said.

"Go ahead," Ray told her. "Nobody's coming for you."

The music and din from the party was loud. A scream wouldn't sound out of place on a holiday where people dressed as the most ghoulish things they could find. She looked toward the back stairs, but no one was there.

A car pulled into the shadows at the entrance to the alley, and Ray loosened his grip for a second. She yanked her arm away and tried to run again. This time he caught her sooner and smacked her across the face.

She tasted blood.

She lashed out and caught his face with her nails, dragging them across flesh. Ray cried out.

"Stupid whore!" he spat. "Carl, get her in the trunk."

She screamed this time, but the hulking one's hand clamped down on her mouth. She tried to stomp on his foot, but his other arm squeezed her rib cage so hard she lost her breath.

"What are you doing?!"

Ruby stood in the doorway of the building and disappeared inside a second later.

"Shit," Ray muttered.

Carl pulled her to the car, but she dug her heels in, doing everything she could to slow him. She heard the snick of a knife and felt the blade at her neck as he twisted her toward the car, away from the building.

"What the hell is going on out here?"

Carl froze, and the knife left her neck. Lupe twisted around and looked over, seeing Tim in the doorway, Jesse right behind him, and Ruby moving aside to let Bill out. Lupe elbowed Carl in the midsection and ran when he loosened his grip.

No one chased her this time.

Jesse came down the stairs and took her hand, swinging her around behind him. Ruby was there a second later, bringing her up the stairs as Tim and Bill stepped into the alley, moving toward Ray.

"I asked a question," Tim said. "What the hell's going on out here?"

"Not your business, Kelly," Ray said.

Ruby inhaled sharply.

"Not my business? You itching to get your head kicked in or something?" Tim asked.

"Or something," Ray said.

"Oh, Jesus," Ruby breathed.

"You've got ten seconds, Roth," Tim said. "What the hell were you doing with Lupe?"

Ray looked at her and gave a slick smile. He had a dangerous look in his eyes Lupe didn't like one bit. Carl and Pete were at the edge of the dark alley, and she remembered the knife.

This might be as bad as Calderón's men coming for her.

8

When Ruby had rushed up to him, pulling him to the door, he expected to hear Lupe had run off. Instead, he found Carl manhandling her and Ray in the alley looking like he was in the middle of something he shouldn't be.

Now Ray stared at him, a look in his eyes Tim couldn't read. Carl's hand was hidden behind his back, so he was sure there was a blade there. Something was wrong.

"I'm not asking again," he said. "What the hell's going on?"

"I think I can answer that."

Jimmy Lewis moved out of the shadows of the alley and into the light. He joined Tim, Jesse and Bill.

"If I read it right, Ray was going to take Lupe out to the Bar S. It's an abandoned ranch out of town. He has a place, just like you thought, Tim."

Tim looked at Jimmy, wondering what the hell he meant. He struggled to keep his face neutral.

"I've been tailing you guys, Ray," Jimmy said. "On Tim's orders. He knew you had something going."

Tim hoped Jimmy would keep talking. He remembered Jimmy telling him he suspected something the other day, and he hadn't listened. Apparently, neither had Jimmy.

"Saw him meet with Johnny Moro a few times, like you suspected." Jimmy took his hat off and handed it to Ruby. "When I followed Carl out to the Bar S, I found the girls. He's got three prostitutes working for him already. Or maybe working for Johnny. I don't think Ray's that high up the food chain."

"Fuck you," Ray snarled.

"So he is working with Chicago," Tim said, making it sound like confirmation rather than surprise. "What do you have to say for yourself, Roth?"

"I don't answer to you," Ray said.

"Nah . . . sounds like you answer to the Outfit."

He could see the look in Ray's eyes change. No matter what, Ray hated being under someone's thumb. Tim had always known it, but he figured the money and opportunity this gun deal would bring was enough to keep him in line. He hadn't thought he'd look for opportunity elsewhere when something big was on the horizon.

He remembered all the whispers—especially the ones about Diana and Ray. He pushed it out of his mind for now and remembered the Outfit learning about things before they should, like the black book operation.

"You selling us out to the Outfit now, Ray?" Tim asked, cracking his knuckles. "If I start asking around about how they got all the information when we were placing bets for the guys in the black book, what am I going to hear?"

"I don't give a shit what you hear," Ray said. "I'll tell you to your face. I told the Outfit what you were up to. You didn't cut them in, and that's a mistake."

"I'm not their errand boy."

"You think that's what this is?" Ray spread his arms. "You think Johnny Moro would work with some punk kid? No . . . he works with people who have promise. Guys who know what they want and how to get it. Guys who don't mind running women and doing what they need to do to get ahead. You were never going to play ball with the Outfit, Kelly. You're always going to be scraping by like a bunch of losers. Street thugs and nothing more."

"Not after this deal."

"A few guns going to Denver won't get you shit," Ray said. "And if you're not cutting the Outfit in on it, it'll get you dead, not that I care. Doesn't get you respect."

"And being Johnny Moro's little pimp will? You're dreaming, Ray."

"Moro's got plans for me. I get made and the world's at my feet."

"He's not gonna make a punk like you. You're not even Italian. They make their own."

"Yeah," Ray said, a shark-grin on his face.

Tim didn't have time to figure out what Ray meant, as Ray charged at him and slammed him back into the stairs. He nailed Tim in the midsection—he'd forgotten Ray was a southpaw. Since he led with his left, Tim used his right to knock him in the side of the head.

Bill had jumped into the fray, fighting Carl, and Jimmy went for Pete, who ducked around the side of the building like a chicken shit. Jimmy chased after him and hauled him back into the alley.

Tim kicked Ray in the shin, then hammered a fist into his kidney. Ray drove him back into the railings on the stairway again, and he heard Ruby and Lupe yelp.

94

Faces appeared in Rett's windows facing the alley, and soon more people were pushing their way onto the porch, others hearing the noise from the side of the building and coming around back.

Ray got two good shots to his face, and that was enough to enrage him. The last thing he needed was to get any uglier.

He held Ray's head and smashed a knee into his nose. The crowd in the alley grew, and Bill and Jesse held Carl back from jumping in to help Ray. Jimmy had broken Pete's nose from the look of it, and Pete was so pale Tim wouldn't be surprised if he passed out any second now.

Ray reeled back, his nose a mess, and spat blood.

"You're dead, Kelly."

Tim waited until Ray came at him, and drove a boot into Ray's knee. He crumpled, but connected with an uppercut to Tim's jaw as he regained his balance. Tim hit him in the face again, then Ray pushed him, catching him off guard with that damn left handed punch.

The people outside were cheering, most in costume, giving the scene a strange, surreal look. Zombies, vampires, werewolves, witches and princesses all egging on a fight in a dark alley. Tim couldn't decide who they were cheering for.

"I'm not surprised you've ended up with a Mexican whore," Ray said, his lip swelling and the words beginning to sound funny. "I mean, it's no surprise with a face like that. Ruby did go looking elsewhere, right? Whores are all that's left for you."

He should've stopped himself so Ray wouldn't know he'd landed a missile with that one, but he charged at Ray, landing two solid punches to his midsection, hoping one of them broke something. He ducked another aimed at his face and hit Ray in the ribs again. Ray wheezed getting air in, but Tim was furious to see him laughing.

He ducked another of Ray's haymakers and slipped on some oil in the alley. He was about to turn and charge at Ray when something came down on the back of his head.

Stars exploded behind his eyes, a riot of brightness that dimmed as his hands hit the pavement. He was too stunned to see where Ray was, but rolled anyway and heard the clang of something hit the pavement where his head was a moment ago.

He reached into his pocket and flicked out the switch.

The clang came again—a pipe. Ray dropped it. The snick of another blade opening made him force his eyes open. He stood, unsteady and willed himself to focus.

"Last time someone pulled a knife on you, it was Wheeler, wasn't it?" Ray sliced the air in front of him. Ray's voice was dim, like it came from much further away, but he came into focus at least. "He about spilt your guts on the pavement. Too bad he didn't finish the job."

"Too bad for you, you mean." It was a struggle to get the words out.

He took in a few gulps of air as they circled each other, his head clearing a bit. Bill and Carl duked it out close by, and Pete had Jimmy in a headlock, Jesse clamped onto Pete's back trying to pry his hands loose.

Tim focused on Ray and got his bearings a second later and slashed out, catching the sleeve of Ray's leather jacket. Ray back-stepped away from him. Ray's arm shot out, aiming for Tim's stomach, but his belt buckle stopped the blade from doing any damage. Jake had already cut him open a few months back from ribs to hip, and the last thing he needed was Ray spilling his guts in the alley.

"You're done, Kelly," Ray said. "Old news."

He slashed out again, but Tim caught Ray's left arm this time with his own left. He bent it back, shoved Ray up against his car, and Ray's knife clattered to the ground.

Tim was about to stab him when Ray headbutted him.

He staggered back and dropped the knife. Ray punched him again, in the same eye that was already swelling. He grabbed at Ray and shoved him back against the car again.

"Diana's found someone better. Like Ruby did. Like they all will," Ray said, his voice so loud it made his teeth ache. "I can give Diana everything you can't."

His vision went a dark red, and Tim hammered Ray in the face again and again, not seeing anything in front of him. The sounds dimmed and the world seemed to fall away. He could hear Bill tell him it was enough, Ray'd had enough, but the anger wasn't gone yet. A moment later Bill pulled him off Ray, hauling him out of reach.

Carl loaded Ray in the car, but a bleeding Pete begged off, moving away from all of them like everyone was on fire and he didn't want to catch. Carl got in the driver's seat and Ray looked at Tim from the passenger seat of his car. His face was bloodied and broken, but Ray smiled like he'd gotten his way. It left him unsettled.

The car left the alley, and the crowd filed back inside, everyone chattering like they'd just left the movies.

Tim found his footing and got Bill off him. He looked around, seeing the pipe on the ground. Ray was a fucking cheat.

Pete looked at him, then Jimmy, Jesse and Bill, and hurried around the side of the building like he didn't want to get his ass kicked if they decided they weren't done yet.

Jimmy retrieved his hat from Ruby and slipped back inside, probably to fix his hair. Bill stayed near him, as if he thought Tim might collapse at any second.

Tim looked over to the stairs. Ruby stared at him, a look on her face he couldn't read for once. He wasn't sure if Ray's voice was loud enough for everyone to hear, or if he was so addled Ray only sounded like he'd spoken through a megaphone. She gazed at him with those doe eyes, and he looked for some sign she knew he'd gone at Ray for what he said, but he couldn't see anything.

She turned to go a second later, and he decided it didn't matter. They were long over, and he had other things to focus on.

Lupe stared at the car as it left. For someone who was beaten in public, Ray looked strangely satisfied. Lupe stood there watching everyone leave with no concern over what had happened. Perhaps they saw this often. Ruby gave her a tight smile and went inside before Tim could approach.

He climbed the four stairs to the back door, looking tired. Blood covered his face, making the scars and lopsided cheekbone look even more disturbing. He looked at Lupe for a second. "Come back in when you're ready."

He went inside with Bill, and Lupe stood there in surprise. She'd expected him to yank her inside, fuelled up from his fight, but there was an air of defeat about him, even though he had won.

She held the railing tight and slid down to sit on a stair, her legs weak.

"Are you cold? You're shaking," Jesse said. She hadn't realized he was there. He took off the leather jacket he wore and placed it over her shoulders.

"Gracias." Lupe smiled at him and was surprised to see him sit next to her.

"Are you gonna come back inside?"

She shrugged. "I will. Soon."

He looked at her and raised an eyebrow.

"I will," she insisted. She looked back toward the door. "I will give him some time. He may need it as much as I do."

They sat together in silence and looked out into the darkness. An alley cat leapt from the pavement to the top of a Dumpster. Lupe shivered as the wind blew. Her nerves were shot, knowing she may have ended up trapped somewhere with Ray rather than Calderón. Small difference.

"Do you hate me?" she asked.

"Nah." He lit up a cigarette. "What's to hate? Tim said himself some asshole forced you to do it, and took you away from your family and all."

He held the cigarette out to her but she shook her head.

"Tim, he hates me."

"No," Jesse said, his voice lower. "He doesn't hate you. If he did, you'd know it. He wouldn't be sticking his neck out like this if he did."

"He is sticking it out because I have made him. I brought this to him. If I had not, he would have nothing to do with me," Lupe said.

"That's not true," Jesse said, a smile playing on his lips. "He woulda kept you around to get that shipment back."

Lupe glanced over at him and tried to keep from smiling.

"Anyhow . . . all this seems to have shown Ray for what he is. It was time Tim knew."

"You knew Ray had these girls?" Lupe asked.

Jesse shook his head. "No, but I saw him talking to Johnny Moro once. I got into the Riviera on a fake ID and saw them in the lounge. Didn't seem right, but Tim doesn't listen to me much, so I kept my mouth shut. I should've used my brain and did what Jimmy did and got proof."

"For what purpose? To impress Tim or to stop Ray?"

Jesse didn't answer.

"What you must think of me," she murmured.

"I think you're a pretty tough chick," Jesse said. "Running from them and all that. It takes a lotta guts, I think."

They were quiet again, and Lupe sighed.

"I liked that you did not know," she told him. "You treated me like a person. You did not look at me like I was . . . you did not look at me as Tim does."

"Tim's gotta problem with stuff like that," Jesse agreed. "I think it has something to do with a girl he met at a ranch. He said she stole from him, but I wonder if there was something more between them and maybe it burned him pretty bad, I dunno."

Lupe doubted that was the reason. She had her suspicions about the real reason he hated prostitutes and her being around made him remember. She looked over at Jesse. "His father, he is your uncle?"

"By marriage. He's a wannabe with the mob here in Vegas. Works construction. He drinks a lot and when he drinks he gets punchy. They don't get along much."

"Would his father take him on trips?"

Jesse frowned. "I didn't move here until I was fifteen, so I dunno. Before he got on with the construction crews here in town, his old man had his own drywall business, used to bid for jobs all over the place."

She looked at him, wondering if she should say something about what Tim had told her. She imagined Tim as a young boy, nine or ten, coming to a place like the zona roja. No, it would be a place more like the Casa, but with women painted up like they were in a club. It was no place for a child.

Still, it was unfair of him.

"Come on back inside," Jesse urged. "Tim has some kind of plan, and he wasn't going to kick me out of the room when he shared it, so I'm hoping to hell it means I get to help out. It'll look good for me if I bring you back. Come on."

Lupe looked over at him. She could see the goosebumps on his forearms. She touched the leather on the jacket he'd given her. It was a nice thing he did, giving it to her. He expected nothing in return, she could see that in his eyes. She struggled not to cry for a moment.

"Alright. We will go in," she said. She was surprised to see Jesse get up and offer her a hand. She took his hand with a smile.

She stood, and he held the door open for her and led her inside.

Tim shut himself in the bathroom when he got inside, the partygoers giving him a wide berth. When he looked in the mirror he realized why. One eye had swelled, the skin bruised and mottled. Blood from a cut above his eye streamed down his face, and his eyes had the look of a cornered wild animal.

The back of his head hurt, and his hand came away bloody when he touched it. He held a ragged towel to it, willing the blood to stop. Ray was a snake, fighting dirty like that. He should have expected it.

He should have expected a lot of things.

Jimmy showing up with that news stunned him. Ray Roth and Johnny Moro. He should've known.

He should have, and he didn't. It burned him Jimmy was smart enough to suspect something . . . but Jimmy shared his suspicions earlier, hadn't he? And he hadn't listened.

He thought about that. Ray bitched about things behind his back, he knew it, but he'd never called him out or questioned him in front of others in a disrespectful way. He'd stuck around, and he assumed that meant he was on board—otherwise Ray would've bailed long ago, hung around the Outfit like Bobby Tafani used to do. Ray would've tried to get associated and make a name for himself.

But Ray hadn't done that. Ray went behind his back, but didn't leave the gang, and he had the sick feeling there was much more behind that than Ray wanting more opportunity.

He remembered telling Ray the Outfit wouldn't make a guy who wasn't Italian, and Ray had agreed. He realized now he didn't know much about Ray. He had no family, never talked about his past outside of the cons he used to run, and Tim wondered for the first time who the hell Ray Roth really was.

He sighed and watched blood wash down the drain, the water like rust.

He'd heard the gossip about Diana and Ray. He thought it was Diana putting out stories to her friends, and Ray trying to get under his skin, but he had to admit it looked like more than that. Way more.

His stomach soured. He would have a good, long talk with Diana when all this got sorted out. Ray was the worst type of guy she could go for.

So he lost Ray, and he lost Carl. He noticed Pete hadn't gotten into the car with them, and that was interesting. Pete was nervous, and maybe Ray and Carl made him more nervous working with Chicago.

So maybe he hadn't lost much but a guy who was overconfident and disrespectful on a good day, and his mute muscle. It was better this way.

He wondered if any of the other guys would want to cash in and go along with Johnny Moro. Moro might have clout, but he liked killing people who crossed him, and sometimes it was his own men. He didn't think guys like Adam or Jesse would risk it, but others like Eddie, Dave or Tommy might.

At least Jimmy was loyal. He'd done a decent thing claiming it was all on Tim's orders, making it look like he was on the ball when he was anywhere but.

He stared at his reflection again, the left side of his face a ruined roadmap of bad decisions. Everything was coming at once, and it weighed on him.

One thing at a time.

Mexican hitmen were the first thing to worry about, and he didn't care if the Outfit was up in arms about it or not. These guys were coming after him, and he needed them out of Vegas and off his case.

He had a plan . . . but Lupe wasn't going to like it.

He left the bathroom and went into the back room. Bill was already there.

"I asked Ruby for some tequila," he said. "Figured it was fitting, and I know how you feel about bourbon."

Tim nodded and sat. His head ached, and his eyes felt like they were going to pop out of his head.

Ruby entered a minute later, carrying a few shots on her tray, along with lemon, salt, and aspirin.

"Thought you might need it," she said.

He nodded his thanks, and she left the room without another word, so maybe she hadn't heard Ray's taunts. He didn't want her thinking he fought Ray for her. He hadn't. Not one bit.

He downed one tequila shot and took two aspirin. A knock sounded at the door, and it opened before Bill could get up and answer it.

Tim wouldn't have admitted it, but he was glad to see Jesse come back into the room with Lupe behind him, Jesse's leather jacket draped over her shoulders.

Lupe sat without a word, returning the jacket to Jesse and looking forward like she was about to face a firing squad. Jesse looked over at him and raised an eyebrow, like he wanted him to apologize or something.

"I was about to tell Tim before, the hitmen were spotted around the downtown place," Bill said.

Tim felt his jacket for his cigarettes. Empty.

"Dark maroon sedan?" Jesse asked. He pulled out a Camel and offered it to him. He lit it and nodded his thanks, his head not happy with the motion. "I saw it circle the block a few times. Got the plate."

"Yeah, well let me run on down to the police station and find out who owns it," Tim said sarcastically. "The plate's useless, we know who it belongs to."

"No, I really got the plate," Jesse said. "They parked up the street near the drugstore last night and set out on foot. Me and Adam were watching from the bushes, we lifted their plates and hubs, figured maybe the cops would stop 'em."

Lupe let out a strangled laugh, and Bill's deep laughter echoed around the room.

"What the hell did you do that for?" Tim asked. "Those guys aren't the type to ask questions before they start shooting. You two rocket scientists ever think of that?"

Jesse and Lupe exchanged a look, and Tim stared at Jesse for a moment. He hated feeling like there was some kind of joke he wasn't in on.

"I told you to keep an eye out, not fuck over some Mexican hitmen," Tim said. "I swear to God, Jesse ..."

Jesse winked at Lupe, who giggled.

"Cut it out," Tim said. These two would drive him to drink.

"We know they've been watching," Bill said. "Far as we can tell they don't know about this place, so I think we're okay for tonight at least."

"What I don't get is how they found Lupe in the first place," Jesse said. "Didn't you say the driver was supposed to let you off over the border?"

Lupe nodded. "He was supposed to let us go along the way, I think. I said nothing when they continued on. I thought the farther I was from the border, the better for me."

"Mendoza's man Juan asked around Mexicali about her," Tim said.

"Rafael Mendoza?" Lupe asked.

"You know him?"

"I know of him," Lupe said. "He works with the Castillo brothers and Manuel on occasion, selling stolen goods. You asked him about me?"

Tim hesitated a moment and nodded. "Your story was shit from day one. I was covering my ass. Mendoza sent Juan to ask about you, since I wasn't convinced you weren't telling the truth. Juan heard through the grapevine Calderón was looking for a girl named Maria."

She nodded. "It is the name I used . . . there."

"Juan put two and two together, and so did the men he talked to," Tim said. "He'd let it slip you were in Las Vegas."

"Don't explain how they knew where to look," Jesse said.

Tim hated to admit Jesse had a damn good point. It didn't explain at all how the men had come to the downtown place.

"El Camarilla," Lupe said. "They have a far reach. It may well have been the drivers. Would they have known where your hideout was?"

"It's not a hideout." Tim was sick of people saying shit like that. He thought for a moment and sighed. "The backup drop."

Lupe looked at him, questions in her eyes.

"What?" Jesse asked.

"They wanted to meet out in the open," Tim said. "I agreed, but said if there were any cops in the area when I headed out there, and I didn't show, they were supposed to come to the downtown place. I told Mendoza to pass that on to them right before they left Mexico in case there was a problem. I forgot all about it."

"The drivers hear Calderón's looking for Lupe, and sell the information to them," Bill said. "Easy pay day."

"Many people do so," Lupe said. "It does not matter how they found me or who told them. For all I know Calderón could have seen Manuel put me in that truck. He would not be above little games."

"The more I hear about this guy the less I like him," Tim said. "Make sure you let Adam and Jimmy know to keep an eye out around here. Don't let them leave until the party thins out."

"Are we safe here?" Lupe asked.

Tim nodded. "Too many people around. They won't risk it, especially in a joint like this. We'll stay the night. In the morning we get this plan rolling."

"What plan?" Jesse asked.

"Lupe and I are going to Mexico."

9

"No!" Lupe stood, knocking her chair over.

"Tim, you gotta be crazy!" Jesse looked as surprised as she felt.

The idea was ridiculous to her. The mere thought of going back made her feel sick. Tim must be crazy to think of setting foot in México with her.

"El Camarilla is everywhere," she said. "We would be kidnapped or killed in an instant. It would be suicide."

"Hear me out." Tim stood. He walked over and righted her chair. He held it out, and she looked into his eyes. The left was dark with bruises and swelling shut, but the other was a clear green, looking at her with such intensity it frightened her more than the scars and misshapen left side of his face did.

She sat, wary of his plan.

"We go there to get the microfiche," Tim said.

"What microfiche?" Jesse and Bill asked at the same time.

Tim looked at her. "Tell them."

"When I left Calderón, I took a microfiche from him. It was his prized possession, but I did not know what was on it. Tim believes it is a record of his criminal activity." She stared at her hands. "That is why they tried to kill me in México."

"They chased after you?" Jesse asked.

"I had gone north from the Casa and hid the microfiche, and continued on to Mexicali when Manuel said he would help me. I hitchhiked there. One man, a farmer, picked me up and left me on the outskirts of town. I went for some food and drink. I had little money I had been given by a woman in la zona roja for emergency. When I came out, two men grabbed me."

"Following you?"

She nodded. "I do not know for how long, but not so long they saw where I took the microfiche. They tried to pull me into a car, and they were yelling about making sure I was alive so Calderón would get the microfiche back. That is when I panicked. I could not face Calderón. I knew too well what would happen to me. I managed to get away and run. They fired a gun after me, but I did not stop. I went into a crowded market to get away."

"This microfiche, what are you gonna do with it, Tim?" Jesse asked.

"Sell it," Tim said. "Exchange it for protection."

"Who can give that kind of protection?" Bill asked. "You need someone with enough pull to protect Lupe *and* you."

"That's why we need Mendoza. We'll stop in San Ysidro and get his take on things and have him help us over the border. He may know of a rival to the El Camarilla."

Lupe nodded. "Calderón is unhappy with many people, men like the Castillos. He has all of the Baja in his control, but there are some from Sonora who may challenge him. There are many in the Baja who would if they could draw together. I do not know who is most able. I hear the gossip in town. Calderón, he does not talk business with us, but he is loud when he is angry. It is hard not to learn things."

"You'll be dodging bullets all over again the minute you two get near the border," Bill said. "Those hitmen will be after you."

"They don't want to kill her, I don't think," Tim said. "They know she doesn't have the microfiche. He's going to want that back."

"That is right," she said, with sudden realization. "They know I did not have it with me. They said so, it was why they were taking me to Calderón, so I would tell him."

"You were smart to hide it," Jesse said.

"It might be the reason you're alive," Tim said.

She shivered. The room seemed cold.

"They might not have much of a problem killing you," Bill said to Tim. "They get you, and she's an easy mark. You're standing in their way. They're not going wait to shoot you, Tim."

"Maybe they will if they think I know where it is." Tim looked at Bill, who nodded. "Guys like this, a woman's nothing to them. If they think I'm in charge, they'll deal with me. I'll tell them I'll make a trade with them to keep Lupe alive."

"You will trade the microfiche for my safety?" Lupe looked at him, stunned.

"And a few other things, if I can manage it," Tim said, his smile unkind. "These boys have disrupted my life an awful lot, I think I'm due some compensation."

"You are crazy," Lupe said. "You will get us killed."

"I want you and Jesse to watch things around here," Tim said, looking at Bill. "I have a pretty good feeling these boys will blow town and come after us, but in case they hang around or send others, you keep an eye open."

Bill grinned around his cigarette. "I'm pretty sure Chicago's going to send some folks here to deal with it if they don't vanish."

"They'll have Moro deal with it. Thing is, I don't know where he stands," Tim said. "For all I know he might want to let the Mexicans take me out."

If Moro was working with Ray, and Ray had a prostitution ring going, that might mean Moro and Chicago were going their separate ways. That could be bad news.

"Let Wyatt know if things get real," Tim said. "He was the one who told Chicago, so I'm hoping he went higher than Johnny Moro. If things happen, call him. He'll change the game."

"You boys are crazy," Lupe said. "This is no game."

"It is. A game we're gonna win," Tim said. "Jesse, you keep an eye on Diana. I don't want them thinking she's leverage. Tell her about this if you have to."

He hesitated for a moment.

"And keep Ray away from her. I should've seen that a mile away, but I didn't," he said. "Make sure she understands."

"Fat chance of that," Bill muttered.

Tim stared at him, but said nothing. Bill withered under his gaze.

"She's stubborn," Bill said. "You know."

Tim nodded at Jesse. "Try, anyway."

Jesse sighed. "Yeah."

"You run things here," he told Bill. "Make sure if Pete comes around he gets the message he's either with us or we'll bury him in the desert."

"Ay, Dios," Lupe said. She clutched the rosary beads in her sweater pocket. She was lightheaded as she thought about going back to México. It seemed so wrong.

"You okay?" Tim asked her. "You look like you're about to pass out."

She shook her head. She was dizzy and each breath was as heavy as concrete.

"Come on," he said.

They all got up and left the room, heading back out into the party, which hadn't thinned out at all in the last hour. Costumed people danced, drank and laughed. Lupe was amazed to see how the people looked at Tim as he approached. Despite the horror of his face, even worse now that the damage from the fight showed, everyone watched him, many with admiring looks. Some people appeared to pay little attention, like Ruby, but Lupe suspected she knew he approached the bar all the same.

"She needs a drink," Tim said, when they reached the bar. Lupe watched in fascination as the people sitting on the bar stools moved away for Tim.

"Here, I got it!" Jesse said, plunking some money on the bar.

Lupe looked over at him and smiled. "Gracias."

"You're welcome," he said.

"Jesse, you better get going," Tim said, glancing up at the clock. "Keep an eye out. And leave me your smokes."

Jesse nodded and put the pack on the bar.

"I dunno if I'll see you again," Jesse said, looking at Lupe.

She turned toward him.

"I will always remember you," she said. "For your kindness."

"And I'll remember to pay attention to how many cards everybody's drawing," he said with a grin.

She smiled at him. She wished he could come with them—she'd rather spend the time traveling to México with Jesse instead of Tim—but the best thing was for him to be as far away from México and her as possible.

He looked at her and frowned, then leaned in.

"Be careful, Lupe," he said, his voice low. "Don't do nothin' stupid and get whacked, alright?"

"I will do my best," she said.

He smiled and left the bar.

Ruby put a drink in front of Lupe, and she took the shot, more to calm her nerves than anything.

México.

Tim was out of his mind.

Tim finished his beer at the bar, and wondered if Lupe would be able to stand going back into Mexico. Mendoza would have to help them with logistics. He didn't want to cross the border with his own papers, and Lupe had none.

Ruby glanced over at him a few times with a strange look on her face. He didn't think it had to do with the fight, since she looked at Lupe as much as him. She knew something was up.

He watched the crowd for awhile, his nerves settling since the fight, but his head feeling worse.

"Anything else?" Ruby asked.

"More aspirin?"

She nodded, and got two out of a bottle in the cash register and put them on the bar. He swallowed them with his beer.

Carolyn waltzed past him, her nose in the air. She was dressed as a nurse, covered in blood.

"Trust her to wear a costume like that after all those nurses were killed in the summer," Ruby huffed. "That girl has no sense."

Knowing Carolyn that's exactly what her costume was. He was surprised Ruby paid attention to the news.

Tim took the room key out of his pocket.

"I'll be back," he said to Bill. "Keep an eye on her."

Tim nodded toward Lupe, who played with the empty shot glass in front of her, twirling it on the wooden bar.

He turned around and moved through the crowd to the stairs and climbed up. He looked at the number on his key and found Ruby had given him the key to the room that was under her bedroom. He wondered about the significance. Keeping him close or punishing him for what he did here in the past?

He unlocked the door and walked in to the smell of stale air. He opened both of the windows to let the night air in, bracing his arms on the window sill for a moment.

"What's going on?"

He should have expected it, but he was surprised.

"What's going on where?" He didn't turn around as he pulled the curtains back from the window.

"Something's up," Ruby said.

He turned around. She stood in the doorway, a dishrag in her hand and an apron tied around her waist. He searched her face for whatever it was Lupe thought she saw there, but she was closed to him right now. All he saw was worry.

"Something's always up." He hoped he could shut her up with some well placed innuendo.

"You know right and well that's not what I mean." She eased the door shut behind her.

He didn't answer.

"What's going on with that girl Lupe? She's scared as hell about something."

"Not your business." He moved toward the dresser and leaned back against it, crossing his arms.

"You can't waltz in here with a strange girl—a Mexican girl who it turns out was a prostitute—and expect me to think nothing is going on," Ruby said, her voice edgier than normal. "I know you don't have a fondness for her occupation. You brought her here, something is going on, and what if something happens? I need to be prepared."

"There's nothing to be prepared for," he said.

"That's bullshit, Tim Kelly, and you know it," Ruby said.

He raised an eyebrow as she walked closer to him.

"I know she's not working for you," Ruby stated, those little wrinkles in her forehead looking so familiar to him.

"You don't like her, feel free to kick her out," Tim said. "But make sure it's for the right reasons."

Ruby's eyes narrowed. "I like her fine, she's nice. I'm surprised at you. I remember the way you looked at Rosa when she came on to you, and how you insulted her—don't think I don't speak some Spanish and know. All this 'nothing's going on' is bull, so don't get me started."

"You sound more than started to me," he said.

"Quit trying to get me angry and change the subject," she said. "Fact is, you've got a girl with you that I don't believe for a second you'd have alongside you unless there was a reason for it. And a girl like that involved in what she is, that reason ain't gonna be a good one. So for the last time, what is going on?"

"For the last time, it's not your business," he said, stepping closer to her.

She was angry, her cheeks flushed and eyes sparkling. He remembered being in a motel room with her, feeling her move underneath him for the first time, her breath in his ear and her throat exposed when she arched her back. He remembered how strong the need to be inside her was, how he didn't want to let her go when it was over—but she'd slipped from his arms, curled up away from him and forced him to move to her and hold onto her. He looked at Ruby standing in front of him and cursed her inwardly for being there.

"Tim," she said, her voice soft. "If something's going on, I need to know. At the very least so I can give you a heads up if something happens. I'll be up half the night cleaning up from this shindig. My eyes will be open when yours aren't."

He hated her even more at that minute because she was right. She would be up half the night cleaning up, and he wanted to get a good night's sleep before they left in the morning. He needed to get to the downtown place so the Mexicans would see them there. It had to be timed right so no one would start shooting. He wouldn't be able to stay awake and stand guard all night just in case.

Despite what he told Lupe, he didn't believe the Mexicans would give a damn if they showed up here and found it crowded with people. The way they recklessly fired guns in the middle of downtown Las Vegas, he suspected they wouldn't care about any collateral damage a stray bullet would cause in a crowded room.

They might not care if they killed Lupe, either. The microfiche hadn't come to light; chances are Calderón knew she hid it and hadn't given it to anyone for safe keeping. Calderón would know Lupe had no one to turn to who would keep it safe. Lupe hadn't trusted her friend Manuel enough to give it to him or tell him where it was. No, Calderón might prefer her alive, but would accept her dead in a heartbeat. The microfiche would be lost forever in that case and never see the light of day.

Lupe wanted to believe she was safe. She hadn't considered they would kill her outright, and he wasn't about to tell her.

He looked at Ruby again, standing there with her arms crossed, as if she could make him keep his distance. He couldn't imagine her running the way Lupe had, crossing borders and avoiding killers. They were different people, yet here was Ruby sticking her neck out for him again.

The Mexicans could show up at Rett's, and Ruby might need the warning in case they were less than friendly when they arrived.

"Lupe's in trouble," he said. "Some men are after her from Mexico."

"What kind of men?" Ruby asked.

"The bad kind, Ruby," he said. "What do you think?"

Ruby was quiet, looking at him with concealed anger.

"The guy that put her to work. She's got something they want, and he sent men after her. We're gonna hide out here tonight, then we'll be out of your hair," he said. "The Outfit didn't sanction this, they know what's going on."

She had softened a little, perhaps realizing he spoke the truth.

"Is she gonna be okay?"

"Lupe?" He thought for a moment, then nodded. "She's tough. She'll be alright. We'll head out first thing for Mexico. You see anyone lurking around here at all, you call Bill, and he'll take care of things. I don't expect them to stick around here, they'll follow us."

Ruby's brows knitted together. She glanced around the room, and he watched as her eyes settled on the double bed.

"Any reason you got the one room?" she asked, not taking her gaze off the bed.

Tim wanted to shake her. Like she had the damn right to ask him that.

"Why not?" he asked.

He wanted to make her lash out and say something, but she looked at the floor for a moment, confused. She looked at him a second later.

"So I guess Ray's not running with you anymore, huh?"

The question caught him off guard. "Ray needed his ass kicked."

"Can't argue that," she said. "Why tonight?"

He shrugged.

"Tim."

She didn't look like she would leave until she got an answer. He sighed.

"Ray has something going with Johnny Moro."

She frowned. "The Outfit enforcer? The one who— "

"Turned my face into Frankenstein's monster? That's the one."

"Jesus," Ruby breathed. "How'd you know?"

"Had Jimmy tailing them," he said, not willing to admit it wasn't on his radar.

She nodded, but said nothing. "You did real good in that fight, even when Ray cheated and grabbed that pipe."

He couldn't read her expression again, and it bothered him. She twisted the dishrag, looking for all the world like she was going to say something else, but he didn't know what.

"I better get back," she said.

She walked to the door and opened it, stepping into the hall. She paused and turned back.

"Be careful, Tim." She paused again, then smiled shyly. "Happy Birthday."

He let out a disbelieving breath and tried not to smile. Some birthday.

10

Lupe sat at the bar for awhile, watching for Ruby to come back downstairs. She had followed Tim upstairs and hadn't returned. Bill shrugged when she asked about it.

"He's not getting back with her, if that's what you're wondering," he said. "Tim's not the forgiving type."

"What does he have to forgive?"

Bill shrugged. "Ruby wasn't faithful."

It surprised her to hear that. She drew circles in the condensation on his beer bottle.

"I think she loves him," Lupe said.

Bill nodded. "I know she does."

Lupe spotted Ruby as she returned to the bar, looking resigned rather than happy. Whatever was going on between Tim and Ruby would not be fixed for her to see.

"I don't think he's coming back down," Ruby said, her manner stiff as she whisked away the tequila shot glass in front of Lupe. "If you're tired, I'd go up on your own. Up the stairs, turn right and right again. It's room 6, faces the front."

"I can show you if you like," Bill said.

"It is alright," Lupe told him. "I will find my way."

Bill nodded, then his face lit up. Lupe looked behind her to see what he stared at—a blonde girl had come in the front door, looking a bit lost.

His smile broadened, and he got up and left Lupe without a word.

"Don't mind him," Ruby said, gazing after him. "He's gone over her. I don't think a bomb going off would distract him when Marilyn's around."

Lupe slid off the bar stool.

"Thank you," she said to Ruby.

Ruby nodded. "Whatever's going on, be careful. Tim knows what he's doing, but he won't tell you what it is he's doing. Just . . . be careful."

"Thank you," she said. She hesitated for a moment, wanting to reassure this girl who was nice to her that Tim was not as lost to her as she thought, but Ruby no longer looked as open to her. Lupe figured it was her. Tim had one room for the both of them it seemed, and she knew how it must look to her. By the way Ruby turned her back to sort the bottles of liquor, she didn't want reassurances.

Lupe headed for the stairs.

The party was in full swing, the crowd thick, and she moved through the throng toward the stairway, mindful of people's gazes. She heard one girl ask another why they were letting Mexicans in, and Lupe steeled herself and went up the stairs with her shoulders back. She would not let them see they hurt her. Why she was not welcome, she didn't know.

She walked upstairs, turned right and then right at the end of the hall, spotting the room Ruby told her about. Lupe saw a bathroom next door, and she went inside and used it, relieved to wash her face and clean up. She tried to brush her teeth with her finger and some water, and felt halfway human again when she came out.

The door to the room was ajar and Lupe pushed it open with trepidation. Tim was on his back on the bed, his boots on, and his jacket hung over a rail back chair in the corner. He blew smoke rings.

"Thought you got lost," he said. "You shoulda followed me right up."

"If you were concerned, you would have come to get me," she said. She shut the door.

He smirked before he took another drag and blew a smoke ring.

She looked at the bed with apprehension. There one double bed in the room.

"What?" Tim asked. "You afraid to share the bed with me?"

"No," she said, lying to herself and him.

"You look scared." He sat up and ashed his cigarette in a cut glass ashtray on the nightstand. "Funny thing, considering."

She didn't reply, but edged closer.

"Were you this nervous in your boy's town? Maybe that was your thing . . . making them think you were a first timer or something."

"Stop it."

"If you're not scared get over here. We're getting outta here early tomorrow. May as well get some sleep," he said. "Unless you can't do that without some action first. Or maybe it's the money that does it."

"Why are you saying these things?" Tears pricked her eyes. "I have done nothing to you. You were nice to me before, why are you saying these cruel things now?"

He continued to smoke, infuriating her with his attitude. She kicked off her shoes, picked one up and threw it at him.

"Hey!" he said, batting it out of the way. The sneaker fell onto the floor. "What the fuck's your problem?"

"You!" she said. "You are acting like an ass."

"So your solution is to throw shit at me?" He stood and walked over to the window and threw his cigarette butt outside.

"It is not my fault if you are angry," she said.

"About what?" He leaned against the windowsill.

"I do not know. Maybe she angered you. Maybe because you love her still. But you have no right to say those things about me." Her voice wavered as she spoke. He stared, his gaze hard and cool, his face battered. He scared her so much with those blank eyes. "Please . . . stop. I cannot take this any longer."

She wiped the tears away with the sleeve of her sweater.

He continued to stare for a minute. She walked toward the bed and sat, feeling a little tipsy.

"You're drunk," he said.

"That is also your fault."

She heard him let out a bitter laugh. "Isn't everything, though?"

She lay on her back, her legs dangling over the edge of the bed and stared at the ceiling. A moment later he sat next to her and lay back as well. Both of them were silent for a long time.

"We'll get up early, stop at the downtown place and go," he said.

She didn't reply.

"You scared?" he asked.

"Of what?"

He shrugged.

"I am scared of everything," she whispered.

She got up from the bed and took off her sweater, folding it and laying it on top of the dresser. She excused herself and went to the bathroom to slip out of her bra, and wore her dress as if it was a nightgown.

She came back into the room and shut the door.

"Lock it, too," Tim said.

She looked over at him and frowned.

"Better safe than sorry, right?" he asked. "It's why I got one room. To look out for you."

She turned the lock, surprised at his reason for the one room. She tucked her bra under her sweater on the dresser and came over to the bed and pulled the covers back, getting between them. She stared at the ceiling again.

Tim got off the bed a moment later and took off his boots. He said nothing as he took off his shirt and jeans.

Lupe swallowed and tried to breathe, remembering the sound of belts being undone and clothing landing on the floor. The nausea roiled her stomach.

She looked at him as he sat on the bed, his back to her. She frowned at the myriad of scars on his back. They were long healed, and she wondered where he got them.

Tim got under the covers as well a minute later.

She lay still, trying to keep her breathing normal.

"Relax," he said, irritation in his voice. "You're acting like I'm gonna attack you or something."

"There are so many things I am remembering. It is not easy." Her voice so low it was a whisper.

"Forget them," he said.

"Is it that easy for you? Can you make yourself forget the things that play in your mind over and over?"

"Sure."

"I do not believe you," she said.

"Believe what you want," Tim said, turning the light off. "But it'll be easier if you don't remember."

The darkness in the room was sudden and overwhelming, and it took a moment to adjust. The thin curtains let in halos of light from outside, and soon her eyes adjusted. She toyed with the thin sheet, threadbare between her fingers.

"What is it?"

"What's what?" he asked. The darkness in the room was like a shroud.

"What is it you try so hard not to remember?" Lupe asked.

"Go to sleep, Lupe."

She turned over onto her side, so she faced him. A sliver of light shone into the room from a gap in the thin curtains, and she could see his profile in sharp contrast.

"Do I make you remember?" she asked him.

Tim didn't move or look at her. "Yeah."

"What is it you remember?" she asked again. "I suspect . . . "

"You suspect what?" he asked.

"You are remembering your father," she said. "Did he bring you to places like la zona roja?"

He was quiet for so long she thought he had ignored her question.

"Not like that. Similar." He paused a moment, his eyebrows drawing together. "A ranch. In the country."

Like the Casa, Lupe thought.

"He went to the women?" Lupe asked.

Tim nodded. "I can't remember much. A house. Some damn painted up women inside, petting me like I was a goddamn dog. I didn't know why he went there. Just knew it wasn't where he was supposed to be."

"Your mother did not know?"

"No. Not then."

He was quiet, and Lupe didn't know what to say next.

"Most of the men that come to you, they're married?" Tim asked.

Lupe shrugged. "I do not always know. Some do not talk much. Others . . . I think that is the reason they come. To talk."

"Not talking with the right head," Tim said.

Lupe laughed. "True enough. But I think many are lonely. There are some you can see are there for the sex, because they need it as if they would die without it. They have a hungry look in their eyes. They are not nice men. They do not care if they hurt you. Some, I think, prefer when they do."

She curled up a little tighter in the blankets.

"Many come because they are unhappy," she said. "They will tell me all their problems, knowing I cannot fix any of them."

"Why bother talking then?" Tim asked.

"Sometimes it is better to talk." She looked at his profile, seeing he didn't realize he was doing exactly what he said he didn't understand.

They were quiet for a few minutes.

"Did she ever know?" Lupe asked. "Your mother?"

Tim nodded. "Yeah. She found out one day."

"How?" she asked.

The silence was long and strained. "I said something I shouldn't."

"What do you mean?" she asked.

"I was ten," he said. "Didn't know any better."

"Any better for what?" she asked.

"Went on one of the trips with my father, but he didn't bother to stop and shower at the truck stop this time. We got home, and I went upstairs. Heard them arguing. She came upstairs and asked me point blank where he'd been."

"And you told her?"

"I didn't know it was bad. Hell, maybe I did. I don't know," Tim said. "I didn't know what the place was called. She asked me if there were women there, and I nodded. Guess she knew what he was up to. They got in a huge fight."

"What happened?"

115

Tim shrugged. "That was the first time he hit her. First time he hit me. It got pretty regular after that."

"How long had he been taking you to this casa?" she asked. "To this house?"

Tim shrugged. "A few years by that time. First time I remember, it was the Fourth of July weekend. I was seven or eight. He would take drywall jobs out of town. I look back now and don't know why, all the construction was here in town. Probably wasn't legit anyway. I figure he did jobs for the mob."

She tried to imagine a seven-year-old around things she had seen at the Casa and la zona. They were things she never should have seen or been a part of, forget a seven-year-old boy.

"He still goes?"

Tim shook his head. "Not out of town anyway."

"It was not your fault," she said. "You told the truth."

He shrugged.

"It was not," she said again, placing her hand on Tim's arm. She was surprised his skin was warm. Somehow she had expected he would feel cold.

He shrugged away from her a little, and she shrank back to her side of the bed, wrapping the covers around her even tighter. Whatever he felt, he didn't want her to be a part of it.

"Good night," she said to Tim, turning away from him and trying to get comfortable on the flat pillow.

"'Night," she heard him say.

She was in the room again. Lupe knew it was a dream. Sometimes, it was these dreams that bothered her the most because she knew they were dreams. Try as she might, she couldn't wake up.

She was in the small room at the Casa in the main house, lying on the bed naked, waiting for Calderón. She could hear him in the other room, arguing with his men, or laughing, the sound of clinking glasses and the smell of Cuban cigars drifting into the room through the ventilation system.

She could never see his face in these dreams, but she would always see him walk into the room, loosening his belt, taking off his pants. She felt sick and violated, yet nothing had happened yet. In her dream, when he touched her, it was as if her soul had grown cold.

Sometimes the dreams disturbed her most because there were times her body reacted to him physically. She would feel him touch her, feel the revulsion, then feel the physical pleasure. She would try to wake up and never could. This man had hurt her; she could not allow this.

She fought through all the fog to wake up, but it was always useless.

* * *

Tim heard Lupe's murmuring. He was on the knife's edge of sleep, one moment conscious, the next in a dream he knew was a dream, yet felt real. He could control what happened, even knowing it was a dream. He wanted these strange moments to last for far longer than they did.

The bed moved, and he turned over, curling the blankets around himself, aware of a draft from somewhere. He fell asleep for a few moments, his dream punctuated with the feel of someone's skin and the taste of their lips. He tried to stop himself from looking in his dream, not wanting to know who the girl was. It couldn't be Ruby. He didn't want it to be Ruby.

His dream turned dark, and the sound of gunfire startled him awake.

The sound was real—firecrackers going off outside. The noise ended a second later and he lay there, his heart pounding and his head aching. He got control of his breathing, ashamed he reacted to a noise in a dream.

He turned over and saw Lupe's side of the bed was empty. He sat up and relaxed as he saw her sitting on the window sill, the window open and the curtains covering her, billowing in the breeze. She had one leg tucked up against her chest. She was in tears, her head over her arms. He could see her shoulders heave with her cries, which she attempted to silence so he wouldn't wake up.

She looked tiny sitting in the window like a doll.

He sighed and tossed the covers off and got out of the bed. She didn't lift her head, even when the springs creaked. He picked up Jesse's pack of Camels from the nightstand and tucked one behind his ear, then walked over to her. She kept her head down, sniffling, attempting to stop her tears.

"You need another drink?" he asked, holding the curtain back.

She raised her head and looked at him, her green eyes rimmed red from crying. She shook her head no. He leaned against the window sill near her and waited. She said nothing.

"What's up?" he asked.

She shook her head.

"Come on," he said. "I didn't get all the way outta bed for a shake of the head."

"I had a nightmare," she said.

"Most folks don't cry over nightmares." He remembered his heart racing at the sound of imaginary gun shots.

"Most people do not have my nightmares," she said.

"What are they about?"

She glanced over. "You do not want to know. One minute you are almost kind to me, and the next you punish me for what has happened to me. It was not my fault. I did not want to be there, and you treat me like I chose it. Well, I did not. I did not choose it, and I would never choose it. It was not my fault."

He took in a short breath. "I know."

She looked at him, the surprise plain on her face, and he almost had to smile.

"Lupe, I'm not stupid. Yeah, I might hate it all, it turns my damn stomach. But I know why it does. You don't have anything to do with that," he admitted.

"You tar us with the same brush," she accused.

"Yeah," he said. "I did."

She wiped her cheeks, and he could see she didn't believe him.

"I've come across my share of working girls," he said. "Some of them, they do it body and soul. You know what I mean?"

"Was Rosa like that?"

"How do you know about her?" Tim asked, his brows drawing together in confusion.

"Your girl Ruby told me," she said. "She said you did not like her. Ruby did not like her either."

Trust Ruby to open her mouth like that.

"She's not my girl," Tim said. "But yeah, Rosa was like that. She used it to get what she wanted, which was a fancy ranch outside of Los Angeles, and from what you've said a lot better than what she would've had in Mexico."

"I know of the women you speak," Lupe said. "They use it. They enjoy it. But I cannot judge them for it. I do not know what they run from."

"Yeah." The sound of raucous laughter echoed through his head. He remembered hearing the women with his father laugh. He remembered their blood red nails, how they circled their arms around his father, with Tim right there watching. He didn't understand how they could do it, knowing he was right there watching.

"I do not enjoy it," she said.

"I know."

"Why do you believe me now?" she asked.

Tim looked at her and thought back over the past few days. He remembered her coming onto him, the look in her eyes. Seductive, yes, but also afraid. She had always been afraid, and he hadn't noticed. There were a lot of things he hadn't noticed.

"I think I always did believe you," he said. "Just didn't know I did."

Lupe swallowed and wiped her eyes again. "Then why were you so cruel before?"

A flash of memory from his dream flitted across his mind.

"It didn't have anything to do with you," he said.

She was quiet, but gave a slow nod.

"I wish I could erase this man from my head," she said. "It is always a dream of Calderón. I could smell his cigars. It is always like I am right there. Even though I know this is a dream, it feels real. I cannot take much more of this."

Tim nodded. "We'll get him."

She smiled, and he wasn't sure if it was because of the idea of getting him or the fact Tim had said "we."

He held his hand out to Lupe. He wanted to be up and out of Las Vegas in a few hours.

"I like you when you are nice to me." Lupe took his hand.

He was surprised when she stepped closer to him and slipped her arms around his waist, hugging him. She buried her head against his neck.

He rested his arms around her shoulders, and she pressed herself closer to him, sniffing back her tears. He didn't feel she was coming onto him like she had before, and maybe that was why he was so aware of the way she felt against him. Her chest was pushed up against him, and he could feel the rise and fall of her breasts as she breathed, her breath hitching a few times from her tears.

His hands made slow circles on her back, and he tried to stop himself, confused about why he was doing this, and with her of all people. He let his hands travel down her spine, resting on the small of her back. He wasn't surprised when she lifted her head to look at him, questions in her eyes.

He bent his head to kiss her.

She froze the moment he moved, and he almost wanted to laugh at the panicked look in her eyes, a split second before she closed them.

Her lips were soft when he reached them, and he was surprised she didn't kiss him back right away. He deepened the kiss, pulling her closer to him, moving a hand up into her hair. Her body went rigid, and she pushed against his chest, backing away with a wild look in her eyes. She was confused. Something in her expression made him stop and stay silent.

He stood there watching her, trying to get a read on what she thought. She inched forward, closer to him, her gaze jumping around the room. She licked her lips and let out a breath, and he realized she'd been holding it.

He didn't understand how she could be so scared. He wanted to ask her why, what scared her about him, but it was as if he knew words would stop her, and at that moment, he wanted to kiss her again. Maybe then he could forget the face in his dream.

He stood still, and a moment later she placed a hand on his chest. Her own chest rose and fell as if she'd run some kind of race. If he didn't know better he would've said she was as nervous as a virgin.

She leaned up and her kiss, aimed for his lips, diverted at the last minute and landed on his jaw, as if her lips were too shy to meet his own. Resisting the urge to pull her to him, he stood rooted to the spot, knowing something odd was going on with her. Her hands ran up the back of his neck and tangled in his hair.

He stood and waited.

She leaned in and kissed him, tentatively at first. He kept pace with her, letting her lead, and felt triumphant when she deepened the kiss this time.

When she pulled back this time, she looked surprised. She looked in his eyes for a moment, then looked at the floor.

"It is late," she said, her voice a whisper. "We should sleep."

She walked past him to the bed, and Tim looked at the ceiling and let out a breath. Yeah, sleep was what was on his mind.

He watched her climb under the covers. Sighing, he left the room and went to the bathroom. There was only one thing that would relax him enough to sleep.

11

Lupe opened her eyes, feeling as if she had slept for one hundred years. Birds chirped outside and noises came from upstairs. Water was running in the bathroom next door, and she turned over in the bed, not surprised to see Tim wasn't there.

He disappeared for awhile the night before, then returned to the bed as if nothing had happened. She lay still for a long time, until his breathing was even and slow.

She couldn't believe what she'd done.

Many men who had come to la zona or to the Casa had kissed her. It wasn't like she had never done it. But there was something about stepping toward him and kissing him that was different from what happened in México.

He was patient with her, and that surprised her. She expected he would be passionate and eager, like the first kiss he had given her. It scared her, brought forth memories of the men who came through her life since she was young. He had sensed it, perhaps. When she stepped back, he didn't say anything to her, didn't move and didn't chastise her. He waited until she stepped forward and overcame her fear.

When she kissed him, he responded in kind. She relaxed, knowing he wouldn't hurt her. Now she wondered why he did it at all. Between the insults and his strange history with prostitutes, she didn't understand why he kissed her. Maybe it was the fight, or maybe he had something to prove to himself. Either way, he had kissed her, and he seemed to understand her fear. She liked the feeling of control he allowed her to have.

She was under no illusions she was in control, though. She suspected a man like him didn't like being out of control. His whole demeanour since the hitmen arrived was agitated, as if he hated being out of control of the situation. Of course a man like him would plan something. He wouldn't sit by and wait for them to come and kill them.

She tossed the covers back and shivered a little in the cool morning air. The curtains were billowing in the breeze, the window open from the night before. She made the bed up, and Tim came in a moment later.

"Leave it," he said. "Ruby can make it."

"She has much to do," Lupe said, tucking the bedding around the pillows.

She glanced over at Tim. He wore his blue jeans, but no shirt. His hair was greased, and there were droplets of water on his shoulders.

"Go have a shower," he said. "We'll get out of here when you're done. There's a towel in there."

Lupe nodded and left the room, her stomach beginning to knot. Soon, she would be going back to the place that scared her most. She hoped Tim was ready for it.

Tim dressed and went downstairs. He went behind the bar, flicked out his switchblade and pried open Rett's cash register. He took forty dollars and two aspirin.

"So you're robbing us blind now, too, huh?"

He looked over at Ruby standing in the doorway to the kitchen.

"I'll pay it back," he said.

"I made you some sandwiches to take." She held up a metal lunch box. "Couple bottles of Pepsi in here, and if Lupe wants, I have some clothes she can wear."

Tim looked at her, wondering what the deal was. Ruby's impatience grew.

"Take it, would you?" she asked. "Don't make me regret doing it."

She set the things on the bar.

"I told you to stay out of it," he said.

"I am," she said. "A sandwich ain't gonna put me in it. Besides, I doubt you've been feeding the girl, she was on her ear after those shots of tequila."

Tim reached out and took the lunch box and the paper bag.

"I'll go get the clothes for Lupe," she said.

He watched her leave the room, not believing something wasn't going on with her. Tim sighed. He didn't have time to worry about shit like this. If she wanted to help Lupe, let her. He wasn't about to feel guilty for what happened the night before. Nothing had.

It confused him the way he'd gone from wanting nothing to do with her to kissing her, but he put it down to adrenaline from the fight. Maybe that pipe to the back of the head scrambled his brain.

Maybe he looked at her differently since hearing her story. Somehow, being forced into it wasn't as terrible as choosing it in his eyes. He doubted she'd see it that way. Lupe made him think of things he hadn't thought of in a long time, but somehow it hadn't angered him like it usually did.

His head throbbed, shaking him out of his reverie. The back of his head hurt, and there was a scab of crusted blood holding the gash shut. He shook a few aspirin out of the bottle in the cash drawer and took them.

He wondered where Lupe's fear had come from. There was a lot he didn't know about what she did in Mexico. Sure, he could imagine, but he couldn't know what it had been like for her. She was afraid. Every fibre of her body was tense and nervous when he kissed her, and he expected her to slap him after that first kiss. She looked like she was on the verge of breaking down and crying again, and he was surprised she had come to him and kissed him.

He wouldn't lie to himself—he wanted more.

It made him uncomfortable, thinking about all the men she must have had. That thinking wasn't right—Lupe called him on it. She hadn't done anything to him. He thought of those women from the brothel. Who the hell knew, maybe they had been like Lupe. To his eyes at that age maybe they only looked his father's age.

The discomfort crawled up his spine at the idea of his father taking a girl like Lupe to bed with him, leaving a few bucks on the nightstand and driving home with his son to his wife and daughter.

All these years he hated those faceless women. Now, they weren't so faceless, and it bothered him more and more he hadn't thought more of them and less of his father.

He shook his head as he heard steps on the stairs. They were heavier, and he wasn't surprised to see Rett make his way into the room.

"What're you doin' here?" Rett asked, his eyes narrowed.

"Clearing out," Tim said. "Stayed the night."

Rett hadn't thawed out much over the last few months. Hell, Ruby talked to him now, but he didn't think Rett Gordon ever would. He was too scared not to show Tim and his gang every courtesy like he always did, but Rett didn't pretend he enjoyed having Tim around at all.

"Who's the Mexican?" Rett asked, pouring himself a shot of whisky.

"Little hair of the dog there, Rett?" Tim asked.

Rett rolled his eyes. "Didn't answer my question."

"Isn't your business," Tim said.

Rett looked over. "Just don't start nothing."

"Now, when have I ever done that?" Tim asked.

Rett looked at him awhile longer, then downed his shot and headed toward the stairs.

"Hope you paid up for the room," he said.

Tim nodded. "Ruby saw to it."

A look flashed across Rett's face. A moment of hatred directed at him. After all Ruby had done, Rett looked at him as the bad guy. Typical.

Rett continued up the stairs, and a moment later Tim heard two sets of footsteps coming downstairs.

Lupe and Ruby both came in the room together. Tim flinched a little when he realized Lupe was dressed in Ruby's jeans and an old western blouse he remembered undoing the buttons on more than once. He glanced at Ruby, but she wasn't looking at him.

She knew. He didn't think Lupe would have told her, but she knew either way. He didn't want to see her eyes.

"Come on," Tim said, taking the lunch box and paper bag. "We need to make a couple stops before we get on the road."

Lupe thanked Ruby.

"Remember what I said if you spot those Mexicans," Tim said, not turning around to look at Ruby. "Bill's number's in the register."

"I remember," Ruby said. He glanced over his shoulder—Ruby had followed them both to the door. He went down the front porch steps, Lupe on his heels, and headed toward the side of the building.

"Tim."

He stopped, took a breath, then turned to look at Ruby.

"I meant what I said," she told him. "Be careful."

He nodded. The last thing he heard before he left was the porch screen door banging in the wind.

Lupe was quiet on the drive. Tim had said they would stop at his house before going to the warehouse.

She wasn't sure why they were stopping at his home and his hideout now that they had some food and she had new clothes. She felt like a new person, clean from the shower and wearing new clothes. She was surprised Ruby had given them to her. She was a nice girl.

Ruby had somehow known something happened between her and Tim. She didn't say it, but Lupe sensed the wariness in her, even as she offered her new clothes. Ruby was in love with Tim, and yet had shown her kindness, and the guilt gnawed at her.

She wondered if Tim knew. Either way, he didn't seem to care much.

They pulled up in front of his house, and he pulled the big gun she had learned on out of the glove box.

"Come on," he said. "We'll be quick."

"Is anyone home?" she asked, looking at the small house.

"No," he said. "Old man's at work, my mother keeps the books at the Catholic church Tuesday mornings, and Diana should be at school."

Tim opened his door and Lupe followed, walking quickly to catch up with his long strides. Tim made sure to pull the curtains, as if they were hiding.

He went down the hall and Lupe followed, ending up in a barren room.
"This is your room?" she asked. She hadn't seen it her first time there.
He nodded.

"It is worse than my room at the Casa," she said.

Tim's smile was grim. "I don't spend a lot of time here."

"Decorating is not your strong suit," Lupe agreed, looking around at the empty walls, the lack of furniture. It looked like a room at a boarding house. Like no one lived here.

Tim reached under the bed and pulled out a lock box, taking a key out of the wallet he retrieved from his back pocket. She looked at the wallet in surprise—he didn't seem like the type to carry one.

He unlocked the metal box, and Lupe's eyes widened at the ammunition inside.

"You are prepared for a war." She kneeled to take a closer look. "Why did we not come here for the bullets before?"

"If those hitmen were following us I didn't want them finding the house." He opened the lunch box and put a few boxes of .38 Special ammunition inside. He put the nine millimetre ammunition in the paper bag.

He opened one box and shook out some bullets, then took the gun she had learned on out of his waist band.

"You do not wear a holster," Lupe said.

"An ankle one for the other gun, but this one's usually in the glove box. I didn't want to bring any guns into Rett's so they were both in the car."

"You had no weapon?" she asked in surprise.

"There's weapons in Rett's if I'd needed them." He locked the box again. "Anyhow, if Ray had seen a gun on me, things would've gotten bad."

"They were not already?"

He ignored her and shoved the box under the bed. He sat on the mattress.

"I'll give you one of the guns when we get to Mexico," he said.

She shivered a little at the thought of heading south. She sat next to him and felt the urge to touch him, to slow this all down and stop it all from catapulting away from her. She reached out and touched his arm.

He paused and looked over.

"No," he said. "Not now, Lupe. I don't know much about what's going on with you, but stow it for now."

She pulled her hand back as if it was burnt. A shadow of a smile was on Tim's lips.

"Aren't used to hearing no, are you?"

Her cheeks felt like they were on fire, and she stared at her hands for a moment.

"No," she said, ashamed. "I am not."

"Don't take it personal," he said. "We've got work to do."

She looked over and was surprised to see he looked at her with concern. She took a deep breath and stood.

"It is moving too fast," she said, trying not to think about where they were headed. "All of this is moving too fast."

He stood and nodded. "Nothing we can do about that."

He left the room first, and she followed him down the hall and out of the house.

Lupe walked to the Charger, expecting bullets to rain upon them at any second. But she reached the door and got inside, letting out a breath when the doors were shut.

"I wouldn't relax that much," Tim said. "The car isn't bulletproof."

They made one more stop—the downtown warehouse. Tim pulled over a few blocks from the place, talking to the one she thought was called Adam. He told Tim the hitmen were parked two blocks over.

She protested when Tim drove by them on a cross street, but was relieved he didn't stop or drive up any closer to them.

They got on the highway a few minutes later, and the drive south began.

The drive out of Las Vegas reminded Tim of all the times he drove out to Insane Wayne's place in LA. All those times he took Ruby with him. He pushed it out of his head.

Lupe was quiet as they headed into the desert.

"It's best we stay on the main roads," he said, even though she hadn't asked him any questions. "I'll stick to the highway. Less chance they'll try something on the road."

"Try something?" Lupe asked.

Tim braced the steering wheel with his knees as he lit a smoke.

"Don't worry about it," Tim said.

"I have been worried for a long time," Lupe said.

She watched the scenery, looking out the window and seeming to shrink into herself. He figured she was scared. The area looked familiar to him, and at first he thought it was the fact he'd driven this road so many times in that damn truck months ago, but he remembered the feeling back then too. It came to him like a lightning strike.

"It was around here somewhere," he said.

"¿Qué?" Lupe asked.

"The . . . whorehouse, brothel, whatever you wanna call it," he said. Images flashed across his eyes. "It was out this way. On the way to Los Angeles. Couldn't have been legal, seeing as we're in Clark County. Dammit, I always thought it was a legal place."

"Do you remember it well?" she asked.

He shrugged. "Some. Flashes of things here and there."

Perfume. Peppermint. The sounds. Always the sounds.

"Yet it made a strong impact on you," she said.

He didn't answer. He closed his eyes for a second and tried to turn off the memories. He focused on Mexico.

"Will we drive to Tijuana today?" she asked. He looked at her, wondering if she changed the subject on purpose.

"No," he said. "It's almost noon now. We'll stop somewhere so I can call Mendoza and let him know we're coming. Best place to find a phone will be in Barstow. He'll know whether it's safe or not and how the hell we can swing this."

Lupe asked no more questions, and they were quiet the rest of the way to Barstow. It was mid-afternoon when he spotted a pay phone outside of a gas station and pulled over.

"Stay in the car," he said.

"Someone could shoot me." She opened her door. "I will stay with you."

"Great, both of us can get shot," Tim said. He didn't protest as she followed him to the pay phone.

He dialled Mendoza's number and the man answered on the second ring.

"I don't know if Bill told you, but I'm on my way down there," Tim said.

"You are a crazy man," he said. "I have heard they sent a hit squad. The El Camarilla has a bounty on her head."

"Yeah?" Tim asked, not wanting to alarm Lupe, who inched her way into the phone booth with him. "What's the word on that?"

"Dead or alive," he said. "And if you know these type of men, you know that means dead is fine."

"Alright," Tim sighed. "I need to meet you in San Ysidro. We may have some trouble with the border. I have an idea of how to turn this thing around."

Mendoza gave a throaty laugh. "You are suicidal I think, sometimes. Very well. Come ahead tomorrow to the junkyard, I will get papers prepared for the both of you."

Tim hung up the phone a moment later. Lupe looked at him, curious and expectant.

"What did he say?" she asked.

"He'll be waiting for us tomorrow. We'll get all the information we need then," he said. "Come on. Let's get back on the road. We'll find a place to stay tonight outside of Los Angeles or something."

After a bathroom break at the gas station, they got back in the car and back on the desolate highway.

Tim looked in the rearview mirror. He remembered his few trips in the truck last year and wished for the CB radio. It would have been a good way to find out if there was anyone following them.

"Your gang," Lupe said, trying to start a conversation. "Have you always been their leader?"

"We're not a gang. As far as the Outfit knows, anyway," he said. "And yeah, I've always run things."

"Will Jesse lead them one day?" she asked. "He is your cousin; the duty should pass to him, yes?"

Tim took a minute before he answered. "I dunno."

"Yes, you do," Lupe said softly.

Tim glanced over.

"He tries hard to please you," Lupe said. "I can see he would like to be like you."

"He's got a long way go," Tim said.

"Perhaps," Lupe said. "But he is loyal and true. I believe he always will be. I think you will find in the end, he will be the one that is there, along with Jimmy and your friend Bill."

Tim nodded. "I know."

"He is smarter than he looks."

"Bill? Hell, anyone can see that," Tim said.

"No," Lupe told him. "Jesse. He is smart, but he doubts himself. He makes mistakes when he tries to please you or get your attention. When he acts of his own will, he is sure and smart. Do not doubt him."

"You gonna lecture me about my family all day?" he asked.

"No," she said. "I am making conversation."

"What about yours?"

"My family?" she asked in surprise. "I have told you of them."

"No, you told me you had a father, mother and three sisters," he said. "And that your father is sick."

"Yes, he has never been well," she said. "I do not know anything more. Ramón would not speak of him to me. He may be dead for all I know."

"What's he sick with?"

"When I was small, he was sick with polio. He almost died. His legs were affected, and he walks with crutches."

"Does he work?"

"Oh yes, we are from a small village, and his family had been there generations, all of them farmers. He would work from sunup to sundown in the fields."

"On crutches?"

"Sí," she said. "He was strong. But he could not fight off Calderón's men."

"I guess you come from good stock if your father's out there farming when he can't walk," he said.

She smiled. "My mother has said that many times. She is a strong woman herself. She worked in factories as a child, and in the fields when she could. She had many brothers and sisters and looked after them all."

"What about yours?"

"My sisters? There are three," she said. "All younger."

"What are their names?"

He could see Lupe touching the rosary in her hands. He hadn't noticed she'd taken it out of her pocket.

"María Luisa, María Teresa and María del Carmen," she said.

"Wait, you're all named Maria?" he asked.

"We are called by what you Americans call a middle name," she said. "Guadalupe, Luisa, Teresa and Carmen."

"Did they call you Lupe?"

She paused for a moment. "No. They called me Lupita. It is a pet name."

"And the others?"

She shifted in the seat, discomfort radiating from her.

"Marisa, Mayté and Mamen," she said. "Mamen was a baby when I was taken. She would not know me."

"And you've never thought about going back when all this is over?" he asked.

"If I am not dead, they would wish it so if I came home now," she said.

"As much as I hate what you've done, I wouldn't turn Diana out if it was her," he said. "She's family."

"You do not understand the shame associated with this in México," she said. "A woman who is raped . . . it is a shameful thing. People do not speak of it. Prostitution and things of that nature are sins. I would be outcast."

"Things aren't easy in America for girls who have been through that either," Tim said. "It's got nothing to do with Mexico or America. It's your family."

"It was."

He said nothing more, frustrated with her attitude. How the hell would she ever know for sure if she didn't try? If they didn't want her back, to hell with them. At least she'd know.

Lupe went through his glove box, and took out a map to follow their progress as they drove.

"Will we stop in Los Angeles?" she asked.

"No," he said. "Somewhere else. If these guys show up, I want to be able to outrun them, and Los Angeles traffic might make that hard."

He figured he'd stop when he saw a decent place. He checked the rearview mirror. No cars behind them. If those hitmen weren't chasing them at least they'd have a day or two head start.

And if they were . . . well, he'd think of something.

He shifted gears and laid his foot on the gas harder.

12

Lupe was half asleep, tired from the rhythm of being on the road and the lack of sleep the night before. Her eyes kept fluttering shut, her head bobbing down before she jerked it back up again. It was like she was in a dream. But nevertheless, when Tim spoke, her eyes bolted open.

"We're being followed."

"Dios," she said. "Are you sure?"

"There's a sedan back there, maroon," he said. "Don't turn around and look, use the side mirrors. It's about a half mile back, a 1962 Oldsmobile. You see it?"

She waited a moment, and Tim let the car drift to the right. The traffic had thinned out and she spotted the one he spoke of some distance behind them.

"Sí," she said. "I see it."

She sat back against the bucket seat and tried to breathe. Her pulse hammered in her throat.

"Relax," he said. "They're following. They want to see where we're headed."

"And when we stop?" she asked. "What will they do when we stop?"

"We'll be ready," he said.

She looked over, trying to see if there was any fear or doubt in his mind, but he spoke firmly, his hands weren't tense on the wheel, and he didn't glance in the rearview mirror every five seconds. He seemed unconcerned and in perfect control.

She sat in her seat and looked forward, trying to mimic his calm demeanour.

"Take a nap or something," he said. "I'll wake you if something happens."

She looked over, and he nodded. "Go on. Better to sleep when you can. I don't know what's coming the next few days."

She thought for a moment, nodded and settled into the seat, trying to get comfortable. She let her mind drift, trying to keep thoughts of México and gunmen out of her head.

Lupe was falling and opened her mouth to scream.

Her eyes flew open, and she was so disoriented she didn't know where she was. She hit the door frame, and her head slammed against the passenger window. A moment later another jerk of motion sent her into the dashboard. Tim grabbed her shoulder and pulled her back against the seat.

"You okay?"

His voice sounded far away. She closed her eyes, then opened them again. "Lupe?"

"I am alright," she said. "I think. What is happening?"

The car jerked to the right and she held on, her fingers grabbing the centre console for leverage. She clawed the side of the seat with her other hand.

"Tim?" she asked.

The sun was low on the horizon. She must have slept at some point, and she didn't know where they were.

"What is happening?" she asked.

"They're making their move. Put your seatbelt on," he said.

She braced herself against the dash as Tim changed lanes quickly. He did his best to avoid the few other cars around them.

"What did they do? Where are they?" she asked, her voice panicked.

"They came up real fast, tried to ram the bumper, but I saw them coming and jerked the wheel at the last minute." he said. "I knew they'd try something here. It's a long, dark stretch of road. The cars have thinned out."

"You said they would not try," she said.

"Yeah, well I lied."

The sedan came up behind them, and Tim changed lanes again. She watched in horror as the car followed.

"Are they trying to run us off the road?" she asked.

"I don't know." His hands gripped the wheel. "I think they might try if they can get close enough."

She took out her rosary and held it, praying in her head.

The sedan roared up behind them and swerved into the passing lane. She gasped as the driver looked over.

"You know him?" Tim asked, gunning it to outrun their car.

"He is from the Casa," she said. "One of Calderón's personal guards."

The sedan pulled up next to them again.

"He has a gun!" she yelled.

She didn't know what happened first—Tim pulled the handbrake as a shot rang out. The brakes squealed and burned as she flew into the dashboard, almost hitting her head. The car spun in a full circle, and the sedan chasing them slowed. As soon as it made the attempt to reverse, Tim pushed the gas and shot forward, rocketing by their car.

"Pays to have a Hemi," he said with a wicked grin.

"You are enjoying this too much," she said.

She held on for dear life as they drove along the highway.

"There's a truck stop a few miles up ahead," Tim said. "Just off the high-way. Keep your eyes open; if there are cars or trucks in there, we're getting off this road."

"Why?" she asked. "They will catch us. They'll kill us!"

"Nah," he said. "They're bear bait."

Lupe didn't understand. The tires screeched as Tim changed lanes, the se-dan gaining on them.

"They must have something big under that hood," Tim murmured.

"I do not care what is under the hood so long as we get away," Lupe said tensely.

Tim floored it again, narrowly missing a car in front of him when he changed lanes.

"That truck stop almost always has the fuzz sitting in the lot," he said. "It's why I avoided the place every time we came by."

"We?" she asked, gasping as the speedometer crept up toward eighty miles an hour.

"Me and Ruby," he said.

The sedan backed off, and she sat back in the seat and tried to calm her breathing. Perhaps they were trying to scare them.

"You would come here?" she asked, desperate for a distraction.

"Yeah," he said. "I used to do runs to LA. I know the road."

Tim eased off the speed as the chase seemed to have died down.

"I do not understand," she said. "Why have they not tried to run us off the road?"

"Because I'd nail their balls to the wall if they even breathed on my car?" he suggested. He looked over, an impish smile on his face.

His grin was full of excitement, and he seemed to be primed with energy he channelled straight into the steering wheel. He was enjoying this car chase.

"Tim."

She glanced in the side mirror—the car was coming up on their rear again.

"Hang on," he said.

He floored it, but the other car kept pace, gaining on them. Lupe watched, her nerves raw, as the car came up right behind them.

"Tim!" she screamed. The car seemed to gain speed as it approached. A moment later she was thrown against the dashboard as the car rammed their back bumper.

"Shit!" Tim swore. He smacked his hand on the steering wheel. "Fuck, it's not even a few months off the damn production line!"

"I am fine," Lupe said, her voice tense. "Thank you for asking."

"Sit back and put the seatbelt on like I told you," Tim said. She looked at his and realized he must have fastened it some time ago.

She clicked the buckle in and clutched her left hand on the seat divider. She turned around to look, and the car came up on them again.

"They will hit us again!" she exclaimed.

"No they won't." His voice was low and angry. He glanced up at the rear-view mirror, then over to the side mirror. At the last second, he jerked the wheel to the right and the car swerved into the slow lane. The sedan was almost neck and neck with them.

"Down!"

Lupe ducked and heard a bang and crash, then felt wind.

"Shit!"

Lupe sat up to see a bullet hole had entered the driver's side window and exited her window, glass shattering onto Tim's lap. He slowed the car to a crawl, and the chase car slowed ahead of them. Tim grabbed the ankle holster and put the gun in his lap.

"This is insanity," Lupe said, her throat dry.

"Hang on and stay low."

As the car almost rolled to a stop, Tim slumped in the seat a little.

"What are you doing?" she asked, afraid he was hurt.

"Playing possum," he said.

"I do not know what—"

"Shut up, Lupe."

She stopped talking, watching Tim gear the car down until it slowed. The sedan following them had stopped fifty yards beyond them and began to back up. She got down lower, afraid bullets would fly into the car at any moment. She tried to envision what it would feel like to be shot and tears pricked her eyes.

"Hold on," Tim said.

She was folded over in the seat, her head near the divider. Tim's hand was on her head for a moment, his fingers in her hair. Nausea rippled through her stomach as she remembered men forcing her head into their laps. She shook her head, and Tim removed his hand.

"Keep your head down," he said. "We'll be outta here in a minute."

She resisted the urge to poke her head up and see what was happening.

Tim's legs tensed, as if he was a cat about to jump on its prey. A second later he slammed the clutch in, shifted gears and stepped on the accelerator. The car shot forward, spinning its tires. She smelled the burning rubber and braced herself against the dash. She glanced up at Tim, who shifted gears and worked the clutch like it was his job. His motions were fluid and quick and seconds later she felt as if she was in a rocket.

She raised her head a little. The sedan was trying to catch up.

"They came back to see if I was dead," he said. "Took them some time to shift out of reverse, but they've got something big under that hood. Remind me to thank Bill for all those times he wanted to drag race out in the desert. It paid off."

Lupe said nothing, her hands shaking as she sat up and back into her seat. As they sped forward, she could see the sedan catching up to them.

"They will do this all night," she said.

"No," he said. "Look up ahead. That's the truck stop."

Lights twinkled in the distance, maybe a few miles away, and her hope soared for the first time.

"Will they follow us there?"

"I hope so."

He must be crazy.

She took the rosary from the floor of the car where it had fallen and prayed it, moving the beads with her fingers and moving her lips with the words.

She gasped when she heard Tim tell her to brace, and the sedan slammed into the back of the car, just as they were feet from the off ramp that led to the truck stop. The sedan took the exit with them, and Tim slowed.

"What are you doing?" she said. "They will catch us!"

Tim pulled into the truck stop at a normal speed, the sedan speeding in behind them. As the car gained on them from behind, Tim pulled Lupe below the dash. Another bang echoed, louder this time, and glass broke behind them.

Tim sat up and steered the car toward a white sedan at the far end of the lot. A light on its dash came on and the sedan behind them squealed as it peeled out of the parking lot.

A siren pierced the air, and as the sedan sped back onto the freeway on-ramp, the white car began chasing it.

"Smokey in a plain white wrapper," he murmured.

"What?" she asked. Her body shook so much her muscles were beginning to ache.

"The police," he said. "That guy sits in his unmarked car at this stop just about every day. They used to have problems here with lot lizards."

"I do not understand."

"Prostitutes," he said. "They stuck an unmarked in the lot to scare them away."

"You knew he was here?" she asked.

He nodded. "I did a lot of runs to LA in the last year. Saw him here every time I drove by."

She let out a breath.

"He'll give chase for awhile, especially if he heard the gunshots," Tim said. "It buys us some time. We need to get somewhere for the night and get the car off the road for awhile. State troopers and the cops might be looking for it, and even if they're not it's going to stand out with all these broken windows. Shit. This is gonna cost a fortune to fix."

He slammed a fist into the steering wheel, the stared out at the road for a moment before he pulled back onto the freeway.

She sat back, trying to let the tenseness in her body release. She swallowed hard again, her mouth as dry as sandpaper, but try as she might, she couldn't keep the tears from overflowing.

Tim glanced over a few times, but he said nothing. He pulled off the highway and onto a small feeder road that took them into the hills. They climbed into the wilderness and the trees and plants changed. The air was cooler. She wished she was able to pay closer attention, since she had never seen a place like this.

"Keep your eyes open for a motel," he said. "We'll stay the night and head to Mendoza in the morning. Hopefully it'll be enough time to lose the Mexicans and the cops."

She spotted the motel first, in the distance. It turned out to be tiny individual cabins tucked away amongst pine, and when Tim returned to the car from the motel office, he drove to the one furthest back from the road, hidden amongst the trees.

"We'll be safe here," he said.

She clutched her rosary as she got out of the car. She was not sure she believed she'd be safe anywhere now.

Tim was tired.

His muscles ached from the tense way he held them during the long car chase, and his head ached from the fight. He was bone tired and wanted nothing more than a hot shower and to fall into bed.

He decided to take advantage of the hot shower, and soaped up his hair and sat under the spray, as hot as he could stand it. When he was done he came out to find Lupe had set out the sandwiches Ruby had made. She set the small table with a foil wrapped sandwich at each place, and the bottles of Pepsi on the table. He opened one of them with a church key and took a long drink.

Lupe had tried hard to make everything normal, and he figured she wasn't used to car chases, even coming from her situation.

She was nervous as a cat, her hands shaking and her eyes wide and scared. He could see bruises forming on her arms from the times she was sent flying in the car with all the sudden stops and starts. He should have known they would try something on the road. He should have had her strapped into the seat from the beginning.

"You okay?" he asked.

She looked over. "I am fine."

"You're awful bruised up," he said, nodding toward her arms.

She looked at them and rubbed a hand over her arms.

"My head is worse," she said. "It feels like my brain will pop out of my skull."

He walked over and placed a hand behind her head, working his fingers against her scalp. He didn't miss how her breathing changed and how it became hard for her to hold eye contact. She tried hard not to look at his chest. He had put his jeans back on, but elected to go without a shirt. She tried to look away, and he didn't want to let her get away with that.

He felt a lump on the side of her head and left his hands in her hair longer than necessary.

"You got a nice goose egg," he said.

She looked at him quizzically.

"It means a big bump," he said. "Like half a goose egg sitting on your head."

She lifted her hand to her head and felt for herself, her fingers tangling with his.

"What was it from?" he asked.

"I believe I hit my head on the window," she said. "I was asleep, I think, so I could not brace myself."

He took his hands out of her hair and sat at the small table. He pulled out a church key to open her Pepsi. Lupe sat across from him a moment later. She moved her lips silently—grace, he supposed.

They ate their sandwiches in silence, and Tim watched her. She seemed nervous, her breathing quick and shallow. He wondered if she would to try and kiss him again, and he wondered if he should let her.

He didn't like thinking about the things she'd done. But she didn't work the streets or anything now, and she wasn't the ones in his head. He didn't know whether he could take her to bed knowing what was in her past. He decided to leave it up to chance. The nervous way she looked, nothing would happen any time soon.

The thought disappointed him. He always felt like this after a fight, a car chase, any kind of activity that involved danger. Usually he ended up with Carolyn in his bed, and he knew she wasn't the most faithful girl in the world. He couldn't hold Lupe to a standard he didn't hold anyone else to.

She finished her sandwich and drained the Pepsi, then excused herself to the bathroom. Tim heard the water running for awhile. He rubbed a hand over his eyes.

He would have to tell her sooner or later there was a bounty on her head. It would scare her even more, but she couldn't be kept in the dark. Knowing would make her vigilant, and he needed her to pay attention to what went on around her.

He smoked a cigarette and stretched out in the chair, trying to relax his muscles from the stressful drive. Lupe came out of the bathroom a few minutes later.

"You alright?" he asked again, wondering why she was so jumpy. Maybe the chase this afternoon had affected her more than he realized.

She stood there for a moment, then came over to him and looked him in the eye before sitting on his lap, snaking her arms around his neck.

"Lupe, what are you doing?" he asked. His mind flashed back to the whorehouse in his memory, his father sitting alongside a bench seat with him in a hallway, a woman with bright red fingernails laughing and sitting on his father's lap, touching him in a way he knew at eight she shouldn't be, and by ten knew was wrong.

She didn't answer, but she did bend her head toward his. He pushed her away and got up from the chair, ignoring the confused and hurt look on her face.

"What is wrong?" she asked.

"This isn't a whorehouse, Lupe," he said harshly.

She looked like she'd been slapped.

"I was not—"

"Come on," Tim said, taking a drag. "You come up and sit on my lap like that? Was it Calderón who used to tell you what to say to the paying customers when he'd make you go up to them like that?"

Her face paled as he spoke, and he knew he hit the nail on the head.

She stood there, her chest heaving with each breath, looking close to tears. He stared at her for a moment, then flinched as his cigarette reached his fingers, burning him. He stubbed out the butt in the ashtray.

"I do not know how to do this right," she said, desperation plain in her voice.

He looked at her again, her breasts rising and falling as she breathed, and he grew hard. He cursed himself for his lack of control. He tried to replay words in his head, thinking about her and who she was, but all he could think about was the way she nibbled her bottom lip, turning it pink.

"You just do it," he said. And if you don't, I will, he thought.

A moment later she had crossed the room and paused before pulling him to her. He was surprised at the urgency of her kiss, so different from the night before.

He kissed her back, feeling her almost collapse against him, and wondered if this was the same girl he had kissed last night, one who tensed up like a statue and pulled away in fear.

She slipped her hands around the back of his neck, her fingers working into his hair at the back.

He kissed her deeper, sucking on her bottom lip, and she pressed herself closer to him. He pulled her tighter against him. He kissed along her jaw and down her neck, listening to the way her breath came in short gasps. Her hands were on his chest, and he expected her to push him away. Instead, she raked her fingers along his chest before pulling him closer to her.

He guided her toward the bed, pushing all images out of his head about how many times she had done this with other men for money.

She broke their kiss before sitting on the bed. He could see the longing on her face. He wondered for a moment if she had missed it, all the sex, and pushed the thought away as quickly as it had come. He couldn't go there; he couldn't think of her like that, not after all she told him.

She looked at him again, her eyes fringed by her dark lashes, her mouth parted. A button had come away on the blouse she wore and he could see the top of her bra peeking from the fabric.

She reached up, her hand grazing his stomach and her fingers playing over the taut scar on his abdomen. She grabbed his waistband and pulled him with her as she moved back on the bed.

When he reached her lips again, all thoughts of her past were gone from his head. Her hands were on the small of his back, and he flinched as they travelled up the myriad of scars on his back. He pushed the sudden thought of Ruby from his mind, wondering if he would ever feel hands on his back and not think of her.

He kissed Lupe again, relishing the heat of her mouth, feeling her move beneath him. Her lips placed hot kisses along his neck. She hesitated as he undid the buttons on the western shirt she wore, exposing her bra. He heard her light moan as he touched her and kissed her again. He undid the clasp on her bra, and she slipped out of it, her gaze watching him as he looked at her body.

He bent his head to one of her nipples and flicked it with his tongue. She arched toward her as he moved his head away.

She responded with more urgency, and he jumped as her hand slid down his stomach, resting near the button on his jeans.

He wouldn't have stopped her even if those thoughts of her past had come into his head.

Lupe felt different than she ever had before.

She was excited, like her skin was on fire, and she kissed Tim back with as much fervour as she could. She didn't think of her previous life—there were no thoughts of the pain and torture she had felt. She had a great need to be in this moment—she wanted it to last forever.

Tim's lips trailed down her neck again and he kissed the tip of her right nipple. She didn't feel exposed or scared in front of him like this. In fact, she was amazed he hadn't stopped this at all.

Perhaps he did see more to her than Calderón had made her. The thought gave her hope for the rest of her life.

She shivered as his lips kissed their way down her chest, hovering around her belly button. She tangled her fingers into his hair, wet from the shower.

She arched up when he undid the button on the jeans Ruby had given her, and let Tim slide them off her. His jeans were already discarded on the floor. She felt a consuming need to have him. She was amazed at the urge she had to do this.

When he was naked in front of her, she looked at his body without shame, let him look at hers and looked him straight in the eye. He covered her body with his, and the overwhelming need to have him engulfed her.

She pulled his head to her and kissed him, feeling him pull her legs around his waist. She gasped as he entered her, then closed her eyes as she began moving with him, feeling as if every nerve was brilliant and alive.

She remembered crying out, not in pain or fear this time, but in pleasure, saying his name over again, her fingers in his hair.

A short time later she was curled against his chest, listening to the occasional inhalation as he smoked. Her body was warm and sated, and he was quiet beside her.

She couldn't keep the tears from coming.

She heard the irritated inhalation of breath from Tim.

"What's wrong?" he asked, not sounding interested in hearing the answer.

"Nothing is wrong," she said.

"Most folks don't cry when nothing's wrong."

She was quiet, trying to figure out how to say it.

He sighed. "I know it isn't like you said out loud you wanted to do this, but if you wanted it to stop you should have said something."

"No," she said. "I wanted this. Very much."

"Then what is it?"

She turned to look at him.

"It has not been like that," she said.

He studied her face, his brow creased, then his expression changed.

"Lupe, have you ever had sex?" he asked. "I don't mean in that boy's town, or that casa, or whatever else they made you do. I mean on your own, because you wanted to do it. Because you liked somebody."

She hesitated, then shook her head. She tried to stop the tears, but it was useless. They overpowered her, just as her desire had.

"I did not know it was different," she said. "It has surprised me how much it is different."

Tim looked at her, a new understanding in his eyes.

"This was the first time you weren't forced to do it," he said.

She nodded. She couldn't understand why she kept crying. She wasn't sad.

Tim reached over and brushed the tears off her cheeks.

"I guess I wasn't too far off thinking you were acting like a virgin last night," he said. "I guess you kind of were."

She curled up against him again, and he let her cry, rubbing her back in soft circles. She fell asleep in his arms.

13

Tim awoke early.

Lupe was curled against his him. Her warm breath feathered his chest, and he stayed still for a few minutes, not wanting to wake her. He tried to roll her over, but she woke up.

"It's early yet," he said. "Go back to sleep."

"I cannot," she said.

They lay there together for a few moments without speaking before Tim got out of bed and got dressed.

"We'll head to Mendoza's," he told her. "He's got a junkyard in San Ysidro near the Tijuana River, and another place over in Tijuana. He's been keeping an ear to the ground. You ever been to San Ysidro? Or San Diego?"

"Never," she said. "This has been my first time outside of México. Before Calderón came for me, I had never left my village."

She got out of the bed, naked and not shy at all about it. Tim remembered Ruby's shyness the day after they'd first slept together. Lupe was different from her in so many ways.

He watched her collect her clothes from the floor and realized all thoughts of what she had done didn't seem to matter to him much anymore. Maybe he slew those demons of his past. At least, some of them.

While she showered, he went outside to look at the car. Glass was all over the seats and he collected as much of it as he could. He knocked the rest of the glass out of the driver and passenger windows. The back window wasn't badly shattered, so he tapped out some of the loose shards and found a roll of packing tape in the glove box. He taped around the hole, hoping it would be enough to prevent further damage.

The back bumper was scraped and bent, and all said and done would cost the most to fix. If he ever caught up with those Mexicans, he'd bury them in the desert.

Lupe emerged from the little cabin a while later, and they got in the car and left the motel and continued to drive through the mountains. They even passed a ski resort.

Lupe stared out the window at the landscape.

"You do not think they will be following us?" Lupe asked, rubbing the spot on her head where Tim had found the bump.

"I think they've gone ahead to Tijuana," he said. "If they're any good, they'll know we're going to Mendoza. I bet they're trying to figure out what the hell we've got planned."

"I would also like to know this," Lupe pointed out.

"Wait until we get to Mendoza," Tim said. "I need to hear what he knows before I make any solid plans."

The drive took them through the mountains and down into towns and suburbs to the southeast of Los Angeles. They connected with the big highway again, and Lupe dozed in the passenger seat. It was hours before they reached San Diego and went on to San Ysidro. Tim pulled off the highway and through a maze of roads before finding the dirt one that skirted the Tijuana River. He stopped the car outside of the junkyard and idled for a moment, making sure no one followed. He pulled around the back and parked.

The sun was high in the sky and it was hot, at least pushing ninety if he wasn't mistaken. Mexico was over the river and a short walk to a fence.

Lupe got out of the car, and he watched her eyes darting from side to side and her hands shaking. He didn't blame her for being scared. She could see Mexico from where they were standing, and when she left she didn't think she'd ever come back. It was days later, and here she was.

Tim walked toward a building that looked to be no more than a large shed with a TV antenna on it. He banged on a corrugated metal door. A moment later Mendoza's right hand man, Juan, opened it. Tim didn't miss the gun in Juan's hand, which he tucked into the back of his pants when he saw Tim there.

"He is in back," Juan said, studying Tim's bruised face. "It is good to see you."

"Good to be seen," Tim said. He followed Juan into the building which housed tools and rusted car frames and toward a small add-on room where Mendoza kept his office.

Rafael Mendoza was in his late forties, a cigar always clamped in his mouth, and his dark hair showing no signs of grey. He had a thick moustache and wore dark sunglasses, even inside, to hide the cataract that had developed in his left eye.

"I am happy to see you're here in one piece," Mendoza said. "Although it looks like you have already met with trouble. Sit. We have much to discuss."

He said a few words in Spanish to Lupe, who seemed to relax a little at hearing her native tongue. Tim hated it when people spoke languages he couldn't understand right in front of him, but he allowed them to share a few words, seeing the effect it had on Lupe's nerves.

"What have you heard?" Tim asked.

"The bounty is still out," Mendoza said, lighting a cigar.

"Bounty?" Lupe asked. "For what?"

"On you, mija," Mendoza said, his voice soft, as if she was an injured animal. "The El Camarilla has a price on your head."

"¡Dios mío!" She crossed herself.

"Dead or alive?" Tim asked.

Mendoza paused. "He prefers her alive."

"They will kill me the moment I arrive," Lupe said morosely.

"She may not be wrong," Mendoza told him. "Juan says the word is out everywhere. Calderón is eager to get his hands on her. They will not say why."

Tim glanced at Lupe, then looked back at Mendoza.

"She has something he wants," Tim said. "A microfiche."

"Ah." Mendoza reclined in his chair and puffed on the cigar. "So the rumours are true. Juan was not sure whether to believe them or not. Some were talking about Calderón's operation being in jeopardy. Even a hint of this getting around the criminal underground is not good for him."

"We need to let him know we'll be in Mexico," Tim said.

"You are crazy," Lupe told him.

"Hear me out," he said. "We let it out I captured you in Las Vegas, and I want to make a trade. I give him you and the microfiche for some cash."

"He would think it's a trap," Lupe said. "He would never agree to meet."

"I think he would," Tim said. "We get the word out we want a meeting. We tell him we'll meet where you hid the microfiche and make a trade. Maybe I can sweeten the deal and tell him I want to work with his organization, get feelers up into Las Vegas, that sorta thing."

"You are crazy," Lupe said again. "He may agree to this meeting, but neither one of us will walk out of it alive. He will kill you."

It stuck out to him she didn't mention herself. That could be a problem.

"We aren't meeting with him," Tim said. "It's just a way to get him to back off. If he thinks we're coming to meet him he isn't going to have anyone kidnap or kill us on the street. We'll have some freedom to move around and find someone to get that microfiche to."

"I can get Juan to put out the information," Mendoza said. "I have facilitated things between criminal groups before, it will not be unusual if contact with him comes through me."

"We'll need a place to hide in Mexico," he said. "Where he can't get to us."

Mendoza looked at him. "That is where you will run into trouble. His men are everywhere, and they will try to kill you if Calderón does not accept this meeting or you are there before he learns of it."

"Well, we need a damn good place to hide," he said.

"I think I may know of one," Lupe said slowly. She looked over at Tim. "But I am not sure you will like it."

Thursday, November 3, 1966

Mendoza provided papers for them to get across the border, and they crossed Thursday morning. Tim was surprised with the relative ease. The Mexican border guards didn't asked them anything as they drove into Mexico in a junker of a car Mendoza had lent them. Tim's Charger was too recognizable, and there was already body damage. He didn't want to risk trashing the entire car. As it was, he could find someone to fix it up when he got home. It'd cut into his take of the weapons deal, but it had to be done.

Lupe looked tense and worried beside him. She kept looking in the side view mirror and glancing out the windows. He was glad she was vigilant.

Tim drove the car in speed with the traffic into Tijuana, then headed into the desert and toward Mexicali on a road that turned to dirt the minute they were out of town. Over two hours later, he was glad to see Mexicali on the horizon.

"Where do we go?" he asked.

She directed him into the thick traffic of downtown, and toward a slum butted up against the busy entertainment area.

"Calderón had this place built with others, but he runs the area," she said. "It was to resemble the zona roja in Nuevo Laredo. I have not been there, so I do not know if it does, but it is similar to the one in San Luis Río

Colorado. It is like a compound, but there is movement in and out. There are a few cantinas inside, and brothels as well. The bars and cantinas of the main zona roja are close by, and customers move freely between them."

"What about the car?"

"I will show you where to leave it. The policía will not take it. Many concessions are given in Calderón's zona."

Tim nodded, his hands tight on the steering wheel. He didn't like being here one bit, so he could imagine how Lupe felt. He turned on a street she pointed out, and they drove over a set of railway tracks. The area to the left contained a walled compound that looked new—at least the wall part. The right side had some small houses back from the road, and the block leading away from it was filled with bars, restaurants, cantinas and what looked like seedy motels.

"We can park the car on one of the side streets here," she said. "It is quieter here and it will be ignored."

Tim was surprised at how close people lived to this place. The high wall that surrounded the place reminded him of prison, and he supposed it was a prison for her.

"We need to leave the car some place we can get to it easy, in case these guys show up," Tim said. "I don't wanna be running all over hell's half acre to get to it."

"There are ways to get out of the compound," Lupe said. "Calderón believed it was under his control. But there are many things here people do not see."

Things they don't want to, he surmised. She directed him to a side street, and he parked the lousy twenty-year-old Chrysler Mendoza had given him. It was rusted in places, but the engine was big and Tim hoped it could outrun people if it had to, even if it was an automatic transmission.

They had to walk around almost the entire compound—and it was a compound, Tim realized—to get to the entrance.

"I'm gonna stick out in here, aren't I?" he asked.

"No," she said. "Many Americans come here. You will be like any other customer. But first, we must meet Inez."

"How will you get in touch with her?" Tim asked. "You said she had no phone."

"When I said Calderón built this place to resemble the zona roja—the Boy's Town you speak of—I was not speaking generally," Lupe said. "He has tried to re-create it. There are small rooms here where girls stay. Not all are under Calderón's control, but they all must pay him for use of the rooms. Many women here live with their boyfriends or husbands."

"You've gotta be kidding," Tim said. "Some asshole would let his woman do this?"

"Some, yes," Lupe said. "But many are what you call pimps. There are few free women here, yes, but many more are said to be free and are not."

"What happens if one of them leaves?" Tim asked. Lupe looked over like he had a screw loose. "I mean ones that haven't stolen important shit from gangsters."

She smiled a little at this.

"If they are not Calderón's girls, many times they go. But trouble often follows," she said. "I have seen many women beaten. It is like their payment for leaving these men without income."

They reached the entrance on the busy street. Tim wished they'd come at night. He felt like all eyes were on them.

Lupe lingered near the entrance, a scarf over her head, and spotted someone. The girl approached her, making like she was cat calling Tim. Lupe spoke to her in Spanish, then turned and joined Tim again.

"We must go," Lupe said. "She will tell Inez where to find us. Calderón's men are inside."

"She'll keep her mouth shut?" Tim asked, taking Lupe by the elbow and walking with her toward a side street.

"Of course," Lupe said.

They walked back to the car and got in, and Lupe closed her eyes.

"Tired?"

"I did not get much sleep," she said, a slight smile on her face. She moved across the bench seat to sit closer to him and rested her head on his shoulder.

Tim shifted in the seat, her action giving him pause.

"Lupe," he said. "You know this isn't . . . this isn't anything permanent? Right?"

She was quiet for a second, and he found himself hoping she wasn't upset. The last thing he needed right now was her upset about something that could distract her.

"I know," she said. "You will return home and I . . . well, I do not know what I will do yet. It depends on so many things. But I know you will not stay with me. I know you would not want me to return with you."

"It's not anything personal," he said, feeling like a jerk.

"I know," she said. "Your heart lies elsewhere."

He looked over. "What do you mean by that?"

"You know exactly what I mean."

"We're not on that again, are we?"

"You do not love me. That is alright, I do not expect you to. Your heart . . . it is free for someone else," she said.

"There isn't anyone else."

"Mmm."

He didn't know why it set his teeth on edge she didn't believe him.

"There isn't." His voice was firm.

"I believe you," she said, sounding like she didn't believe a word he said. "We should rest. It may be some time. She will find us."

Lupe drifted off to sleep. Tim kept his eyes open.

Lupe woke up when Tim shook her.

"Is that her?"

Inez stood against a tree outside, looking at the car and waiting.

"Yes," Lupe said. "That is her."

They both got out of the car and Lupe went to Inez, who hugged her.

"They are after you, mija," she said in Spanish, stroking Lupe's hair. "Calderón is angry."

"This is Tim," she said in English. "Tim, this is Inez."

They nodded at each other, and Lupe could see Inez didn't trust him.

"Is it bad?" Lupe asked.

"His men are around la zona roja all the time," Inez said, her Spanish rapid, perhaps because she thought Tim could understand. "He has offered money for information. No one will speak. We were hoping you would not come back. And not with someone who looks like he takes beatings for a living."

"I had to," she said. "He will chase me forever."

Tim's agitation showed the longer they spoke Spanish to each other.

"We need a place to hide until we can arrange a meeting," Lupe said, switching to English.

"A meeting with Calderón? Are you crazy?" Inez asked in Spanish. She stared at Tim.

"No, we're not crazy," Tim said laconically. "The two of you mind? Hablas inglés."

"Calderón will kill you both," Inez said, switching to English.

"We will not meet with him," Lupe said. "We will try to trick him into leaving us be for awhile."

"Lupe's got something he wants," Tim said. "We're gonna find someone who wants it and has the power to keep Lupe safe."

"Tim will trade protection for the information I took," Lupe said.

Inez looked over at Tim. "Meeting with Calderón would be foolish. All he would want is to kill you."

"Making him think we want to meet buys us some time to get the information into other hands. Hands that'll help Lupe." Tim looked at Inez unflinchingly.

"We should not involve you," Lupe said to Inez.

"I am involved," Inez said. "Come. We will get you inside. Meeting or not, these men will try to kill you if they know where you are. They will not search the rooms. They are too stupid to think you would come here."

Inez led them across the street to the back wall that surrounded the compound. A cluster of trees and vegetation climbed up the wall and she moved the brush aside to reveal a crumbling section of the wall. Tim was surprised gaining entry was that easy.

"The policía do not know about this entrance," she said. "Nor does Calderón or his men."

Inez led them through back alleys, past people huddled in the doorway of small rooms, then into the open, past cantinas inside the compound. They approached a building that looked like an apartment and went up a small flight of stairs to a hallway. She opened a door and led them into a small apartment, then closed the door, leaving them inside.

"She will go and make sure we were not seen," Lupe said. She looked around the room and felt sick. She had stayed in one like this many weekends.

The apartment was one large room with a half kitchen on one wall, a window on another and bedding was piled on the floor against the other wall.

"She live here alone?" Tim asked.

Lupe nodded. "She travels to Hermosillo once a month to see her children."

The door opened and Inez entered, shutting it behind her.

"It'll be safe here?" he asked her.

"Calderón and his men have little idea what you look like," Inez said to him. "You can move around with some freedom. You will blend in with the tourists at the cantinas and the brothels. Lupe will have to disguise herself if she's to go out, they will be looking for her."

Tim nodded. "What's this place like for cops?"

Inez sat on a small crate turned over to make a seat.

"The policía have a small office across the street," she said. "They will not do anything but look for tourists who are too drunk and people buying drugs. The Army will raid this place if that happens, so the policía maintain order. They are supposed to look for underage girls, and they do not. They are paid by many different people to look the other way."

"Has Ramón been here?" Lupe asked her in Spanish.

Inez nodded. "A few times. He asked about you. I believe word of the trouble has gotten to him by now."

Tim watched her.

"There are El Camarilla guards here as well," Inez said in English. "I will take you around and show you. I am furthest away from the apartments the El Camarilla has for the girls from the Casa. Calderón built this compound surrounding these two buildings. They should not come here. But I will show you each man and tell you the schedule. Calderón is stupid, for a man in charge."

"Why?" Lupe asked.

"Because he has a schedule," Tim supplied, looking at Inez for confirmation. "He's consistent."

Inez nodded. "Yes."

Lupe thought back and realized they were right. Calderón had things done at a certain time, a certain way. It was the reason she was able to escape from the Casa—she knew when the guards were changing and knew when the most vulnerable time was.

"There are many men you have to worry about," Inez said. "I wish you would run back to America."

"They followed her there and tried to kill her," Tim said. "It's not an option."

Inez looked at him, then Lupe. "Manuel was by to tell us of your success in getting across. I have heard the El Camarilla questioned him at length."

Lupe was worried. Manuel was her closest ally. She didn't think he would give her up, even if there was torture involved. He was loyal to her.

"Get word to him," Lupe said. "We need to meet with him."

Inez nodded at her and turned to Tim.

"I will take you now to show you the guards and Calderón's zona, and where each brothel and cantina is here," she said. "If you like, I will show you the cantinas and brothels down the road as well."

"Stay here, Lupe," Tim told her. "I'll be back."

Lupe nodded, and watched them both go. She looked around the desolate room, one she never thought she'd see the inside of again, and tried not to cry.

Inez knew her shit.

Tim was wary of her—hearing she had kids had surprised him—but Inez was damn good at paying attention to things. If he was stupid enough to let girls get involved in his business, she would've made a first rate lookout.

"What're you doing here anyway?" Tim asked, sitting at a table in one of the local salons that allowed women, which was deader than a doornail in the early evening. Inez said it would look less suspicious if they drank together.

"I am here because I have nowhere else to go," she said.

"So you're under Calderón's thumb too?"

"No," she said. "Calderón built this zona to control his girls better, but it's become a place busy with tourists, so many of the women who work come here as it's harder to get on with the brothels down the road. He takes a cut for use of the brothel rooms here, and if you stay as I do in the apartments, you pay him again. It is expensive, but this zona is popular and the work is steady."

"Some work," he said.

She turned and faced him.

"I have a primary school education because my father did not believe that girls should go to school. I found myself pregnant with my son when I was Lupe's age, and my father made me marry the man. My husband drank and beat me. He was killed in a bar fight when my son was two and my daughter days old, and I thanked the man who did it. But I had nothing, no place to go. My cousin told me to come here to work because the money was good. But it meant I had to leave the children with my aunt. My mother and father are too poor, and now that they know what I do, they do not speak to me. This was all I could choose. It allows me to send money for my children."

Tim took a long drag of his cigarette.

"You think Lupe's gonna choose this when she gets out?" he asked.

"It is possible," Inez said.

Tim didn't think so anymore. Not for her.

"You can't sew or work in a factory?" Tim asked.

"Why are you so eager to change my life?" Inez's dark eyes were probing.

"Doesn't look like much of a life to me."

"It is not your business. You are as bad as the people who come to tell us God loves us."

Tim smirked. "Yeah, it's not my business. I'm just wondering why someone who isn't looking for the exit is trying to help Lupe find one."

Inez's expression softened.

"The girls who come from the Casa have been through more than most of us," she said. "Calderón allows some of us to work out of here, and if we pay him, he pays us no mind. But the girls and women under his control have a different life. They suffer as children through his cruelty, and when they have grown they have nothing but him and this life. They did not have a chance to choose as I have."

"So you'll give her that chance now?" Tim asked.

Inez nodded. "Her and as many others who have been forced to this. I have gotten four girls out since Christmas. Two were Calderón's. If he knew, I would be dead. But it would be worth it."

Tim picked up his pack of cigarettes and got off the bar stool.

"You're good with information," he said.

"I know."

"Keep using it." He left the bar and found his way back to the apartment.

14

By the time Tim returned to the apartment, Lupe had made a small dinner. The hot plate in the apartment was nothing special to cook on, and Inez didn't have a lot of food, but Lupe made do.

They sat down on overturned crates to eat.

"We're not waiting on Inez?" he asked.

"She will stay in the cantinas until she works," she said. "The zona does not fill up until nine o'clock, but many of the other cantinas do not get busy until later. The cantinas here allow the women inside. The brothels are always busy after ten o'clock. When the women are off work, they often go to the clubs to drink or dance, sometimes with their boyfriends or husbands."

"I've never seen shit like this before," he admitted. "How the hell can you live in this shit hole?"

"I do not," she said. "I only exist here. And I fear, not for much longer. What is our plan?"

Tim took a swallow of a beer Lupe pulled from a small icebox for him.

"Mendoza's got the word out I want to trade. It'll back Calderón off a little if he thinks I'm gonna bring you to him," Tim said. "I've thought more about it, and we don't have enough people to risk meeting with him. Instead we'll get the microfiche and get it in someone else's hands."

"Who?" Lupe asked. "I do not think the Federales will care. Calderón has bribed them."

"I'm not talking about the cops," Tim said. "The day I work with a cop is the day they bury me in the ground. Mendoza is looking into another criminal group or something."

"So you trade me from one criminal to the next?" Lupe asked.

"No, we trade for your safety. They get the information in exchange for protecting you," Tim said. "We set that up, then we schedule a time to meet Calderón, only they show up and take him down—it won't take much to

153

topple this El Camarilla with the info on that microfiche. Calderón will be a bad dream."

"He already is." She shuddered at the memory of her dreams. As she thought that, she realized she hadn't dreamed the night before with Tim.

"Inez said she'd get word to Manuel you're here," Tim said. "Are you sure you can trust him?"

"Of course," Lupe said. "He risked his life to get me out. The Castillos are owed some thanks for that as well."

"I want those weapons," Tim said. "Don't think I've forgotten about that."

"Perhaps if you give the information to them, they will help you get the weapons across the border," Lupe said with a smile.

"I don't think the Castillos run a big enough outfit to take down a gang of criminals," Tim said. "And those bastards owe me the weapons over the border anyway. That was the deal. I'm not trading anything to get it, either."

"You are very stubborn," she said.

Lupe washed up the dishes while Tim stretched out on a mattress on the floor, looking out the window. They could hear the music drift in from the cantinas and smell the food cooked in some of the stalls.

"What are you gonna do when you get out of this?" Tim asked.

Lupe sat on the mattress near him and shook her head. "I do not know. I have not allowed myself to think that far."

"You should start thinking," Tim said. "Inez thinks you'll stick around here. Seems to think it's the only thing any of you know how to do."

Lupe leaned her head against the wall. Inez was right.

She couldn't cook much, and she didn't have any sewing skills. She supposed she could work in a factory if they would hire her. But she wasn't even eighteen yet. If she got away from the El Camarilla, she was on her own.

Despite the terror they had put her through, there was one constant—they took care of her. She had a place to sleep and a little food. The prospect of having to find this for herself frightened her.

"Manuel may have an idea," she said. "He will come tomorrow. He would not let me stay here, this much I know."

"Good."

Lupe lay near Tim and cuddled up as much as he would let her. He continued to smoke his cigarette, and when he was done, he pulled her closer to him.

"Would it bother you doing it here?" he asked.

"Doing what?" she asked.

"Having sex here," he said.

She looked at him and thought about it. The smells, the noise . . . it all reminded her of the past, how the men would walk up the stairs with her, the El Camarilla guards watching. It reminded her of men she would never want touching her doing just that.

She closed her eyes and remembered how Tim's hands felt as they touched her.

"No," she said. "I do not think it will. And if it does, I must stop it."

Tim kissed her. "I'm going to have to teach you how to say don't. You sound like a school teacher."

Lupe laughed. "Your language is strange."

Tim kissed her again and looked her in the eye.

"Get out of here, Lupe," he said. "Doesn't matter where to. Just get out of here and don't come back."

Friday, November 4, 1966

Tim woke up at noon the next day to find Inez moving about the small apartment. He tried not to think about what she'd been doing and where she'd been doing it, but was curious enough to ask anyway.

"I work at the brothel downstairs," she said. "They have their own rooms there."

Lupe woke up after him, and they showered in a small bathroom down the hall and dressed.

"Manuel sent word," Inez told them. "He will come this afternoon."

Tim noticed Lupe break out into a smile. She trusted this guy, but he would have to have his eyes open the entire time. A bounty on someone's head was a good reason to turn them in for a reward. Old Manuel may like the lure of El Camarilla cash more than he liked Lupe.

Inez had a small black and white television with huge antennas sticking out of it, and it received two channels, none of which were in English. Tim thought he'd go crazy.

Inez left and came back with a pack of Mexican playing cards.

"I need to know where you hid the microfiche," Tim told Lupe. He shuffled the deck of cards, the pictures different than he was used to.

"No," Lupe said, shaking her head.

"What the hell do you mean 'no?'" Tim asked, incredulous. "That thing is the whole reason we're here, I'm gonna need it if you want to live."

"It is safe," Lupe said. "We will get it when we need it."

"No," Tim said shaking his head. "We get it now."

"And give the El Camarilla a chance to kill us?" Lupe asked. "They will follow us from here, and they will kill us and take it."

"You saw yourself I can shake a tail," he said.

Lupe looked at him in confusion.

"The guys following us," he said impatiently. "I outran them, didn't I?"

"You may not be so lucky next time," Lupe said.

"Lupe, we need the microfiche," he said. "I don't care whether or not you think I'll be lucky. Tell me where it is, I'll get it and bring it back. You won't even have to go."

"No," she said, standing up, her eyes blazing. "You will be killed. I will not tell you where it is."

"Fuck!" He stood and tossed the cards around the room. "This isn't some kind of game, Lupe. You don't get to decide what happens here, that's why you brought me."

"Brought you?" she asked. "You dragged me here against my will."

"Bullshit," he said. "You want this over as much as anyone."

"Yes, but I do not want you dead to do it," she said. "If you have it, you will be in danger."

"I can handle it."

"I cannot," she said. "If they were to hurt you because I was stupid enough to give it to you, I would never forgive myself. No. I will not tell you."

Tim quelled the urge to slam a fist against the wall. The rage washed over him, and he tried to contain it.

"Stupid bitch," he spat.

He walked out of the apartment, slamming the door behind him, his boots heavy on the floor.

"That was stupid," Inez said. "You should have told him."

"No. He can call me all the names he likes. He would be killed. I know they would follow him and kill him after he retrieved it," she said. "They cannot hurt him. Manuel will know what to do. If we must get the microfiche, we will get it together. One person can look out while the other retrieves it. At least there is a chance we will get out alive. Oh, I wish I had burned the thing."

"Then you would have been killed already," Inez said.

Lupe sat on one of the crates and cradled her head in her hands.

"This is a nightmare," she said.

Inez sat across from her.

"Do you love this man?" she asked.

"Tim?"

Inez nodded.

"No," Lupe said. "But I do care for him. He has turned out to be a true friend, and I would not have thought that from our first meeting."

Inez looked at her.

"Are you sure, Lupe?" she asked. "The way you look at him . . . "

Lupe looked at the floor, her face hot.

"He is not mine to have," she said. "He will deny this, but I know. For now he is with me. It is not like it was here. Everything is different."

Inez smiled. "I know. I can see in your face. So will Calderón's men, so you must hide this from them. He can take care of himself."

"I cannot let him go after the microfiche alone," she said. "No matter if he can take care of himself. We must go together or I will not forgive myself if something happens."

"Lupe," Inez said softly. She ran her hands over Lupe's hair. "I know you will not forgive yourself even if you are there and something happens. You cannot fix this alone."

"Neither can he," Lupe said, her eyes brimming with tears.

Tim spotted her a mile away.

She weaved through the crowd with purpose, having spotted him at the table. She hadn't gone to much trouble to disguise herself. She wore a dress which was a little big on her—probably Inez's—and had wrapped her hair in a scarf. Men looked as she passed.

"You want Calderón to show up here?" he asked. "That's not much of a disguise."

"I came to find you," she said. "You left so angry . . . "

"Because you're making a mistake." He stubbed his cigarette out in the ashtray and took a sip of his beer.

"Maybe so," she said. "But I cannot let you go after the microfiche alone."

She looked around, and he spotted one of the guards Inez had pointed out to him the day before. Lupe also noticed and scooted her chair closer to him, placing a hand on his thigh in an effort to look like a working girl chatting up a client.

"We need it, Lupe," he said.

"I know," she told him. "And we will get it. But we will go together."

"A lot of help you'd be if Calderón or his men show up," Tim said. "You couldn't hit the broadside of a barn when I tried to teach you to shoot. Literally."

"Tim, please," she said in desperation. "I promise you we will go together for it."

He didn't have any choice. He had no idea where she had hidden it, and without it, they wouldn't be able to bargain with any other criminal bosses. He was at her mercy, and he hated it.

"Fine," he shot. "But you've gotta listen to what I say. Anything I say, you have to do it. I'm not going to have you trailing along behind me fucking everything up. I can take care of things, as long as you let me."

"These are dangerous men," Lupe said, leaning in closer and speaking in a whisper. "If you were to die because I—"

"No one's dying."

"But if you were to die," she said, her voice insistent. "If you were, I would feel responsible. It would be . . . I do not want anything to happen to you."

She covered his hand with hers. He took a breath.

"Come on," he said. "Back upstairs. Make it look like you picked me up. You shouldn't have come down here anyway."

"Stupid bitch, sí?"

He looked away from her. "I didn't mean that."

"You did," she said. "You have a bad temper. But I have been called worse."

"Still," he said. "Shouldn't have said it."

He stood and held his hand out, and she took it without question, leading him through the walkways and stalls, waiting until no guards were around before they went back upstairs.

The time crawled until the afternoon.

She and Tim played poker, and she was startled to find out how good he was.

"You should have taught Jesse," she said. "He did not even know the basics."

"Yeah," Tim said. "I never got around to it. He'd blow all his dough on a game anyway."

"You are so hard on him."

"I have to be," Tim said. "He doesn't use his head half the time. He needs to learn. If I go away, he has to step up and be Bill's right hand, and he's not even close to that right now."

"Go away?" Lupe asked.

"I'll be locked up sooner or later for something. No use in pretending that won't happen with the things I do."

Staccato raps at the door made them pause. Tim got up without a sound and padded toward the door, looking out a crude peephole. He waved at Lupe to come over.

She walked over, trying not to make any noise, and peered out. She gasped and flung the door open before Tim could stop her.

"Lupe," Manuel said with relief as the door opened.

Lupe was shocked at his appearance. His face was beaten; there were stitches in his lip and above his eye, the yellow and brown bruising standing out even against his tanned skin. One arm was in a sling, and she felt sick when she saw it.

"Don't cry," Manuel said, when she couldn't help but let the tears fall. "It would take much more than this to hurt me."

She ushered him into the room and shut the door. She noticed Tim put the chain lock across.

She made quick introductions between Tim and Manuel.

"What happened?" she asked, switching to English so Tim could understand.

"Some of Calderón's men showed up the day after we shipped you out," he said. He sat on one of the crates, wincing as he did. She wondered if they broke his ribs. "They accused me of helping you, and I denied it. They didn't believe me and beat me until the Castillo brothers showed up."

"The Castillo brothers," Tim said. "I only met one brother, Arturo, and only once. Tell me about them. Are they any kind of challenge for the El Camarilla?"

"Perhaps," Manny said. "There are three brothers— Arturo, Ruben and Pedro. They are involved in weapons trade now, but they have a small drug operation. The El Camarilla controls much of the region in that respect. They have been butting heads more frequently because of that."

"Where do you fit in?" Tim asked, offering the man a smoke. Manuel lit his cigarette by striking a match on the wall.

"I have contacts in America. They need workers, cheap labour. So I find people to send to them. The Castillos provide the transportation to get them across the border. They have some guards paid off if I can't get enough paperwork in time."

"And what do you provide the Castillos?" Tim asked.

"Whatever they need," Manuel said. "Workers, connections in America and throughout México, and papers if they need them. I have the benefit of years on them."

Lupe never asked Manuel his age, but he had to be close to forty. He had come to her so many times in the past and each time she had taken him upstairs, he paid her the money and asked her questions. She was so confused why this man would pay and do nothing to her, but she didn't want it to stop. She looked forward to his visits.

One night, he came to her beaten much like he was now. She asked what was wrong, and he confessed. He was drunk then, and she wouldn't know anything about him if not for that. He told her about the men who saw him with the man he loved. They beat them both, and Manuel escaped. His friend was not so lucky. Manuel never spoke of him again.

She knew he felt some safety in la zona roja as a few cantinas catered to men like him. Lupe never understood it, but what she did understand was it meant Manuel would never hurt her like the others. She kept his secret, and he kept coming to her to keep up appearances. She looked at him and could only see a man who had to hide his love for someone else. It caused him pain, and she could find no reason to condemn him.

"What do you plan to do?" Manuel asked. "Calderón is thinking you have something of his. If you don't contact him soon, he will send men for you. And they will kill you."

"Sounds like word travels fast," Tim said.

"Manuel, he knows," Lupe said. "Tim, Manuel knows about the microfiche. I told him before I left."

"He knows where it is?" Tim asked, his voice irritated.

"No," Manuel said, with a slight smile. "That is the one thing she would not tell me. It was too—"

"Dangerous," they both said at the same time.

Lupe made a face, sure they were making fun of her.

"I may be able to help you in this," Manuel said. "Lupe, your cousin Ramón Delgado came to me two days ago."

"He did?" she asked, her hopes soaring.

"He was . . . distraught," Manuel said. "Word of the El Camarilla's contract on your life had reached him. He was sure I had helped you escape, but I told him nothing. He wanted me to get a message to you that he would help you."

Lupe swallowed a lump in her throat. Ramón. He was like a brother to her when they were children. When he turned away from her before it was like a knife in her heart, and to know he was worried for her made the pain lessen.

"He knows about the microfiche," Manuel said. "I do not know how, although there are many rumours about why Calderón is after you. That is one of many. Ramón said there were rumours of a microfiche for years, and the Federales and policía have been eager to get their hands on it for some time. He said he can get the microfiche to the proper authorities and have Calderón and his men arrested. He is eager for you to be free of this place."

"This guy's a cop?" Tim asked.

"Policía," Lupe confirmed. "Who would he get this information to? He does not have the power to change anything himself."

"The commissioner and the state police, I suppose," Manuel said. "Perhaps the Federales if there is evidence of wide-scale criminal activity."

"I don't like it," Tim said.

"You do not like anything today," Lupe commented. "Where is he? Does Ramón know I am here?"

Manuel shrugged. "I do not believe he knows yet, although there are rumours Calderón knows you are in the city. I'm sure your cousin would want to meet, he said as much to me. He wants to help. I believe he feels guilty for turning you away. Perhaps he thought you were here of your own volition."

"He knows why I am here," Lupe said, her voice trailing off. "It still shames him."

"I don't like it," Tim said. "The guy's a cop. He could scoop Lupe up and lock her away for a dozen different things."

"He would not," Lupe said. "He could have arrested me when he saw me before, but he did not. For fear of Calderón, I think. I believe what Manuel says. Tim, you do not know Ramón. He is as close to me as a brother."

"It's a cop, Lupe," Tim said.

"You can meet with him," Manuel said. "Talk with him. See what the impression of him is before you make your decision. It may be easier to operate with a member of the municipal force on your side. Things are not the same here as they are in America."

"You can say that again," Tim murmured.

"Please, Tim," Lupe said. "He is my cousin. My family. If you do not wish him to help, he will not. But I would like to speak to him, to know he does not hate me."

Tim looked at her, appraising her words. He nodded tersely.

"Fine," he said. "We meet this Ramón. We talk. If I don't like him, he's out of this. I don't care whether he's a cop or not."

Lupe launched herself at Tim, and he caught her and stumbled back a step.

"Jesus Christ, don't get so excited," Tim said. "I said we'd talk, that's all."

"It is all I need," Lupe said. She was excited now. Even if she was to die tomorrow, at least she would die knowing someone in her family wanted to help her.

15

That night Lupe lay beside Tim on the thin mattress, listening to the *ranchera* music being played at one of the cantinas. Tim shifted beside her again.

"You are restless," she said.

"I don't trust this guy."

"Manuel?" she asked.

"No, not him, your cousin," Tim said.

"You have not even met him, how can you distrust him?" she asked reproachfully.

"He's a cop, that's why," Tim said. "You may not have a lot of experience with the law, but I do. He's gonna arrest you, throw me in jail for getting across the border illegally and who the hell knows what else."

"He could have arrested me before I left México," she said. "He would not do that to us."

"You can't promise that, Lupe," he said. "This is a guy who told you that you were dead to him a few months ago. What changed between now and then?"

"Manuel would not lie to me," Lupe said. "If he believes Ramón feels bad, then I believe him. Perhaps you do not."

"He was alright," Tim admitted. "Sharp, knew what he was talking about. Seems to care about you enough."

"He is my closest friend," she said.

She was quiet for a moment, then felt around until she found his hand. She placed her own over it.

"I would like to think he is not my only one," she said.

He turned toward her, and she leaned over to kiss him.

"You're eager," he murmured. "Can't seem to slow you down."

"I want to remember this," she said, running her hands up his torso. "I want to remember how this feels. The good. I know you will be gone when this is over, and I want to remember."

He pulled her on top of him, and she bent her head to his and kissed him. The thrill of attraction and an eagerness to be with him coursed through her. The feeling of wonder that something that had hurt her for years could make her feel so good now hadn't worn off. It gave her hope there was a way out and hope that things would be different moving forward.

They slept together to the sound of the music, and Lupe replaced the multitude of memories of the zona roja with memories of Tim. How his hair felt, how she thrilled to his touch, how there was no pain, only pleasure. She tucked these new memories away, hoping it was not the last time she would experience them.

Saturday, November 5, 1966

They slept late again the next morning, and Tim lay in bed thinking. The desert air from the open window chilled him, but it also kept him awake and alert. He needed to go over every detail in his mind.

"You are quiet this morning," Lupe murmured into his ear.

"I'm quiet every morning. How far away is the place you've hidden this microfiche?" he asked.

She frowned.

"I'm not going to run off and go looking," he said, realizing the reason for her hesitation. "I want to know how long it'll take to get there, things like that."

"It will be about thirty minutes by car, I think," she said. "It is in the country, outside of Mexicali."

Tim nodded and factored the time into his plan.

They would meet with Ramón, retrieve the microfiche and then the plan deviated. If he agreed to work with Ramón—and he was pretty damn sure he wouldn't—they would meet somewhere neutral to exchange it. Tim couldn't see any benefit in that. Even if Ramón could keep his word to have Calderón locked up, it could be months before that could happen the way the police moved about things.

The other plan would be to contact Mendoza afterwards and see where he would suggest selling the microfiche. He knew Calderón would want to meet, but that was a meeting they wouldn't come out of alive. Their best bet was to sell the information to a competitor, or someone who wanted to compete. They would need to have the ability to protect Lupe.

If that couldn't be done . . . Tim turned over, facing the wall. If it couldn't be done, Calderón's men would have them killed. He didn't aim to be on the run. Calderón would have to be taken out.

Tim ran through the names and faces of guys he met in the joint, wondering if any of them would have the connections to help. It all hinged on what Mendoza found. He needed to find someone who could take on the information and use it to shut down the El Camarilla.

He closed his eyes. His head ached. The plan had so many damn holes in it, and it wasn't like this was gang turf and shit like that. Even the Outfit had rules, and knowing them helped when you went up against them. This was his life and Lupe's life. Calderón wouldn't let them walk away alive.

So they were going to have to kill him first.

They got word after lunch that Ramón would meet them in a cantina down the road, one for locals, at least according to Inez.

When they got there, Tim wasn't happy to find out it was a cantina for queers.

"It is safer this way," Lupe told him. "They will allow me in and will not bother us, and the guards will stay away, as they always do. Calderón's men do not come to these places. I believe they are afraid."

As smart as he thought the idea was, Tim was nervous walking in, even though he'd never admit it. A few of the local men looked over, surprised to see a foreigner, but Lupe took his hand and led him to a table, and the men went back to their drinks and games, paying no attention to them.

Lupe chose a table in the back corner. Tim made note of the exits and made sure he had a sight line on the door. In Rett's he was comfortable without a view of the door, but he knew Rett's. This place was an unknown, and he needed to give himself every advantage.

He had the Colt in the ankle holster, and the Browning in a shoulder holster Mendoza had given him. At any minute a bunch of Mexican cops could flood the place, and he didn't aim to spend the next few years in a Mexican prison, that was for damn sure.

Lupe bounced her leg and fidgeted with her hands.

"Would you relax?" Tim asked. "You're so on edge you look like you're ready to spring a leak. Calm down."

"I am scared," she said. "It will change everything if he will forgive me. It may mean my family would as well. Ramón is the only male cousin I have. He suffers much shame himself because of what I have done. It is his responsibility to look out for me, like a brother would. He was not in our village the day I was taken. He had been a policía member for a few months, and had come back to see Gabriela. She lived in the next village, they were . . .

how you say, sweethearts? From school? They were to marry. When he got back, I was gone. I cannot imagine . . . "

Neither could Tim. He had no idea how this Ramón could've sat on his ass and not gone after Lupe when a guy like Calderón came along. That's why he didn't trust the cops. Even when it was their own damn family, they didn't do shit.

Lupe glanced at the door, and her posture stiffened.

The man striding toward them had to be in his late twenties, with straight dark hair cut close, and a shifting gaze that swept the room. He didn't wear a uniform, but Tim could see the badge on his belt and the gun strapped to him. He looked like a cop, even out of uniform.

Lupe was frozen next to him. She stood, and Tim followed suit. The man stopped a few feet away.

"Lupita," he said.

"Ramón," she said, her eyes brimming over with tears.

He said something in Spanish—Tim thought it was 'I'm sorry'—and Lupe flung herself into his arms, crying in earnest. Ramón stroked her hair and murmured something to her. She pulled herself together a minute later, stepping away from him and wiping her eyes.

"Ramón, this is Tim," she said, making the introductions.

They shook hands, both sizing the other up. Tim moved behind the table again and sat, and Ramón took a seat across from Tim. Lupe sat between them.

"When I heard the El Camarilla had a contract on your life, it was a horrific discovery," Ramón said.

"What is the contract?" Tim asked, lighting a cigarette. He already knew the terms thanks to Mendoza, but wanted to see if Ramón had heard the same.

"Capture her alive," Ramón said, tapping his fingers on the table. He wore a thin gold wedding band. "Although, with Calderón, that means dead is fine as well. A large reward. It has generated much interest."

"I suppose I should be honoured," Lupe said wryly.

"Is it true?" Ramón asked. "Is there a microfiche?"

Lupe glanced at Tim, and he nodded, hoping Ramón hadn't picked up on it.

"Yes," she said. "There is one."

"What does it contain?"

"I don't know if you noticed, but it's not like she's carrying a microfiche reader around with her," Tim said, looking at Ramón.

Lupe's brow creased as she listened to him.

"There are many people the El Camarilla deals with, here in México and in the United States," Ramón said. "We have some information on the El Camarilla, but nothing to put Calderón away. If there is account information, banks, identification . . . anything that can get us solid evidence, it could change everything."

"I do not know what is on it, Ramón," Lupe said. "Tim is right. I could not read it. All I know is Calderón kept it will him at all times."

"Until you," Ramón said.

Lupe nodded.

"We are so close," Ramón sighed. "So close to putting him and his men behind bars forever. The commissioner is eager to get his hands on this information."

"Can they protect me?" Lupe asked. "If I give this microfiche to you, can they protect me? I do not want to run forever, and Calderón will kill me if he can."

Ramón nodded. "The commissioner will give protection to you until Calderón is in jail."

"Not good enough," Tim said. "I'm not stupid. I know your police force is crooked as hell, and Calderón has a long reach. He had hitmen after us in Vegas. He'll be able to give orders from prison."

"No," Ramón said. "The commissioner is already making arrangements to have him held in isolation because of the danger he poses to those who have given us information on him already."

Tim took a long drag on his cigarette and exhaled the smoke in a long breath, blowing a few rings.

"You don't give a lot of guarantees," Tim said.

"You know as well as I do, there are no guarantees when a criminal like Calderón is involved," Ramón said. "I was not always policía. I got into my fair share of trouble. There are never guarantees."

Tim had a feeling Ramón's idea of fair share was pretty different from his own. He looked at Lupe, who was glowing sitting next to Ramón.

"I can promise you she will be safe," Ramón said, his voice strained. "Safer than with you, from the look of your face."

Tim took a drink of his beer and a drag of his smoke, thinking things over.

"How can I know you won't turn around and throw me in jail after you get what you want. You may have loyalty to Lupe, but you don't have any to me," Tim said.

And I don't have any to you, Tim thought.

"He will keep his word," Lupe said.

Ramón nodded. "It is the only way. I want Calderón gone as much as you. I want him away from my family and away from here. I have been trying to make this happen for many years, and you will be helping me to do it. I would owe you."

Tim looked at Lupe and indicated for her to follow him. He got up from the table and walked over to the bar.

"I don't like it," Tim said.

"You have not heard from Mendoza," Lupe pointed out. "He may not know who to contact for the microfiche. But we have Ramón here, and he can help us now."

"I don't trust him, Lupe," he said.

She looked crestfallen, but he didn't have time to feel sorry for her.

"He's come out of nowhere trying to make things right," he said. "I know from experience it's usually to cover your own ass."

"Do you not trust me?" she asked.

Tim looked at the ceiling. "It doesn't have to do with trusting you."

"Please, Tim," she said. "If they can arrest Calderón, I can be free."

"Prison isn't as locked away as you might think, Lupe," Tim said, his tone serious. "I know, I've been there. Your reach can be just as long from behind bars."

The fear in her eyes was plain.

"I trust him, Tim," Lupe said. "Please. Let us give the microfiche to him."

He thought for a moment.

"Fine," he said. "But we do this my way."

She hadn't liked the sound of "my way" when he said it, and she didn't like hearing his plan.

"Lupe and I will get the microfiche, and we'll call you and set up a time and place to meet," Tim said.

"And how do I know you won't retrieve it and vanish into the night?" Ramón asked. "For all I know, you are using Lupe as leverage. Perhaps you want to trade the microfiche and Lupe for a position in Calderón's gang. I have heard rumours you run a gang of your own."

Lupe looked at Ramón, surprised at his information.

"You'll have to take my word," Tim said.

"No," Ramón said. "I can see you don't trust me, but that is a two way street. I want to know that you are not going to give that microfiche up to Calderón."

"He would not do that, Ramón," Lupe said. "I trust him."

"And he might be lying to you," Ramón said to her in Spanish.

She looked at Tim, and saw he understood Ramón's Spanish. She knew Tim wasn't lying to her, but it was impossible to put how she knew it into words. There was an honour about him, despite his gun running and other activities.

"Well, I guess if you don't trust me, we've got a problem," Tim said.

They were quiet for a moment.

"We will all go," Ramón said. "We will get the microfiche together, then travel back to the station and give it to the commissioner together. You will see I can make sure Lupe is protected."

She studied Tim, trying to figure out what he would do. It was so hard to judge him by his looks—he gave away nothing in his face. She wished he was a little more like Jesse, unable to hide what he thought. Tim's blank expression hid everything he thought and felt, and she was lost trying to determine if he'd agree to Ramón's plan.

"Alright," Tim agreed after a long pause. "We all go. We'll meet outside of this zona at nine tonight and go from there. Lupe and I take my car and you follow in your own."

Ramón shook his head. "We go together. We travel together in the same car. That way I know you will not try and lose me on the road."

Tim stared for a moment before nodding his assent. They shook hands across the table, and Lupe smiled in relief.

Lupe didn't understand why Tim made her change into the blue jeans. It was hot out, and she would much rather wear a dress.

The clock showed eight thirty, and she was nervous as it crept closer to nine.

"Here," Tim handed her his ankle holster, the Colt .38 Special inside. "Put this on."

"What? Why?" she asked, taking the leather holster. The gun was much heavier than she expected from its size.

"Just in case," he said. "We could be followed, who knows. I want to make sure we have our asses covered."

"But I have never fired this one, you said it was too hard. I could not even shoot the other!"

"I can't hide the Browning on you, but I can hide this one," he said.

She looked at him for a moment, then sighed and struggled to put it on. She sat on the mattress, and Tim approached and took the gun out of the holster to tighten the holster around her leg. He put the gun back in when he was done.

"Stand up," he said.

She stood, and he struggled to cover the gun with the cuff of the jeans.

"You have any other jeans to wear?" he asked.

She gave him a look. "Your Ruby did not give me a suitcase full of clothes."

"Yeah, yeah. Hold on a minute."

He flicked out a switchblade and slit the seams on each side of the jean cuff, allowing it to flare out a little and hide the gun. He did the same to the other cuff so they matched, and when he was finished it was impossible to tell she wore the gun.

"Take some time to practice drawing it from the holster," he said.

"Tim, I will not need this, you are being paranoid."

"You don't know, Lupe," he said. "I always tell my boys they have to be prepared for any situation. Practice. It'll be hard to get the gun out fast, especially if something goes wrong. You'll be scared and nervous, so it's best to get used to the motion, so you can do it without thinking. And practice loading it too. It's a revolver, it's not like the Browning."

She sighed, but took the gun from the holster and figured out how to release the cylinder. She took the bullets out and put them back in again. She snapped the cylinder shut and put the gun back in the holster and practiced taking it out. It kept getting caught on the cuff of her jeans.

Tim gave her a look.

"Alright, it is not as easy as I thought," she said. "But we will not need this."

"Practice," he said.

As the clock approached nine, she watched him load the Browning's magazine. He popped it into the gun and tucked it into a shoulder holster on his left side.

He must have noticed her confused expression.

"Got it from Mendoza," he said. "I didn't want to risk the gun falling out or being taken off me."

He put his leather jacket over top and it was no longer visible.

"The jacket will stand out," she said.

"It'll be cool at night," he said. "Especially if we're going into the country. Are you going to tell me now where you hide this microfiche?"

"No," she said. "It is in the desert at a barn. That is all I will tell you. I will give you instructions to get there when we are on the road."

Tim stared for a moment, then shook his head.

"Fine," he huffed. He handed her a strange round object with bullets for the .38 Special.

"What is this?" she asked.

"A speed loader," he said. "You can load all six chambers in the time it takes to load one," he said. "Put it on the holster."

"You are being ridiculous," she fumed. "Nothing will happen. And why do I have to carry extra bullets? You have none."

"I have thirteen rounds in here, and an extra magazine in the car. You can't hit a target if your life depended on it, you need all the bullets you can get."

"We will not need them." She tucked the speed loader in the holster. "You are treating Ramón as if he is a criminal, and he has done nothing to you."

"I don't trust anyone, Lupe," he said. "Only myself. I may trust in a few other people a little, but the only one I can rely on is me. I don't care if you don't like it. You're carrying the damn gun and the damn bullets, and if things go south, you'll use it, got that?"

"You cannot make me," she said, crossing her arms.

"Yeah? What if we get followed, and Calderón's men pull me out of the car to put a bullet in my head? Are you saying you wouldn't fire that gun?"

She looked at the floor, then up at him. "You know I would."

"Good," he said. "Because if I'm gonna put my ass out on the line for you, you sure as hell better be doing it for me. Now come on, let's go. It's almost nine o'clock."

16

Tim had stolen a cowboy hat in the cantina, and Inez tucked Lupe's hair under a scarf and lined her eyes with heavy makeup in an effort to disguise her. He and Lupe left Inez's room separately and met in a bar downstairs, and he wandered outside with her as if he picked her up.

They found Ramón outside the zona roja in his full police uniform, and Tim was pissed.

"Real great job looking inconspicuous," Tim said.

"It will help us," Ramón said. "If someone spots us, I can use my uniform and job as a cover."

Tim grudgingly accepted his explanation. They walked the few blocks to Mendoza's car, and Tim had a prickly feeling between his shoulder blades again. He didn't like this one bit.

He opened the door to the backseat and Lupe got in, then Ramón climbed in the passenger seat.

Tim got in the car and started up the engine. He took a breath and turned to Lupe.

"Where to?"

"We must go south. We will find the road to San Felipe, it will take us there," Lupe said. "We are going toward Cerro Prieto. A small town close by there called Agua Seca."

"Dry water?" Tim asked. Lupe shrugged, a tiny smile on her face. "How far?"

"By car, it is about thirty minutes," she said. "Probably less, the way you drive."

"Where is this casa you talk about?" he asked. He wanted to know how close they were to Calderón's lair.

"It is further south, where the river meets the mountains," she said. "There is no town there, only the compound hidden in the hills. The people in the closest village call the place La Casa."

171

"How far is it from where we're going to get the microfiche?" he asked.

"About half an hour," she said. "Where I hid it was half way to Mexicali. I became scared, thinking they were following me. I thought it better to be caught without it, because he might keep me alive until he got it back."

"So it's along the same highway?"

"Yes," Lupe said. "Where I hid the microfiche is away from the highway, as is the Casa. Both are quiet places in the desert."

Well, that made it a little better. He didn't like the idea that it was right on the way between the two places. He wished Lupe could have thought about hiding it better, maybe gone out of her way.

"How'd you get out of there, anyway?" he asked.

"I have told you," she said.

"Tell me again," he insisted.

"I left the compound on the laundry truck. It went north to a small village where the women do all of the laundry. I slipped out and hid until the night, and walked until I reached Agua Seca. I called Calderón from there and hid the microfiche. I was afraid, and I called Manuel to ask him what to do and he said to come to Mexicali. I hitchhiked my way there, in the night, but it was at great risk. Any of the people who stopped could have taken me straight to Calderón if they had known who I was. I thought Mexicali would be the first place they would look for me. I was right." She took the scarf off and shook her hair out. "I was almost caught right as I came into town and stopped for food."

"How did he know where you were?" Tim asked.

"I do not know," she said. "It is possible he has men in these towns watching things for him."

"We should take a back road," Ramón suggested. "It will make it easier for us to see if he is following, and if he has men on the road they will not see us."

"You'll have to tell me where to go," Tim said.

They turned off the highway at the next exit, and Ramón and Lupe directed him as they drove toward Agua Seca.

"It was an old barn," Lupe said as they drove toward the area she thought it was in. Tim was already frustrated with her. She had been to this barn during the night and couldn't tell him what colour it was, or where it was on the road. All she knew was it ran perpendicular to the highway.

"There were no wooden fences," she said. "And it was abandoned. There used to be a house nearby, but I could see it was in shambles, it had been destroyed."

"That narrows it down," Tim said. Everything around them looked like it was in shambles.

"Well, I am sorry," she told him. "But I was too concerned with not being killed to look at where I was. There were no road signs to tell me."

Tim headed up and down each dirt road he came across, and soon she recognized some of the buildings they passed.

"Yes, the cotton field," she said. "I remember this. It was close to here."

Tim slowed as they approached a building.

"That is it," she said.

The barn was dark and loomed at them from the road. A barb wire fence half-heartedly surrounded what used to be paddocks. Scrub brush grew into the fields, and it was as abandoned as she had said.

Tim glanced into the rearview mirror again. No headlights followed them, but he was still eager to get the microfiche and get out.

Tim pulled up to the barn and cut the engine of the car. The barn and area reminded him a little of Rett's where he used to stash the trailer.

They all got out of the car and listened. It was quiet but for the howl of a distant coyote.

"Come on, let's get inside," Tim said. "I don't like being out in the open like this."

He walked toward the doors and found them shut with a rusted bar latch. He lifted it up, and swung one of the doors open with a creak.

"You're sure this is the place?" Ramón asked.

"Yes," she said. "I remember the doors. I had trouble getting them open."

They stepped inside, and the darkness closed in around them. He was reminded of sharing his first kiss with Ruby inside a darkened barn at Rett's.

Tim took out his Zippo and flicked it open. It lit about a foot in front of him, but it was far enough to see an old fashioned lantern hanging on a peg. He lit it and saw there were lanterns on each post in the barn. He lit a few more until there was enough light to see by.

The barn was filled with hay. It spilled over from the loft, and was loose around the floor and piled up inside the stalls. It smelled musty and didn't look like it had been disturbed in a long time. He hoped they were in the right place.

He turned to Lupe. "Do you remember where you hid the microfiche?"

"Yes," Lupe said. "Turn around."

"Turn around?" Tim asked, incredulous. "You've got to be kidding me, Lupe, come on."

"You too, Ramón," she said. "Both of you turn around. I told you I would not tell you where it was."

"Technically, you're showing us," Tim said.

"Turn around or we will stand here all night," Lupe said. A smile danced at the corner of her mouth.

Tim rolled his eyes and turned around, watching as Ramón did the same. He smiled to himself when he was sure Lupe couldn't see him.

Lupe crept over to the corner of the barn where a small door was and took ten steps diagonally from the door, then knelt and dug through the hay. Her fingers hit the old metal box, red with rust. She opened it and picked out the microfiche inside its small envelope.

It was four inches by five inches and fit in the palm of her hand. It was hard to believe something so small might topple the monster that had made her life so miserable.

She slipped the envelope into the pocket of her jeans and crept back toward Tim and her cousin.

"Alright, I am done," she said.

They turned around.

"Let me see it," Tim demanded.

Lupe pulled the envelope out of her jeans and handed it to him. Tim opened it and took out the microfiche, holding it to the light. He popped it back in the envelope, then looked at her and handed it back to her.

She smiled.

"Give it to me," Ramón said. "Now, please."

"Let's wait until we're outta here for that," Tim said.

"No," Ramón said. "You will give it to me now."

She stared in confusion as Ramón drew his service weapon and pointed it at her. His hand shook.

"Ramón!" she exclaimed. "What are you doing?"

Tim stood rooted to the spot next to her.

"You!" Ramón said, gesturing at Tim with his gun. "Take off your weapon and lay it on the ground. I know you have one."

"Ramón, what are you doing?" she asked him in rapid Spanish. "I will give it to you, let's go! There's no need for the gun."

"No," he said in English. "Calderón will be here soon. I must be the one to hand it to him."

"What?" she asked, her voice a strangled sob. Her breath hitched in her throat.

Tim said nothing and took the gun out of the holster and laid it on the hard packed dirt and stood again. Lupe looked at him forlornly, then back at her cousin.

"Ramón, what are you talking about?" she asked, trying to stop the tears. "Ramón! What have you done?"

"Can't you see?" Tim asked coolly. "He's sold you out."

"I had no choice," Ramón said. "The minute I heard it was you who took it, I knew what would happen to us. You never should have run! I told him I would get it back for him."

"In exchange for what?" Lupe asked. "Me?"

Ramón's hand quaked as he held the gun. "You? He doesn't care about getting you back. He will probably kill us all. But he has promised me she will be safe."

"Ramón, what are you talking about?"

"He's too far gone, Lupe," Tim said, his voice low. "Maybe he's too busy seeing dollar signs."

Lupe looked over at Tim, her chest hurting when she inhaled.

"You mind if I have a cigarette?" Tim asked. Lupe couldn't understand why he was so calm.

Ramón nodded and watched as Tim pulled out his pack of Pall Malls and his lighter. He lit his cigarette and tucked the lighter back in his pocket. Lupe stared.

Ramón's hand was shaking even more. "All of those years after Calderón took you, there was nothing to do. He has bribed everyone to look the other way, no one will do anything. I cannot do anything! Do you know the shame when the rest of the men on the force knew of you? Some came to you, did you know that? All the times I came home with that knowledge, Gabriela would always say to have hope for you, to have hope someone would stop him."

"What are you saying?" Lupe asked.

"He tried to bribe me, did you know that?" he asked, his laugh hollow. "Gabriela told me to say no, she told me to be strong. And I was. He laughed, but he didn't retaliate. Not then anyway. Not until you ran. Not until you took the microfiche. Then he took everything from me!"

"Ramón," she said, her voice strained. "We can stop him! We can finally stop him with this."

"No!" She was shocked at the vehemence of his reply. "We can do nothing but hand it over, it is her only chance."

The sick feeling of dread grew in the pit of Lupe's stomach. Lupe paused when she heard the sound of car tires on the dirt, and she shook. She was unable to control herself. She edged closer to Tim, watching how Ramón straightened the arm holding the gun. Tim's gun was a few feet in front of them. He couldn't reach it without Ramón shooting him.

"Stay cool," Tim said, his voice low. "We're gonna get out of this. Be ready to run. Whatever you do, don't wait for me."

"But—"

"Don't wait. Promise me."

She nodded.

Car doors slammed, and men's voices approached the barn doors. Lupe took a deep breath. She recognized Calderón's large frame in the doorway, silhouetted by the moonlight. He was dressed like he always did, like a ranchero, a whip on his belt and heeled cowboy boots heavy on the hard-packed dirt.

"Well," he said, his voice a booming echo in the barn. "Good job, Ramón. And both of them, too."

"I told you," Ramón said. "Just as I promised, the microfiche is here, you can let Gabriela go—"

A gun roared, the flash lighting up the inside of the barn for a split second. Lupe screamed. Ramón collapsed on the floor, shot in the head. She touched her face and came away with blood.

"No!" she screamed, her scream bouncing off the walls and intensifying. "No!"

She tried to run to Ramón's prone body, but Tim grabbed her at the waist and held her back, drawing her toward him. She sobbed, fighting him, but she could feel the energy draining out of her as she stared at Ramón's dead body.

"No, no, no," she repeated, sinking toward the ground. Tim tried to pull her up.

"Stay with me, Lupe," Tim murmured in her ear. "He wants you over there, the closer you get, the closer the microfiche. Keep it together."

Lupe bit her lip so hard she tasted blood.

Tim hauled her to her a standing position, and she stood there shaking. Anger bubbled up in her chest like a red hot poker. He had taken so much from her.

"¡Chinga tu madre! You are a pig," she said to Calderón. "A fat, disgusting pig of a man whose prick is so small he can only do it with little girls."

She heard Tim chuckle beside her, and it steeled her nerves.

"You will regret those words, mija," Calderón said.

"Do not call me that," she said.

"Why not, mija? Have I not been your father? Have I not been everything? I give you a roof over your head, and food to eat, nice clothes to wear . . . "

"Men to come and fuck her when she doesn't want it," Tim finished. "Yeah, you're a real prince, buddy."

"You are Tim," he said, stepping into the light. Lupe realized with dread she remembered every line in his stinking face. "I have heard much about you. Perhaps you are smitten with our little María."

Lupe went rigid as she heard him call her that.

"Give me the microfiche," he said.

"No," Lupe responded, her mind reeling. "You will have to kill me first."

"You leave me no choice."

Calderón raised his gun, but a split second later the hay beside her erupted in flames.

"Run, Lupe!"

The fire from Tim's cigarette spread rapidly, and she turned and ran for the small door at the back of the barn. She struggled to get through the deep hay and could feel the heat from the fire already. She looked over her shoulder, but the smoke was already thick, and she couldn't see Tim. She hesitated a moment, tempted to go back, but she had promised him.

The fire spread through the dry hay fast, crawling up the dry beams. Lupe turned back toward the door and struggled to it, pushing her way through dry, musty hay. She reached the door and pushed it open, praying it wasn't locked. She felt the door give, then it flew open. She got only a few steps before Calderón grabbed her.

Tim hadn't expected the hay to go up so fast, but in seconds there was a raging inferno in the barn.

The fire blocked his view of Calderón, but he saw Lupe run in the opposite direction, away from the fire and away from all of them, the moment he had told her to.

He jumped forward, trying to get his hands on his gun before the fire reached it, but as he grabbed for it, he got a boot in the gut.

He doubled over as someone hit him on the back with something. He rolled out of the way, seeing the gun kicked away from him.

One of Calderón's men, a tall cowboy, loomed over him, a piece of wood in his hand. Tim rolled out of the way again and swept the man's legs out from under him.

Tim got up, then ducked as the other man, a short, stocky moustached man, took a swing. Tim punched the man in the midsection as hard as he could, hearing the whoosh of air as the man lost his breath. He staggered back, and Tim went for the gun again. As he neared it, a shot ripped through the ground next to his hand.

He rolled to the left and found himself pinned against a stall door. The tall cowboy levelled his gun again. Tim reached up for one of the lit lanterns, threw it at the man's feet, and scooted to the side to avoid the flames.

The cowboy leapt back and almost into the fire behind him.

Tim's other attacker jumped on his back, his arms around Tim's neck. He was squeezing his air off, and Tim fought to throw the man as his vision grew darker.

He could hear the tall cowboy yelling in Spanish, wanting to get a decent shot. He tried not to think about Lupe and where she was.

Tim threw the man on his back over his shoulder and into the hard-packed dirt, sending embers and pieces of lit hay into the air. Tim dove for his gun again, but the cowboy was there and kicked it out of the way. Tim rushed him and reached him before the man had a chance to cock the hammer on his own gun. He grabbed the man's wrist as they tumbled onto the ground, trying to smash it against the ground so he'd loosen his grip. He noticed it was a single action revolver and thanked his lucky stars, otherwise he'd be dead.

The fire raged up into the rafters of the barn and an owl screeched above, the sound making an already horrific scene even worse. Tim smashed the short man's hand to the ground again and it broke his grip on the gun. It spun across the ground into the fire.

He kneed Calderón's man in the groin, then stood and stomped him in the stomach. He was about to turn to look for the other one when the metal gun barrel was pressed against the back of his head.

"Turn around," the man said in English. "Slowly."

Tim turned, beginning to cough as the smoke built in the barn. He turned, seeing the tall cowboy held Tim's own gun to his head.

A moment later gunfire erupted from the gun that had been kicked into the fire. He got down and kicked out at the cowboy's knee, watching the man go down in sudden pain. He jumped on him, trying to wrestle the gun from his grasp.

The man was strong, and the gun was pointed at Tim's midsection and not moving. He grunted with effort as he tried to turn the barrel around, right as the man tried to find the trigger. Tim dug into the dirt with the toe of his boot and gave one final push.

The gun jumped in his hand as it went off.

Warmth spread against his stomach, and for a moment, he thought he'd been shot.

He moved off the man and saw the blood flowing from Calderón's henchman and not him. The Browning was in his hand, blood on it.

Something came down hard on his left shoulder as he went to turn around, and he collapsed to his knees. He twisted around and fired two shots, both wild, then attempted to roll out of the way, his shoulder burning with pain. The short man had a shovel raised high, the sharp edge aiming to come down on his skull.

Tim rolled to his back and fired.

The man didn't move at first, and Tim fired two more times, his eyes tearing and throat burning from the smoke. The man's gaze locked with his own as he fell to his knees, the shovel falling to his side. The man fell next to him, dead as he hit the ground.

Tim got up, choking and coughing at the heavy smoke. Ramón's body was engulfed in the flames, and the fire licked at the pant leg of the other man he'd shot. He stood for a moment in the inferno, looking at the bodies. He had killed two people.

His eyes stung from the smoke, and he coughed, then stumbled back toward the door Lupe had run for. Calderón was nowhere to be found in the barn, and Tim had sudden visions of him capturing her. Of course he'd go for her—he knew she had the microfiche.

He braced himself against a stall, coughing violently and wanting nothing more than to fall down and rest. His lungs burned, and he struggled to suck in air where there was none. He heard a loud creak and looked up.

The roof of the barn was on fire. One end was engulfed, the smoke billowing toward the end he was in, the flames licking over the beams and easily catching. It was hypnotic, the way the fire and the smoke were moving, like snakes in the grass.

He coughed again, his lungs burning. He tucked the gun in his waist band, feeling the blood smear his skin from the barrel of the weapon. He looked at the red on his shirt, touching the other man's blood. They were dead. He couldn't do anything about that.

He moved toward the door, but a wave of dizziness stopped him.

He looked up at the fire and the smoke, his eyes watering so bad he couldn't see.

He had to get out. He wouldn't give that fucker Calderón the satisfaction of knowing he died in a fire he started himself.

He struggled through hay and tripped as he headed for the door. His head swam, and he wondered if he'd ever want to smoke again after this.

The awful heat of the fire was at his back, and he stumbled toward the door, the deep hay slowing him down.

He reached the door and pushed—it was locked shut.

Lupe never would have locked it behind her.

He panicked for a moment, the flames ripping from stall to stall, the dry hay igniting from the heat alone. He was penned in now, with nowhere else to run.

He covered his mouth with his jacket, trying to find some clean air somewhere, his lungs heavy and sluggish. He clawed at the door, trying to find a latch, a loose board, something. He banged his good shoulder into it over and over, but it didn't move.

He stopped when the jolt of ramming the door started hurting his bad shoulder. He took the gun out and shot three times, splintering the wood.

He kicked at it, feeling dizzy, like he would fall over any moment. Thoughts of his body burning like those men spurred him on. He tried to ignore the smell of burning flesh.

Every cell of his body screamed for air. He kicked at the door once, then twice. On the third kick the wood splintered. He fired three more shots.

A fourth kick made the door come off one hinge. He ran at the door with his shoulder and it burst open, and with it the fire was sucked toward the air. Tim dove through the door, the flames surrounding him.

He rolled as he hit the ground and was relieved to feel the cool night air. He crawled away as far as he could, the flames shooting out of the open door into the air, the creaking of the failing wood getting louder.

He took in giant gulps of air, his throat swollen and raw. He lay on the dirt, dizzy and sick. He needed water. He needed oxygen.

He gasped, coughing and sputtering, his throat feeling as tight as a drinking straw. He struggled to suck the air in. His head cleared a little as he breathed in, and he put all his energy and concentration into breathing. This must be what drowning was like.

A few moments later he struggled, but not so bad. The fire was behind him. Part of the barn entrance collapsed, and Tim wondered if anyone in town would come to investigate.

He lay on the dirt and closed his eyes, wanting nothing more than to sleep.

A scream pierced his consciousness.

Lupe.

He struggled to his feet, feeling weak.

"Lupe!" His yell came out as a strained and strangled voice, not audible over the sounds of the fire. "Lupe!"

He looked around, trying to see where she was, listening for her voice. He heard her crying out a moment later and grasped the gun in his hand tighter. He stumbled through the scrub brush, calling out her name, but his voice was too hoarse to be heard. He checked the gun as he moved. He had one last round, and the extra magazine was in the glove box of the car.

Lupe screamed again, and he tried to run toward the sound, but a moment later the pop of a gun and the flash of a muzzle lit up the desert.

He swallowed soot and ran as fast as he could toward the place it had come from. He approached, seeing a shape on the ground. The fire threw long shadows, and he couldn't see where she was. He pointed the gun toward the figure on the ground.

"Lupe," he said again, his voice sounding unnatural. "Lupe!"

He moved toward the figure, his boots slipping on the ground. Lupe rolled Calderón's body off of hers and crawled away before sitting up. Tim held his gun on Calderón.

"He is dead," Lupe said. "And you were right."

"About what?"

"He would have to be on top of me for me to shoot him."

Tim looked at her. Her jeans were unzipped and her shirt was ripped open. There was blood covering her chest and face.

"It is the last time he will try that," she said, her voice strong. He watched her zip her jeans up and fasten the button, her gaze on Calderón, and the Colt in her hand.

He looked down and noticed the chunk missing from the side of Calderón's head.

He coughed violently, his throat raw and the air thin. The last thing he saw was the desert rushing up to meet him.

17

"Tim!"

Lupe rushed forward, and caught Tim's arm, but it did no good, he was already passed out on the hard pan.

"No, no, no," she said, scrambling toward his head. She bent her ear toward his mouth and let out a relieved breath when she could hear him breathing, albeit with effort.

She looked around. The barn fell, embers swirling in the air. Someone would come soon, and she didn't want to be here when they found the bodies. Lupe spotted the car Mendoza had given them near the barn and looked at Tim.

"Dios," she said.

She picked up the Browning where it had fallen when Tim dropped it, and she tucked it in her waistband. She grabbed the Colt she'd laid down and stared at it for a moment.

Blood covered the barrel, and she shuddered. She looked over her shoulder, Calderón's body still prone on the ground. Some part of her hindbrain thought he might rise up and come after her. But he was dead.

Truly dead.

Her hand quaked for a moment as she contemplated that. He was dead and gone. That wouldn't mean much if one of his men decided to come looking for him.

And the girls. The girls were still at the Casa.

She took a deep breath as her vision swam. She needed to focus.

She looked down at Tim and felt his pockets and found the car keys, then ran to the car. She opened the door and started the engine, and tried to remember what Tim did when he drove. She had never been behind the wheel of a car, and she cursed herself for not paying closer attention.

She put the car in gear and stepped on the gas, lurching forward. She pressed the other pedal—the brake. Getting the feel of it, she pushed the gas again and drove as close to Tim as she dared. She threw the car in park and got out, then opened the back seat door as wide as she could. She hurried out to him.

She shook him. "Tim! You must wake up!"

His head lolled. He mouthed something—her name, maybe.

She muttered a string of curses, then stood and hauled him under the arms as best she could. She got into the backseat, pulling him inside with effort and slumping him across the seat. She shut the door, then got in the car and put the car in reverse. It made a grinding noise, and she panicked and threw it back into drive. Wherever she went, it would be forward.

The roads were deserted, but it wouldn't stay that way for long. Someone would have called the policía, and a fire brigade would come to put out the fire licking the grasses.

She drove along the road, unsure of where to go. Tears blinded her for a moment, and she wiped her eyes with the back of her hand. Smeared blood and soot covered her hand, and she shuddered.

A gasoline station appeared ahead. It was closed, but there was a pay phone at the side of the building. She looked for change and resorted to searching Tim's pockets. His breathing was laboured.

She found a dime and rushed over to the phone, dialling the one number she knew. Manuel answered on the second ring.

"I need a doctor!" she said, near hysterics. "Tim is hurt, there was a fire."

"What has happened?" Manuel asked. "Where is Ramón?"

"A doctor, Manuel! I need a doctor. Ramón is dead. They are all dead. Something terrible has happened. I need a doctor!"

"Lupe . . . Lupe," Manuel said. "You must calm down. I know a doctor. It will be alright. Where are you?"

"South of Agua Seca. There was a fire. He was coughing so much, and he is not awake."

"Alright," he said. "This man, the doctor, he is in Zakamoto, you are not far."

"He is dead," Lupe said.

"Tim?"

"No," Lupe said. "Calderón. He is dead. I killed him."

She stared at her hands. The blood was dried and crusted around her nails—Calderón's blood.

Manuel was quiet for a moment. "I will meet you at the doctor. Do not leave there."

He gave her directions, and Lupe raced back to the car. She drove along the road until she reached the turn off, and took an unpaved road toward the small village. At the church, she turned and followed a road that ended at a small clapboard house.

She banged on the door for a good few minutes until it was opened by a man with a shock of white hair and a grey moustache. She pulled him to the car, unable to speak, and he looked at Tim.

"Help me with him," the doctor said.

The doctor hauled him out of the back seat, and Lupe supported one side. Inside the small house was a makeshift hospital, a single room with a bed and some supplies, and beyond it, a kitchen and a small addition to the house.

They placed Tim in the bed and the doctor shined a light in Tim's eyes and listened to his heart and lungs. Lupe shivered.

"How long since the fire?"

"Not long," Lupe said. "Twenty minutes."

"Good," the doctor said. "You are just in time."

He placed a mask over Tim's face and twisted a tank of oxygen on. Lupe turned away when the doctor reached for the needle.

Lupe sat on the front stairs shivering. The stars were shining in the sky, and the half moon winked through wispy clouds. It was cold, and her sweater was back at la zona roja.

Gabriela. Her cousin had mentioned her at the end. "You can let Gabriela go" were the last words he spoke.

It wasn't possible.

It was. It was Calderón, after all. He would have seen the best way to pressure was with family. He would take everything to get what he wanted, and it seemed he had taken Gabriela.

She swallowed when she spotted three sets of headlights moving toward her. She reached for the Browning and held it in her lap.

One was a car and the others were Jeeps filled with men. The car stopped, and she let out a relieved breath when Manuel got out of the driver's seat.

"Oh, Manuel." She flung herself into his arms, her hand gripping the gun.

"What has happened?" he asked. "Why is Ramón dead? Are you bleeding?"

"And is Calderón dead?"

She looked toward the other voice. The man standing near the closest Jeep had a moustache and longer hair. He smiled, revealing a missing front tooth.

"Arturo Castillo," Manuel said. "And the others are Pedro and Ruben and their men."

Lupe looked at Manuel in confusion.

"Is it true?" one of the other brothers asked.

"Yes. Calderón is dead." She looked at Manuel. "I shot him in the head."

"Good." His reply was quiet and only for her.

"It is a day to celebrate," Arturo said. "If we can work fast."

"Work fast for what?" Lupe asked.

"The Castillos mean to take over his territory," Manuel said.

Lupe paused for a moment. "The girls. We must get the girls."

"What girls?" Arturo asked.

Lupe looked at him. "You are not a stupid man. You have heard and know what Calderón does and who he keeps at the Casa. There are many young girls there. When Calderón does not return and his men go looking and find he is dead, what happens to them?"

She looked behind her at the house, then at Manuel. Tim was safe, and she was not a doctor. He would think rationally about this, and so would she.

"We must go."

Arturo laughed. "Mija, we do not need you. We have men here and more coming."

"I do not care," she said. She raised her arm, pointing the Browning at him. "Those girls are my responsibility. They will listen to me. I will keep them out of your way while you do what you must, but I am going for them. With or without you."

"Lupe . . . " Manuel began. She turned to look at him, and he paused, looking her over. She realized she was covered in blood and soot, and it gave them pause. Manuel turned to the Castillos. "She is right. She has more right than any of us to go."

Arturo shrugged and moved toward his Jeep, yelling at his brothers. More cars were coming up the road. Lupe lowered the gun.

"Go straight to the girls," Manuel said. "Let the Castillos lead the charge."

"I do not care about their charge," Lupe said. "I care about the girls. And if these men are good men, they will leave them to me, and perhaps I will leave them with something too."

Manuel stared for a moment until the realization dawned.

"You have the microfiche."

"I suppose we will see when my girls are safe."

Lupe walked toward the car Mendoza had given them.

"Lupe," Manuel said. He looked at her with a strange expression. "Do you even know how to drive?"

She smiled. "I learned tonight. I have learned many things tonight."

Sunday, November 6, 1966

The Casa was near the Colorado River, hidden up in the desert hills. There was one road in and out, and guards posted everywhere.

The Castillos were parked near the river, a mile down the road, discussing their plans for storming the main house.

She didn't care at all about the main house, filled with Calderón's men and Calderón's cigars and Calderón's bad taste in furniture. What she wanted was in the outbuildings, the casitas dotted around the property.

The men argued their plans. The hour crept toward one, and she knew time was running out. They would have expected Calderón back before now and if men weren't out looking already, they would be soon.

The Castillos stood around, pointing, yelling, stamping their feet. She checked her back for the Browning and secured it, then pulled the Colt from her ankle holster and slipped across the road and into the scrub brush of the hills.

She hiked up parallel to the main road into the Casa, the moon lighting her way, and got to the barbwire fence before she realized she was not alone. She ducked behind an ocotillo.

The footsteps crunched closer. She held the Colt with her finger sitting over the trigger. She thought of Tim for a moment, telling her to carry the Browning locked and loaded. She liked this gun better. It was ready at all times and it had done the job she asked of it. She shut her eyes for a moment, sending up a quick prayer that Tim was alright.

She opened her eyes and stepped out from the ocotillo, levelling the gun at the figure.

"Lupe! Don't shoot!" came the insistent hiss.

She lowered the gun. "Manuel, what are you doing? I thought I was alone."

"Never," he said, a smile playing on his lips. "One day you will see this as clear as I do."

"You cannot stop me. I am getting to the girls to protect them."

Manuel looked at her, deep understanding in his eyes. "I would not dream of stopping you. But you will need these."

He held up wire cutters and began cutting through the barbwire fence.

Many small casitas dotted the property, but only two mattered. One was where the newest girls were kept, tied up until it was time to entertain guests at the main house. It was small and away from the rest. The others were kept in a large casita, crammed to the rafters. Others around the property were for guests. Although they were full on holidays or special times of the year, they sat empty now.

Two guards were stationed outside the smaller casita, both patrolling with weapons.

"We will go to the other girls first," she said. "They will be unguarded."

She slipped through the underbrush, moving around the perimeter until she was close to the large casita. One of the guards at the other casita was faced her way and she waited until he turned away to rush to the door. She opened it and slipped inside.

It was dark. The casitas had no electricity, and she had no flashlight.

"Juanita!" she whispered. "Flora!"

She heard the rustling of blankets.

"Lupe?"

"Shhh! Shhh!" she cautioned, moving into the room. "Where are you?"

"Lupe, is it you?"

A match flared to life and a small lantern was lit. A moment later she was surrounded by six girls, the oldest fifteen. Juanita gaped.

Lupe looked down. Her clothes were covered in blood and soot. She couldn't imagine what she must look like.

"Are you hurt?" Juanita whispered.

"No," she said. "But Calderón is dead. He is dead."

The girls all gasped, and two cried. Lupe understood the fear—as much as they hated the man, who would take care of them now? What other monster was hiding under the bed?

"I have friends coming," she said. "They will overtake Calderón's men. We will be free."

Juanita made a strangled laugh. Lupe grabbed her hand and squeezed it.

"We will figure it out," she said. "But you must listen, we have little time."

She made them each put on warmer clothes. No shoes were in the casita—Calderón kept their shoes from them unless they were needed. Too easy to escape when it was made more comfortable.

"How many are still in the other casita?" Lupe asked.

"Three," Flora said. "Gloria, Ana María and Joséfina."

The three youngest. Gloria was nine and the most timid.

"Is there another here? A woman? She would be older than me. She was very beautiful when I knew her. Is she here? Gabriela?"

Flora shook her head. "It is only us. There is no one else."

Calderón could have killed her the moment he took her. Lupe was about to ask another question when the gunfire began.

The shots were far away, up at the main house. It had begun.

She eased the door open, watching the other casita. One guard hurried up the path to the main house. The other turned toward them.

She eased the door shut and urged the girls to the east wall. She stood behind the door, waiting for it to open, the Colt in her hands. Steps approached, but before the door opened, shots rang out.

She paused a minute before stepping out from the door and pointing the gun outside. The guard was dead.

Manuel stepped from the shadows. "Hurry!"

"Now girls, now!" she said.

One by one, each of the six girls filed out of the casita, running toward Manuel and slipping down a small embankment. Lupe shut the door behind them and hurried toward Manuel.

"Take them to the road," she said. "I will get the others."

"Lupe—"

"Manuel, no," she said. "You must go!"

He looked back at the small faces, then at Lupe. He nodded.

She gripped the gun and turned toward the other casita. She glanced around for the guard, saw no one, and ran toward the building.

The door was unlocked, and she eased it open and was plunged into darkness again.

She called out, but there was no answer.

"Ana? It is Lupe. Can you hear me?"

"Lupe?"

Lupe felt around, knocking into a chair, and finding the wall. She ran her fingers along the wall until she hit the eye bolt in the wall. Following the rope attached, she found a small pair of hands. The girl whimpered. Gloria.

"It's okay, mija," she said. "I am here to take you home."

She holstered the Colt while she undid the knots, then felt around until she found each girl, none of them talking. She untied each girl and pushed all three of the girls toward the door. Before they reached it, a figure filled the space. She could see him silhouetted, but his eyes hadn't adjusted yet.

She reached for the Browning at her back and shifted the safety off.

A flashlight clicked on, and she kept the gun behind her back as the beam passed across them.

"You!"

She knew the voice. Calderón's personal guard. The man who shot at them from the car.

She didn't think twice. She aimed the gun and fired a shot.

It was loud in the small casita, and the muzzle flash lit up the interior for a moment. She fired again, but the gun was empty.

Her ears rang, but she could hear the girls screaming behind her.

She grabbed the flashlight rolling across the floor and pointed it forward—the man was dead.

188

"Come!" she said to the girls. She grabbed at them, ushering them to the door, trying to block the man's body from them. She followed behind them, stepping over Carlos's body, blood seeping from a wound in the upper left of his chest. An unholy laugh bubbled up—she might not be able to hit the broad side of a barn, but her aim was true here.

She eased the door shut and hurried toward the girls, who were huddled together in thin nightgowns with no shoes. She looked toward the scrub brush and guided them to the path. She stopped and tucked the Browning in her waistband, burning her skin, and pulled out the Colt from the ankle holster, pointing it toward the trail when a head moved between the scrub. She lowered it when she realized it was Manuel. She pushed the girls toward him.

"He is a friend, come on! He will not hurt you."

Whether scared by the gunfire or believing in their rescue, the girls ran toward Manuel. He led them all down a pathway to the hole in the barbwire fence.

"Where are the others?"

"On their way down to the road. I could not leave without you."

She glanced back at the house. Her nerves were frayed, and she was beginning to shake. If Gabriela was here, the Castillos could find her. Her eyes stung with tears—there was no more she could do. Lupe held the gun tightly and scrambled down the hill, hearing the gunshots at the main house get quieter with more time between them.

"I believe we are winning," Manuel said.

She slid down the bottom part of the hill onto the road and crossed toward the clearing where the other girls were gathered. She ushered them to the car, and they sat behind it, sheltered from the road. Joséfina's foot was bleeding badly, and Lupe tore the edge of her own shirt to tie around the girl's small foot.

A few minutes later, a Jeep tore down the road toward them from the Casa, horn honking. The girls huddled with hands over their ears, but Lupe stood, watching the Jeep.

Pedro Castillo jumped out of the passenger seat, yelling something to the few waiting men, who jumped in another car and raced up the road.

He pulled a woman out of the back of the Jeep. She was heavily pregnant, her hands tied in front of her, a gag on her mouth.

Lupe stared in shock. "Gabriela?"

"You know her?" Pedro asked. "She was tied up in the main house, heavily guarded. We had only time to take her and go. I must return. We have taken the house, but many of the guards went to ground like rats. No matter! We will hunt them down like cats."

Pedro laughed and got back in the Jeep.

Lupe approached Gabriela and loosened the gag.

"Lupita?"

Lupe nodded, tears spilling over. She tried to work the knot at Gabriela's hands, but it was tight and her hands were shaking.

"Here." Manuel came over with a knife and cut Gabriela's bonds.

Gabriela hugged her, and Lupe stared at the scrub, hardly able to raise her arms.

"Ramón? Is he alright?" she asked. "Calderón said he told Ramón I was dead."

Lupe looked at the ground for a moment, but it was too long of a hesitation.

"Oh no," Gabriela choked. "No. Not Ramón. No."

Gabriela's legs almost gave out, and Lupe braced her, helping her toward the car where the girls were. She was heartened to see the young ones come over and help her sit Gabriela down inside the car.

Lupe walked to the edge of the embankment, looking down at the river, slow moving and dark.

Ramón had been put in an impossible position.

Awhile later Jeeps came careening down the hillside, men whooping and cheering and guns firing. They pulled onto the gravel side of the road.

"Is it over?" she asked, her head spinning and her throat dry.

Arturo Castillo jumped from the back of the Jeep. "You are free to go, and we are free to take all of what was Calderón's!"

A cheer went up among the men, but she held up a hand and looked at her girls.

"Almost all."

Arturo nodded his agreement. She looked at Manuel, then at the Castillos.

"If you want all that was Calderón's, you will need this."

Lupe slipped the small envelope out of her jeans pocket and handed it to Arturo.

"So it was true." He stared a moment before he reached out to take it.

Lupe nodded. "You have this as long as we have our lives and our freedom."

Arturo looked over and held up the envelope. "You would have that without this."

"And that is why you have it," Lupe told him.

Arturo laughed, called to his men and they mounted up again, careening back up the road to the Casa.

She looked at the girls, then Manuel.

"The doctor," she said. "I must get back. Tim did not look well."

"Go," Manuel said. "I will watch over the girls."

"No," Lupe said. "They will come with me. Joséfina needs her foot tended to. Gabriela needs to be examined too. They will stay with me until we know what to do."

Lupe ushered the girls into the car and started the engine, her hands steady.

18

Tim opened his eyes, feeling as if he had been hit by a truck.

He looked around. He was in a bed in a room that didn't look familiar at all. It didn't look like a hospital room either, so thank God for small favours.

He winced as he tried to move and noticed his shoulder was wrapped up. His throat was raw and sore, and when he took in a deep breath he began coughing.

The door opened, and Lupe stood there. It seemed like he hadn't seen her in years.

"You are awake," she said smiling. She wore a chambray dress and looked clean. Her face was bruised, and he could see cuts, scrapes and bruises all over her arms. He looked at his hands. He was clean.

"What happened?" His voice was hoarse.

"You do not remember the fire?"

He closed his eyes, and it came flooding back. The fire, the smoke and the two men he had killed. He remembered the feeling of the gun in his hand, slick with blood. He remembered seeing Lupe crawl out from under Calderón, his brains in the dirt. He remembered the smoke most of all.

"I remember," he said. "Where are we?"

"The Casa," she said. "Well, it is a casita on the property. Like a guest house."

"What?" he asked, struggling to sit up. "What the hell are we doing here, he was dead. Isn't he dead?"

Lupe pushed him back.

"Yes, he is dead," she said, a smile on her lips. "Will you be still? I will tell you everything that happened."

"How long have I been out?" he asked.

"Almost thirty-six hours," she said frowning. "You were beginning to worry me. The doctor said you would be well. He had to give you much oxygen. He put a tube to help you breathe that night."

"Why? What happened?"

"What is the last you remember?" she asked.

He remembered the barn falling and told her.

"You do not remember being in the car? I had to drive it."

He shook his head. "I don't remember any of it."

"Small wonder."

He was quiet for a second and looked at her. "Can you even drive?"

"I figured it out," she said.

"Thank God my car's in San Ysidro," he said.

"You were very sick," she told him. "I drove to a pay phone and called Manuel, and he gave me directions to a doctor. While you were unconscious Manuel told the Castillo family what had happened. We stormed the Casa and took out the rest of Calderón's men. We moved you here to hide from the policía."

"Wait, 'we' stormed the Casa?" he asked.

"I had to go, for the girls," she said, smiling. "I could not leave them."

"Why am I hiding from the police?" he asked, his head swimming with information. Lupe stormed the Casa. Well, alright then.

"They believe you killed Ramón," she said. "Some loyal to Calderón have spread the story."

"What?" he asked in disbelief. "Christ, I would have for what he did."

"No," Lupe said. "It is not like you think."

He closed his eyes, his thoughts swimming. He was wanted in Mexico for murder. Fantastic.

The door creaked, and Tim opened his eyes to see Manuel enter with a tray.

"It is good to see you awake," he said.

"Good to be awake. I think," Tim said. "Why do they think I killed Ramón?"

"The men loyal to Calderón have told their superiors that Ramón went to stop a meeting between you and Calderón, and you killed him to protect Calderón," Manuel said. "You are a wanted man in México. You are very lucky the papers Mendoza gave you give the name of Thomas Blaistock of Sacramento, California. Mendoza's papers may save your life."

Tim coughed again, and Lupe poured him a glass of water, helping him sit up to take a drink.

"The Castillo brothers have taken over much of the El Camarilla's organization," Manuel said. "They have used the microfiche wisely."

"You gave it to them?" he asked Lupe.

"Yes," she said. "They earned it with their actions. They would not keep me or the girls, even without the microfiche."

"Your friend Mendoza called me late yesterday when he heard the news of you," Manuel said. "He had made contact with a man in Sonora. They have ties to the Castillo family. It was in their interest to allow the Castillos to take over. They are providing help to quell any rebellion from Calderón's men."

"Where are we exactly?" Tim asked.

"The Casa," she said. "South of Mexicali. Remember, I told you? The policía will not come here. We brought you here after the Castillos liberated it. The casita is comfortable and quiet."

"You're staying here?" he asked.

She looked at the bed linens, then at him.

"I am staying in another casita, next door," she said. "Not in the main house. I cannot stay there. And I cannot stay in the other casitas. The girls set fire to them."

Tim choked out a laugh, which set off another coughing fit. His lungs felt like someone had stomped on them.

"I will leave you two to talk," Manuel said. "We will get you back to America as soon as you are well."

Tim nodded, feeling like things had spun out of control.

"You're okay?" he asked Lupe.

"Yes," she said.

"What happened? After you ran, I mean" he said. "I couldn't see shit."

"Calderón caught me as soon as I left the barn. He dragged me into the scrub to shoot me," she said bitterly. "He told me he did not have to take the microfiche now, because he could pluck it off my body whenever he liked. I . . . I taunted him. He hit me, many times."

Tim reached up to touch a bruise on her cheek.

"Should've kept your mouth shut," he said.

"I have spent too much time around you for that," she shot back with a smile.

He grinned. Something had changed in her. She looked happy and free, but the change was bigger than that.

"I knew I could not get the gun and shoot him. He paid too close attention," she said. "So . . . I did what I must do. He threatened me and said he would have me one last time. I tried to get away, he stopped me. I realized it was what I needed to do to have a chance to shoot him. He pinned me with his body, he undid his pants and mine. He concentrated so hard to do this, because I was moving to get my hand to the gun. He had not yet . . . he did not have a chance to rape me. I got the gun from the ankle holster, and I shot him before I could think."

"Are you sorry you did it?" Tim asked her.

"No," she said, her eyes defiant. "I am glad. The moment I felt his blood on me, I felt free."

He nodded.

"I killed another in the casita. I did not feel sorry then, either." She paused for a moment. "I killed him with the Browning. He was not on top of me, either."

Tim managed a wry smile. He remembered the barn and his smile faded.

"I killed the other two," he said. "In the barn."

"Are you sorry?" she asked.

He looked her in the eye. "I didn't have a choice."

She nodded. "Oh, we did. But it was the right choice. Rest, Tim. I will come for you later, and we will walk so you can get your strength."

She left the room, and he fell asleep the moment he closed his eyes.

It was late afternoon when she came back. She held something—the guns.

"I kept them for you," she said. She put the holstered Colt on the floor next to the bed, and laid the Browning next to it.

He looked over at them, and her. He reached over and picked up the Colt, sliding it out of the holster.

"Keep it," he said, holding the gun out to her.

"What? No, I cannot."

"It's yours," he said. "You know it as well as I do."

She took the small gun and held it. "Is it terrible I'm glad to keep it?"

She stared at it a moment longer before tucking it in the holster and placing it on the chair.

"Come, sit up."

She helped him into a sitting position, his left shoulder screaming in pain the entire time.

"What the hell did I do to my shoulder?" he asked, trying to catch his breath.

"It was dislocated," she said. "I do not know how."

Tim paused and thought about the fire. "A shovel. One of those guys hit me with a shovel."

"You will heal in time," she said. "Come, stand up."

He looked up, and he tossed the covers off. He wore only his underwear.

"Who cleaned me up?" he asked. Lupe helped him to his feet. He struggled not to sway, waving off her attempt to help.

"I did," she said. "I thought you would rather me than Manuel."

Tim grinned.

"There was much blood," she said. "I feared you had been shot at first."

"Almost," he said, thinking of the fight over the gun, the blood on his shirt. "Almost."

She helped him get into his jeans, which had been laundered, and she presented him with a plaid work shirt. She buttoned it around his injured arm, which was in a sling. He had his right arm in the arm of the shirt.

"At least it's my left arm," he said. "I can drive without my left."

"Come," Lupe said. "You need to walk, you have been lying down too long."

His legs felt like jelly when they began to walk. His face was pale, the bruises fading, and there were fresh stitches in the back of his head and above his eye. They left the small casita, whose main room contained the bed and some furniture and there was nothing more. Lupe showed him the small outhouse right outside.

A few other small casitas like the one he was in were near, and a large house loomed in the distance. Two scorched areas near the edge of the property held charred wood, and the smell of smoke was still in the air. It made him feel sick.

Steep hills covered in scrub surrounded them, and the view down the side of the hills looked over a small, lazy river.

"You've spent a lot of time here," he said. "Where are you gonna go?"

"I do not know yet," she said. "Manuel has offered me a place to stay with him in Mexicali. We have much work to do."

"Work?" he asked. "Doing what?"

"We will try to return the girls to their homes. If they will not be accepted at home, Manuel has arranged for the Sisters of Charity to take them."

"Nuns?"

"It is an orphanage run by the nuns, yes," she said.

"How many girls?"

They were approaching a larger casita and a girl rushed outside.

"Lupita!" she exclaimed. The girl came running up to Lupe and began speaking rapid Spanish. She slowed as she noticed Tim, looking at him with large eyes.

Lupe said something to her, and she smiled and walked back to the house. The other girls crowded in the window, staring.

"How old are they?" he asked, looking at their faces. Every one of them looked younger than Lupe.

"Juanita is the oldest, she is fifteen. Gloria is the youngest, she is nine. She has been here six months. But six months too long," Lupe said.

Tim watched as the oldest one came out and directed the other girls in Spanish. They were packing things up around the house and yard.

"Jesus Christ," he said, watching some of them, who looked so damn young. "If you hadn't killed him, I would have."

Lupe touched his arm and they walked on.

"We will try to return them home," she said. "But I do not think they will ever forget."

Tim walked with her for awhile, both of them quiet. She took him back to his room and settled him in bed, making sure he ate something. His throat was so raw and his voice so hoarse he thought he'd never feel better again.

He tried to sleep, but all he could think about was how young those girls were.

Lupe slipped into Tim's room trying not to make any noise. She stood near his bed, watching his even breathing, relieved he didn't choke with every breath.

"You gonna get in the bed or stare at me all night?" he asked, not opening his eyes.

She smiled, not surprised he heard her come in. She lifted the covers and got in the bed, mindful of his injured shoulder.

"I'm not well enough for any fun," he said.

"I know," Lupe told him, her hand resting on his midsection. "I just want to lie with you."

He tried to circle his good arm around her, and she snuggled closer to his chest.

"I will miss you when you go," she said.

"Really?" he asked. "You're gonna miss being shot at, barn fires, being followed, run off the road . . . anything I left out?"

She smiled. "Yes. I will miss you."

"Are you gonna go home?" he asked.

She ran her fingers across his chest.

"I do not know."

"Won't kill you to try," he said. "You can always come back to Manuel if it doesn't work out."

Yes, she could.

She didn't know why she hadn't told Tim about Gabriela yet. Maybe she needed to get everything settled in her own mind first.

She took in a breath and kissed his collarbone, working her way up his neck to his jaw. He tasted like burnt embers and the smell of burning wood was still on his skin.

Friday, November 11, 1966

Four days later, Tim was in a warehouse in Mexicali, his arm in a sling.

"Your weapons," Arturo Castillo said, gesturing toward the truck. "We will hide you inside, the border guards in Tijuana will not check, we have paid them off. The driver will take you to Mendoza and you will unload your weapons, and our driver will return."

"Don't how I'm gonna fit 'em all in the back of a fucking Dodge Charger," he said, looking at the crates of weapons.

"Not my problem, my friend," Arturo said. "We will work together in the future, perhaps. You have done us well bringing us the microfiche."

"That was Lupe," he said. "She better be kept safe because of it."

"No one will harm her," he said.

Tim looked around the warehouse. "The cops gonna be knocking on your door looking for me?"

"No, no," Arturo said. "They are too busy looking for Thomas Blaistock."

He gave a hearty laugh and bit off the end of a cigar, lit it, and moved over to the back of the truck, yelling instructions at his men.

Tim shook his head and sat near the office and lit up a cigarette. It had taken a few days before he'd had a craving for one.

"You are crazy, inhaling all that smoke after what you have been through," Lupe said.

"It's different," Tim commented.

Lupe swatted him with the papers she held.

"You'll be okay?" he asked.

"I will, I think," she said. "Manuel has said no one is after me, and I believe him."

"What about your family?" Tim asked.

Lupe sat next to him.

"They will have heard about Ramón," she said. "I do not know what they will think of me. They may blame me for his death. In a way, it is my fault."

"He was on the take, Lupe, that isn't anyone's fault but his own," Tim said.

"He was not," Lupe said. "There is something I did not tell you."

Tim raised an eyebrow at her.

"Do you remember what Ramón said before Calderón shot him? He said Calderón could let Gabriela go. Gabriela was his girlfriend back in our village. For many years."

"I remember. High school sweethearts, you said."

She nodded. "Calderón took her when I left the Casa. To pressure Ramón to find me."

Tim let out a breath.

"Did she get out okay?"

"The Castillos rescued her in the house. She was not harmed."

"Does she know?"

Lupe stared at the floor. "I didn't have to say it. She knew."

Tim didn't quite know what to say about that.

"She is pregnant," Lupe said. "This baby will grow up without a father because of me."

"Lupe, it had nothing to do with you."

"It had everything to do with me." She stared at him, her eyes pained. "He had to choose. Of course he chose his child. His wife. He would not have had to choose if I had not run."

"You think he would've wanted you to stay there your whole life?"

She looked away, shaking her head.

"Gabriela does not blame me. I do not understand her. But my family, they may see me as the reason he is dead. No matter. I will find out and be done with it."

Tim looked over. "You're gonna go back?"

She nodded. "I will go, and I will see what happens. But no matter what my family says, I will come back to Mexicali. Gabriela's family is here. She wants me to know this child, to tell it about Ramón. So I will return."

"You scared?" he asked.

She shrugged. "I am trying not to be. I am trying to be like you. I cannot understand how you thought to light that cigarette before Calderón arrived. What if you had not? He would have killed us."

Tim hesitated before speaking.

"I had a feeling, Lupe," Tim said. "I knew something wasn't right."

She looked over, her brow creased. "What do you mean?"

"It didn't make sense. Ramón was nervous in that meeting we had, too nervous," Tim said. "It didn't wash. What he said didn't make sense."

She frowned.

"What do you mean?"

"You said he felt all this shame and turned away from you, then he's suddenly okay with it and wanting to help. You know how I felt about it all . . . I got past it, best I could. But it took time."

"You have known me for fifteen days."

His eyes widened in surprise. It seemed a lot longer than that.

"Look, I can't say what it was, but he was nervous in that meeting. He knew way too much about me. Where do you think he got that info?

"But what did it was making us drive that back road. I expected any minute they'd pull us over and shoot us. He had them following us since the minute we left Mexicali. They drove with the headlights off so we couldn't see them. When I saw the barn, I hoped to hell I could use something in it before Calderón got there."

She was quiet for a minute, and Tim took a long drag of his cigarette.

"Is it wrong I miss him?" she asked. "Is it wrong I love him still? He was good to me when I was younger. I did not lie when I said he was like a brother. He was given an impossible choice."

It reminded him of the Outfit and Johnny Moro. Leveraging family was something Moro loved to do, but it wasn't how Chicago used to be. He thought of Diana and his mother. He thought of Ruby. Choosing could break someone easily.

A moment later Arturo shouted something in Spanish and waved at Tim.

"He is saying they are ready for you to go," she said.

They both stood and walked toward the truck, which was parked outside, the open back of it sticking into the warehouse.

He sure as hell wasn't looking forward to the ride over the border in this. Thank God he didn't have to ride that way to Las Vegas.

He turned around, facing Lupe. Her eyes teared.

"Don't you dare cry, not after all that's happened. You're too tough for tears," he said. "Anyhow, this isn't something to cry over."

"You are so stubborn."

She stepped toward him, running her hands up his chest, and around his neck, careful not to hurt his shoulder. He bent his head to her and kissed her. She kissed him back. He wondered if the Castillos would hold up leaving for a half hour or so, and thought they'd shoot him for asking.

He broke the kiss first.

"Be careful, Tim," Lupe said. "In everything. You are so much trouble."

"You're not exactly a breeze either," he said.

"Will I ever see you again?" she asked.

He shrugged. "I won't be allowed in Mexico again."

She shook her head. "No, Thomas Blaistock, he will not be allowed in México. Maybe you will visit one day?"

"Maybe," he said, lying through his teeth. He wanted nothing more than to get out of Mexico for good.

He looked at Lupe, her hair clean and curled, her outfit new. For a moment he thought she looked like a regular girl, but there was something in her eyes that was changed. She had grown somehow, something had changed in her for keeps, but he wasn't sure if that was good or not. But she could live a different life now, although she looked far too comfortable with the gun strapped to her ankle, surrounded by gun runners and criminals.

"Take care, Lupe," he said.

He leaned over and kissed her on the cheek.

"Adiós," she said.

He got inside the cube van, sitting between the crates, and listening to the men in the warehouse talk in Spanish. He watched Lupe smile and wave.

The doors closed on him and it was pitch black. He listened to the engine start up. He had his shipment, a potential to work with the Castillos again, and he was headed home.

He leaned back against the wall of the van and closed his eyes, willing the truck over the border and home. It was the beginning of everything—he would have money, and from there he could build something of his own.

If you enjoyed this book, please leave a review on Amazon and/or Good-reads.

Acknowledgements

Lots of thank yous are owed, as always.

Thank you to Hannah Minger for all her thoughtful comments on the series, and her TVTropes skills.

To my co-writer MB Miller for expanding the Sin City world and making it a place that I really love to visit—it's more fun when someone else is playing in the sandbox with you.

To my cousin Bret Collins, who showed me Google Docs way back when (I mean *way* back). Without it MB Miller and I would take even longer to release books, and we're slow enough as it is.

For the research purists, there has never been a compound-style zona in Mexicali, so I constructed one. If you're interested in reading about the history of some of the zonas and border towns in Mexico, I used *The Mexican Border Cities: Landscape Anatomy and Place Personality* by Daniel D. Arreola and James R. Curtis in my research.

About The Author

Jennifer Samson (she/her) is the author of the coming-of-age *Sin City* saga (currently at four full length novels and two side novellas) and co-author of the dark comedy/thriller *The Final Cut*, the first in the *Billie and Diana* series. She has been published in the literary journals *Thursday* and *The Lyre,* as well as the BoldPrint book *Friends.* Her work has been featured in the Brookline TAB, Toronto Star, Ottawa Citizen, and Edmonton Sun.

She enjoys fine-nibbed pens, Hilroy loose leaf paper, corner store candy, adorable cats, and beating her Goodreads Reading Challenge every year. Being Canadian, a love of hockey goes without saying.

She is a member of Gamma Xi Phi, a predominantly African American, anti-racist, non-hazing, all-gender professional fraternity for artists and creators where she currently serves as National Secretary. She is also a member of Alpha Phi Women's Fraternity.

She currently lives on the unceded traditional and ancestral territory of the Sḵwx̱wú7mesh (Squamish), səlilwətaɬ (Tsleil-Waututh) and xʷməθkʷəy̓əm (Musqueam) Coast Salish peoples.

You can find her on Goodreads, Bluesky and Pinterest. She's probably there instead of editing.

* * *

Sign up for my newsletter and receive free ebooks and information on new releases - https://tinyurl.com/arieswriting

Arieswriting - www.arieswriting.com
Goodreads - www.goodreads.com/jennifersamson

Jennifer Samson Book List

The Sin City Series
(Crime/Love Story Saga)

Piece of Work
Sin City
Tilt*
The Dead Woman
Neon and Tinsel*
Bayou Bound

Coming Soon:

Under The Gun

*With MB Miller

The Billie and Diana Series
(Comedy/Thriller)*

The Final Cut

Coming Soon:

Curtains

*with M.B. Miller

Join my newsletter at https://tinyurl.com/arieswriting for free ebooks and news on my latest releases.